Praise for *Hunter's Secret*

When I finished J. C. Hager's first book, Hunters Choice, *I asked the author, "Where's the next one?" I finally got my eyes on* Hunter's Secret *and got by on little sleep until I'd read it. The locales depicted are bang-on, the human characters are well-crafted and many return as the reader's old friends. Now, John, where's the next one?*
Joseph Greenleaf
Publisher, Swordpoint Intercontinental Ltd

Hunter's Secret *has action, intrigue, spot-on descriptions, unique Michigan settings....an entertaining and logical sequel to* Hunter's Choice.
Aubrey Golden
President, Michigan Karst Conservancy

Praise for J. C. Hager's *Hunter's Choice*
The first Matt Hunter Adventure

John Hager knows the outdoors, he knows the human heart, and best of all he knows how to tell a hell of a story!
Steve Hamilton
author of the Alex McKnight novels

In his debut novel, J. C. Hager has employed his expertise as a hunter to offer us quite a yarn that could probably easily make a great movie...What also shines in the novel is Hager's familiarity with the finer points of all things pertaining to hunting and boating that he cleverly interweaves into his plot.
Norman Goldman
Editor, BookPleasures.com

Superbly crafted, Hunter's Choice *documents Hager as a master storyteller whose attention to detail insures the reader's rapt attention from beginning to end.*
Midwest Book Review

Hunter's Secret

Also by J. C. Hager
Hunter's Choice

Hunter's Secret
Wreck of the Carol K

J. C. Hager

A Matt Hunter Adventure

Greenstone Publishing
Rapid River, Michigan

Hunter's Secret
by J. C. Hager

First Edition

Manufactured in the United States

Book and cover design by Five Rainbows Services

Print ISBN:	978-0-9797546-6-1	$14.95
e-Book ISBN (PDF):	978-0-9797546-0-9	$4.95
e-Book ISBN (ePub):	978-0-9797546-1-6	$4.95
LCCN:	2010905660	

Information: www.GreenstonePublishing.com
              1-906-280-8585

Publisher's Cataloging-in-Publication Data

Hager, John C.
   Hunter's secret : wreck of the Carol K / J.C. Hager.
     p. cm.
   ISBN 978-0-9797546-6-1
   1. Corporations—Corrupt practices—Fiction. 2. Conspiracies—Fiction. 3. Shipwrecks—Fiction. 4. Superior, Lake—Fiction. 5. Michigan—Fiction.   I. Title. II. Series: A Matt Hunter adventure.
PS3608.A44 H87 2010
813`.6—dc22

                                2010905660

To Ann, who does so much

Stuck

S tuck, fouled, hung-up…the anchor was down there and wouldn't be hoisted. Matt Hunter held the half-inch, three-strand nylon line in his hands as he stood wide-legged at the bow. After he and Tanya had spent a half hour using every skill they knew, the anchor still defied their wishes to end the beautiful day on Lake Superior and motor back to harbor.

Finally warm, even sweaty, from exertion and frustration, Matt had donned a hooded sweatshirt and lined jogging pants to bring his body temperature back to normal after a day of jumping in and climbing out of Lake Superior. Three days on the boat had introduced Tanya, a Florida native and expert ocean diver, to the cold, fresh water of Gitche Gumee, the anchor being the only problem yet encountered.

Tanya came forward from her role as helmsman. Just the sight of her barefoot, in cutoff jeans and nylon jacket over a long-sleeved t-shirt, took the disappointment of the moment away and filled Matt with a glow of happiness and love.

Tanya gave him a hug. "We're out of tricks. Someone needs to suit up and get wet. I'll make some coffee and watch for sharks." She ducked under the line that Matt was chocking with both hands and came up inside his arms, pulling his head forward, kissing him and snuggling her head into his chest.

Matt fought for balance as a light afternoon chop made the boat rock slightly. He looked west at the low September sun dancing off the wavelets. "It's that damn plow anchor, I've never liked them—like a big fish hook and hard to store. I should have bought a Danforth, but was too pissed at the cost of filling the gas tank. I bought whole fishing boats for the cost of…"

Tanya kissed him again, "It's only money, and you've worked hard on the house all summer. I love being on a boat again, alone with you. We've got two more nights if someone can get his anchor up." Her eyes sparkling, she quickly ducked under Matt's arms and worked along the side of the boat to the stern and into the cabin.

Matt felt like cutting the rope and leaving the whole rode and anchor to rot on the bottom. He didn't want to get into a cold wet suit, then 40- to 50-degree water, but knew it had to be done. He was using the boat for free but had to replace anything broken, and it was Friday afternoon—he wasn't sure if he could find an open ship chandlery store until Monday in Marquette or Munising. Getting a cab to shop at Gander Mountain or Wal-Mart didn't sound like a good idea. He let out 50 feet of line, enough for the dive, secured it and worked aft to the cabin.

The generator was running and the microwave dinged as he entered the cabin.

Tanya poured steaming water into a larger plastic pitcher half full of water. "I heated some water to put into your suit, I wouldn't want anything to get frostbitten."

Matt put on his cold, wet long underwear, then pulled up, wiggled into, and finally zipped his quarter-inch-thick wet suit. Before putting on the rubber hood, he opened the top zipper and poured in the warm water. It felt like peeing your pants, but it did fight the frostbite Tanya was worried about. He climbed onto the diving platform, put on his tank; it showed over 30 percent full. He had a small needle-nose pliers and a screwdriver secured in the zipper pocket of his buoyancy vest.

"If I can't get it free, I'll unscrew the shackle and save the rope and chain."

Tanya handed him his flippers and mask, "I'll watch you from the bridge. Be careful."

Matt held the bottom of the tank attachment and stepped off the platform. The warm water in the suit did its thing and the cold water only slowly seeped in as it warmed to near body temperature. Matt swam under the 34-foot Silverton, noting the twin stainless steel props and the pristine condition of the antifouling paint: a plus for the cold, fresh water that was already making his fingers dumb. He had rubber diving gloves but, if he needed to snip the thin wire that secured the clevis screw, bare hands, even cold ones, would be best.

He grabbed the anchor line and followed it down. The earlier 80-foot visibility had dropped to half that as the sun flattened across the surface. The line went out of his sight as he paused to pressurize. His depth gauge read 40 feet. He could see a large, gray rock shelf before him, with the white anchor line disappearing into the gloom toward it. As he slowly kicked downward, the monotone grayness of the surroundings enhanced the silence and loneliness. The only sound, his breathing and bubbles from the regulator. At 65 feet he saw the anchor chain. Fifteen feet of chain protected the rope from fraying against rocks and kept the line lower in the water, increasing the anchor's holding power. Matt finally held the chain and pulled himself slowly downward, the cold of the metal almost painful to the touch. At last he saw the damn plow anchor, upside down among several large, gray boulders, and it looked securely linked to a log stuck between two smaller boulders, just like a fish hook. The whole scene formed a shallow cave-like grotto containing rounded gray rocks against a gray rock wall.

With no little satisfaction and with full knowledge of what awaited the successful raising of his anchor when he returned to Tanya, Matt wrestled with the old plow hook. He brought it upward, then sideways, turning it until it came free. He pushed off the offending log in the final struggles. The plow anchor, now free, moved across the rock and stopped of its own weight and the lack of much pull from the boat above. Matt gripped the four—or five-inch-diameter log, a thin coating of slime floated away—he touched uniform and round—hard and cold—metal. The large rock on the right side became a massive anchor fluke.

Matt checked his old Rolex—he had set the bezel to the minute hand when he put the mouthpiece in just before diving. Six minutes of diving so far, now at decompression depths; he didn't have his computer, and if he stayed any longer he would be into repetitive dive calculations. There wasn't much time for fun-and-games with the big anchor. Also, the light was quickly fading.

Matt swam around the fluke, finding the shaft and following it to a large chain: old, forged links led away down the steep slope of the main rock cliff, out of sight. He pulled himself down the links, cold forgotten, adventure and discovery beckoning: each handhold bringing him two feet lower into the darkness. He descended, remembering to breathe steadily, the chain leading down and across the rock wall.

The pressure increased, his ears popping, suit compressing, insulating factor going down, cold increasing, leg muscles starting to cramp from the freezing water. Watch face hard to read—not quite dark enough for the radium dial but too dark to read the hands. He could see the second hand moving—it was comforting to have an instrument working for him down here. Something down there wanted to be found; it called to him. He would descend ten more grips. One, two, three, four, five, six little Indians...

Shit, I'm getting numb and dumb, and dumb is death down here.

Matt turned around and headed slowly back up the chain, returning to the big anchor. Looking up, the water seemed warmer, more light; he breathed easier. Eight feet away lay the plow anchor. He worked at bringing it back; there wasn't much slack, but enough to just hook the plow point over the old anchor. It would hold, but could be freed from the boat.

Matt made two decompression stops and finally threw his swim fins onto the diving platform. Tanya offered him a beach towel, steaming coffee and a very worried look.

"Why so long? I could see you moving down the white anchor chain, then I lost sight of you. I could tell you were going deeper by the bubbles, but you were too long and deep for the anchor work. I was getting my gear on when I saw you coming up and decompressing. Are you alright? What's down there?"

"Adventure and discovery is down there. Let me get warmed up and we can make decisions about what we can do," answered Matt as he pulled off his gear. Coffee, sugar, brandy and his sweat clothes brought the color back to his lips.

"I found a ship's anchor, followed its chain down another forty feet." Matt went on as he pulled out scrolled maps from an overhead shelf. He pointed with pencil stub. "Here it is, Granite Island, here are the rocks on the west end, here we are, and there is the slope and shelf, then the steep drop-off. Unless we are dealing with just an abandoned anchor and chain, or chain and cable, we may find a sunken ship right about there—in one hundred sixty feet of water and resting against the cliff wall. I went down the anchor chain, it was tight and strained on the rock, going down at an angle toward the cliff face, either there's a hundred yards of chain caught on an outcropping or there is something at the other end."

Tanya brought Matt half a sandwich left from lunch and freshened his coffee. "Are we going in or can we stay over night?"

"It stays light until almost 10:00, so we can think awhile. Check the Coast Guard UHF weather channel, and I'll make a phone call to the marina. I think the southwest wind is going to stay gentle and the lake will be a pond for the next few days. We have shelter from the south and we know our anchor is solid, even though our scope won't be perfect we can let out most of our two hundred feet of line, set a second anchor on the shallow reef and let the GPS be our anchor watch."

"Planning to dive tonight?" she asked.

He shook his head slowly. "Morning would be better. Maybe a short midmorning dive down that anchor. We can figure out how much time we have with the tanks aboard. If there is something down there we will need more and better equipment."

Tanya and Matt busied themselves with weather, diving tables, anchoring and, finally, dinner tasks. They had salad, fresh lake trout fillets, fresh green beans and rice—all with chilled Chablis from a gallon jug kept in the big ice chest. They transported their plates and glasses to the flying deck and enjoyed the view of the desolate rocky island, the soft reds and oranges of the Lake Superior extended sunset, and finally the twilight and evening of the northern latitude.

While Matt did the dishes, Tanya organized the cabin space, loaded the Bunn coffee maker and prepared the forward berth. With the center support in place, covered by the fitting mattress pad, the whole bow space became a bed. The opened bow hatch framed uncountable stars. The fall moon would soon outshine the stars. The temperature was perfect for their light sleeping bags, which they zipped together. Making love on top of this soft, quilted expanse, they took joy in each other and the freedom of their isolation. The stars watched but didn't comment. The lake, as satisfied as they, slept with them.

2

The Dive

T anya's hair touched his shoulder, her breath made regular pulses on his arm. Matt lay on his back, snuggled in the double sleeping bag; he slowly moved from under Tanya's leg and worked his way out of the forward berth area. The moon had traveled west, out of sight, and the sun was just thinking about making them another perfect September day.

Matt slipped into his sweat suit and a pair of Top Sider loafers, took a plastic glass from the drying rack and quietly opened and closed the door to the aft deck area. The large ice chest yielded orange juice and a four-day-old Danish. Glass in hand, roll in mouth, he one-handed the ladder to the bridge.

The seats were all wet with dew, Matt dried off the helm seat, put down another damp towel and swiveled the seat to face the island. A mist had formed over the water and extended onto the island. They anchored 100 yards off the northwest corner and just north of some exposed rocks that framed the west side. The GPS on the bridge had stood silent sentinel all night, ready to buzz if they had moved more than a few yards. There wasn't a ripple on the water. Matt had patrolled several times during the night to ensure the boat was secure. The anchor line was short for the depth of the anchorage, but hooking to a massive ship's anchor should have eliminated any problems. Matt still worried while being so close to boat eating granite rocks. Lake Superior can change in a hurry, megalithic rocks and some gravel on the bottom are accompanied by many ships and crewmembers offering mute testimony to the dangers that await the freshwater sailor.

Matt sipped the OJ and nibbled on the dry pastry, the reddish pink sky was changing to yellow as the sun fought with the mist. The optimistic, Pollyanna persona he showed to Tanya on these waters, meant to make up for the water temperature, lack of color, plant and animal activity, buoyancy and a hundred other differences from diving in the Keys, were now on hold. Matt felt a foreboding presence; a heavy sinister feeling seemed to accompany the mist he could look down on from his bridge height. He saw movement on the island—birds maybe. He pulled the binoculars from their ledge under the instrument console, wiped them semidry, and scanned the island. Two figures stood on the island facing him, one raised an arm in greeting. Matt couldn't focus the resteaming lenses well enough to see clearly. He wiped, focused and watched intently as the two figures seemed to dissolve with the increasing sunlight and the dissipating morning mist. Looming, it had to be looming, Matt had seen it all his life on the lake waters—different surface temperatures make the air magnify and transpose images. Trees seem to grow from the water, boats to float above the water, and in the winter, ice shacks miles away seem very close in the morning sun.

Matt felt the boat move and heard the coffee pot make its morning burping sound. He kept watching the now clear island as the lake sucked up the last of the mist. He smelled the coffee before the two stainless steel VacuCraft mugs popped up at the top of the ladder, followed by Tanya coming to the bridge.

"Isn't this beautiful?" She handed him a mug. "I do love sleeping on a boat—with you."

He sipped the coffee and nodded. "Me, too."

"You want eggs for breakfast?"

"Sounds good."

She pointed at the binoculars. "What were you looking at?"

"I saw what looked like people on the island, but now they're gone. It must have been shadows or birds." Matt put down the binoculars and took another sip. "Last night I did some checking, we have two full and two low tanks. I'm glad we did as much snorkeling as we did."

Tanya zipped up her down vest and shivered slightly. "Yeah, snorkeling keeps you above the thermocline in that balmy 65-degree water. Ten more feet and you're swimming in the ice age. And you get more exercise snorkeling."

"True enough." He set the mug down.

Tanya took a long drink and said, "I can't believe how preserved all the wrecks are. We even had a hundred-foot visibility a few times— plus no sharks, barracudas, urchins, man-a-war, stinging coral. And if you're thirsty, you can drink the water."

Matt dried the back bench for Tanya and put another damp towel on the seat and back. "The dive computer and I figure we can make about a fifteen-minute dive at one-fifty and have two decompression stops. We can put the two partial tanks at ten feet for backup at the last stage. This will be our deepest and coldest dive. Are you up to it or would you rather we get better suits and go to mixed air?"

"I can make one cold dive, as long as it's warm when I come up." She grinned. "And if I've someone to get my blood flowing again."

After breakfast Tanya made a cell phone call to her parents who were busy doing the finishing work on Matt and Tanya's new home at the quarry, Matt's 360 acre property where they had worked all summer on a retirement home. They checked in everyday when cell phone availability permitted. Their present location twelve miles from Marquette and within sight of the Huron Mountains gave a good signal. Mr. Vega, her father, wanted to talk to Matt.

"Matt?" began George Vega, retired Air Force Tech Sergeant, retired marina owner, diver, fisherman and now consummate carpenter, mechanic, painter and fixer. "I want you to know I'm enjoying myself, the time I lost figuring how to wire this SIP panel stuff is being made up with not having to find studs—the whole place is a stud. I've never worked on a house made of 4x8 panels with insulation between two plywood sheets. The channels for the wiring take some getting used to. I've done almost all the oak trim on the doors, and all the windows are done."

"You've been busy." Matt replied.

Vega laughed. "That's not all. I'll have the floor trim all cut and stained, waiting for the tile and carpet people. I even bought a table saw. Your radial arm is fine, but I like the table for fine trim work."

"Nothing like having the right tool for the job." Matt quipped.

"Indeed. So, you taking care of my only daughter?"

"She's fine, loves boats, says this water is so cold you don't age in it." Matt thought, *over*.

"Well, you won't get me in it." He paused "Tanya's mother told me to tell you that this front room with its cathedral ceiling would make a great place for a wedding. She's over at your aunt's having coffee with the ladies and learning all about your sordid past."

"Which one? Rose, Hawaina or Pearl? I've got three in driving range."

Vega thought a moment, or was waiting for Matt to end the thought, then continued, "The one that makes the great wheat rolls."

"That's Hawaina. She thinks I'm very nice and won't tell about anything bad. Between the three sisters-in-law are families of seven, nine and eleven children. Everybody in the county is related, or probably should be, Anita will learn a lot from those ladies. Would you keep the phone near you this afternoon? We may need some supplies brought to Marquette."

"Sure," said Vega, "I hate leaving all the good projects I've got going, but I could use some things from Menard's I guess."

"Good, here's your daughter."

Matt gave the cell phone to Tanya and went down to the cabin to check the diving computer, their equipment and the charge on the underwater lamps they would carry. He also rigged two spools of braided nylon string, securing strong plastic snaps to their ends and putting a match to the cut ends to eliminate fraying.

Tanya returned to the cabin. "Sorry. My folks are always talking about a wedding. I thought this would keep them happy for a longer time." She held up a multi-carat, princess-cut engagement ring. "The world will never know this was nearly the runt of the litter and we sold a handful of its shiny brothers and sisters to good homes in Nassau."

Matt nodded. "Cashing out the diamonds, expensing the whole Bahama charter and paying tax on the profit seemed the best way to deal with a gift of diamonds from a gangster."

"And it's nice knowing the money is growing in gold, bonds and the worldwide money market: all offshore, all legal."

Matt took her hand, kissed her fingers and held the ring in the sunlight streaming in from the window. "Well, I only gave it to you so we could smuggle it into the country. But you do wear it well."

"Yes, don't I?"

"Ever wonder how ex-crime boss Mr. Webb, our former captor then benefactor and now cocoa farmer is faring in the Dominican Republic?"

"I showed you the letter from his daughter Carla last week. She just enrolled at the University of Michigan. She thinks everywhere in Michigan is a quick drive and will send us her address in Ann Arbor when she knows it. She'll be on their gymnastics team and plans to study dancing and drama."

"She seemed too nice and thoughtful to pick a school so far from her folks just to exasperate them?"

"I agree, her dad wanted her to go to a European girls' school; it's ill-advised for him to come to the States. However, I have the feeling we will be seeing Carla and the Webbs again. Your diamond reward for saving his life and the lives of his wife and daughter and helping him escape the long arm of federal law is nice, but the best thing he did was bring us together."

"As I recall, it was a blizzard and a plane crash that united us, a much more godlike intervention than that of Mr. Webb," said Matt as he laid out their polypropylene underwear, started the generator, put a pan to heat water on the single hot plate that augmented the electric fry pan. He added, "The sun will be about right in a half hour, we better get cleaned up and ready."

Almost an hour passed before the two divers were emotionally and physically ready for their deep dive. They rode down on the anchor line, put down another small anchor with the two partially full tanks attached, adding hand and foot loops to help the decompression stage.

The weather was perfect, mid-70s, light wind from the southwest; they dove in the lee of the island and assorted rock outcroppings to its west. They could clearly see the anchor chain at over 60 feet. Matt tried to imagine a ship at the end of the chain, but couldn't see anything but gray rock.

They used the warm-water procedure, even though they were warm from the sun, suiting, and activity of getting all their paraphernalia and gauges checked. Matt had a small underwater slate and marker—their only means of communication beyond grunts and gestures.

With a final check that all was secure, turned on, calibrated, set, zipped, and their regulator mouth pieces secured by a band around their necks so their soon-to-be very numbed lips wouldn't lose the link to lifegiving air, in they went.

They swam to the second anchor line, checked all their equipment, did a buddy breathing exercise with each other's extra hose, checked the pressure in their main tanks, then swam to the main anchor line and began their decent.

Conditions were as perfect as could be for a Lake Superior dive. The visibility was better than 80 feet—maybe more as the sun got higher. The water temperature was in the 50s, but they anticipated low 40s at their destination. Their only exposed flesh was a few square inches of cheek and lips. They had both been at greater depths than this dive—the only variables were the temperature of the water and freshwater's 3.5% lower density than seawater. They had both adjusted their weights and equipment for this difference.

Inspecting the old anchor gave them time to acclimate to two atmospheres of pressure. The biggest change in water pressure is in the first 30 feet, standard gas volumes are halved, the next 30 feet only halve that again, so it is relatively only a quarter of the initial change, so subsequent depths cause smaller and smaller relative volume changes. Matt watched his suit thickness decrease as the air pockets in the rubber became three-quarters their surface size. He also knew pressure changed his blood. Nitrogen, which makes up nearly 80% of regular air, dissolved into his blood like bubbles in Coke. If he came up too fast the bubbles would form in his vessels and give him the bends, also the air in his lungs would expand like an overfilled balloon and his lung tissues would rupture and bleed or even burst. Then there was the ever-popular nitrogen narcosis, where the nitrogen under pressure combines with oxygen to form nitrous oxide—laughing gas: getting high under water can make you forget all the deadly forces in play around you as you explore a fascinating but deadly environment.

Tanya was the first to break away from the anchor site and head down the big links of chain. Matt caught up with her and together they swam slowly down the rock face, intermittently touching the chain for luck. Matt could see where he had stopped by the disturbed slime on the chain and rocks. They went another 40 feet and the chain lifted off the rock wall. Holding the chain they moved away from the gray rock wall. At the same time they lost sight of the gray-on-gray wall they saw the chain lead into a ship's hawsehole.

Tanya let out an underwater, "Yippee."

The ship was big, they went above the anchor chain, grasping the thick wooden rail, Matt began wiping the film of slime from a carved white and guilt edged name plate—*Carol K* seemed to glow from the disturbed cloud of algae and the light from Matt's diving light, looking up they could clearly see a pilot house. It was gray, with white trim and glass windows, easy to see from 30 feet. The ship's length rested about 30 degrees from vertical, leaning toward the cliff wall and seemed to be in the 200-foot range from what they could see.

Matt's heart raced, Tanya gave him a high-five with her three-finger glove. Matt showed her his watch and depth gauge. They had 15 minutes. He wrote their go-back time on the slate and circled it twice. Tanya checked her watch and nodded. Matt could see the excitement in her eyes. She had an undiscovered ship to explore. A unique adventure she'd never had in her lifetime of diving experiences. Lake Superior was giving her a wonderful treasure.

They went together to the pilot house near the bow, it could be entered from either side, the starboard side was close to the cliff wall and they decided to enter from port. Matt snapped his line on the rail a few feet from the open door to the pilot house, Tanya did the same. They entered. All the control components of a steam vessel were before them. Their lights made the various brass and glass instruments seem to come to life. They noted the telegraph at ALL STOP, the binnacle and wheel were ready for a captain's orders. Charts were still in their pigeonholed wall cabinet. They explored the whole room. There was a doorway on the far bulkhead.

Tanya headed in, Matt reached her, pulling her back and printed, SLOWLY, on his slate. They both knew a submerged room can be a black, silt filled, disorienting death trap. They checked their lines,

Matt motioned he would stay just inside the doorway, and ushered Tanya in.

Tanya entered the cabin, it had a bunk bed, large desk, more chart holders, and various slotted wooden lockers. Tanya opened a locker—foul weather gear, small boots; child or women's size. She glanced up, their air bubbles were pooling on the ceiling and forward bulkhead, due to the angle of the ship. The growing bubble reflected their lights, the room got brighter. Looking up, both Tanya and Matt spied a box floating lid down at the edge of the air bubble. Matt retrieved it. It was a strong box two and a half feet wide, eight or nine inches high and maybe ten inches deep, fold-out handles at its ends. Tight enough to hold some air, making it float. The sides and top concaved by water pressure.

Matt checked his watch, they had three more minutes. They both searched for booty. Tanya took a parallel rule with writing on it; Matt held the box and felt he would be glad to get it to the surface. Desk drawers were warped shut, and he saw no other easily claimed treasure. There was no ship's log or material on the desk that readily identified the ship.

They left by mutual agreement and swam over the bow, working forward until they came to the name: *Carol K.* Matt wrote it on the tablet.

They went back to the anchor line and slowly followed it upward.

At the anchor they stopped. Matt showed the box to Tanya, pointing out how the sides were becoming square and straight again. Tanya didn't understand. Matt went through his best Marcel Marceau effort, finally drawing on the cluttered slate depictions of the expanding box and how it might leak more. It would certainly pop at the surface if they didn't put it into a waterproof, plastic bag. Matt finally figured Tanya understood he was concerned with the box, but not particularly why. Maybe she thought it would explode.

They went through their decompression stages; Matt motioned for Tanya to stay with the box while he went up and returned with a covering for the box.

With the box tightly double-layered with plastic garbage bags, the two divers bobbed up next to the dive platform.

Tanya pulled out her mouthpiece and effervescently said, "That was the most exciting dive of my life. We have to go back. The ship is huge! How old do you think it is? Let's get that box open."

Matt had tied his nylon string to the old anchor, tying the string to the diving platform. "We'll put a float on this."

They got out of their gear, made some coffee, ate peanut butter sandwiches and called Mr. Vega.

"Dad, we found..." Matt took the phone. "Sir, we need your help getting some diving equipment..."

Matt gave George Vega a list of equipment for mixed-gas diving and cold-water dry suits. Also the weekend number of the dive shop owner whom Matt had known for 20 years, explaining that, if the owner wouldn't rent them the equipment for Tanya, Mr. Vega could use his cards and certification to get the equipment. Matt said he would also call the diving shop and talk to them. They agreed to meet the Vegas at the Marquette marina and go to dinner together.

All the time he was talking, he and Tanya looked at the black garbage bags containing the box from the *Carol K*, curiosity taking over all their emotions.

When the cell phone snapped shut, they both raced for the box. Tearing away the wet plastic bags, placing the black box on a towel on the boat's deck, on their knees, they held hands, pausing to savor the moment.

3

Strong Box

Not only didn't the strong box pop open as they brought it up from over 150 feet, but it was determined to remain closed: WD-40, screwdrivers, a small pry bar, hammering, shaking, Anglo Saxon and Spanish invectives proved useless.

Shaking provided tantalizing proof of mysterious, dry contents inside its black sides. Cleaning the outside provided information: *K&L Shipping, Fort William, OT* in gold leaf that matched the pinstriping around the box's top and edges.

In frustration, Matt and Tanya finally placed the metal box on their galley table and prepared to return to Marquette. They took multiple sightings on the lighthouse and rock points, noting everything and marking the site on the GPS and recording the numerical coordinates. Matt secured a gallon, plastic milk carton to the nylon string tied to the sunken ship's anchor. He tied it three feet under the water, easy to see if you were close but not something likely to lure fishermen motoring by the rocks that sheltered the island on the north and west.

With relief, they were able to free their anchor. Storing the old plow in the forward locker, Matt resolved to replace it at the first opportunity. The calm weather began to change as the wind shifted. The northwest breeze was cooler and brought gray, low clouds that made the rocks look mean, the water choppy and a warm sweater an intelligent addition while at the upper helm.

As Matt carefully motored around the island, he looked back at their former anchorage. It wasn't the sparkling, sunlit cove of yesterday; there was a foreboding feel to the place. Lake Superior never was a very happy body of water to Matt; in minutes it could get nasty, always feeling lonely and vast. Like it didn't need or want people or boats: a big jungle cat fascinating to look at, but that might eat you.

The run to Marquette's larger marina took 40 minutes. As they were tying up, a call came in from George Vega: "I'm having poor luck with the diving equipment, most is rented or signed out for tomorrow, or Monday. I figured you would want it for a few days. They don't have some of the deep diving equipment you should have. What should I do?"

Matt took a deep breath. "Schedule it as soon as we can get it for a couple of days. We can talk about what we still need. Can you pick us up in Marquette?"

"Sure, gas is too high for joy rides, I've got a list of a few things I need from the big city. See you at the downtown dock in two hours."

Tanya came into the cabin, cleaning the parallel rule she had taken from the ship. "It says Captain Jud Livingston, and a 1900 something date, I can't read the last two numbers."

They had thought about staying overnight, using the various local libraries or going back home to share their discovery. George Vega would know how to open the box. Opening the box won over scholarly pursuits. Besides, the Shipwreck Museum at Whitefish Point would probably be a better source of information.

They secured their borrowed boat—*Ferr Play*—made ready the box, their rented diving equipment, and foods that might spoil for transfer to the Yukon when Vega arrived. Matt checked with the harbormaster, who knew the boat well but not Matt. The old Silverton was owned by the Ferr brothers—who inherited it from their father. The whole family was in some aspect of the fur business. The patriarch, Silie Ferr, started the family business by building one of the largest fox and mink farms in the state. When his boys got old enough to run the farm, he branched out into multiple downstate stores. Now two boys, Will and his older brother Sam, ran the farm and the third, Tom, ran their stores. They were too busy to work with the boat for the last several years—but were more than glad to have Matt clean it up, get it into the water and make it available for their use for a few days in the summer. Their cabin on Grand Island had been in their family for 50 years, their home harbor was Munising. Most years, Sam and Will were regulars at Matt's deer camp. Matt had planned to motor back, but their discovery made for a change of plans. They would keep the boat at Marquette for the time being.

George Vega brought the Yukon to the dock area. Materials were loaded. They didn't discuss their find or treasure—ears are everywhere in a marina. After two quick stops for more project materials they were finally heading east toward home.

In the back seat, the box was on Vega's lap, over an old beach towel. After 20 minutes of Matt at the wheel, and George scrutinizing, tapping, scraping and shaking the box, Mr. Vega gave his opinion, "There is a key hole here—totally filled in with crap, the piano hinge is solid rust, the top metal is a thinner tin, we need my 90-degree grinder with a carbide disk."

Matt put on the cruise control as they hit open road on Highway 28. "You know we're law breakers. We removed material from a wreck, we haven't reported our discovery. I don't know all the salvage laws— except the government wants to be involved with everything."

Tanya turned to her dad from her front passenger seat. "You knew Mel Fisher who discovered all kinds of treasure?"

"Yes, and he spent years in courtrooms and fortunes on lawyers. Let's just keep our mouths shut, be good detectives and understand our options."

They stopped at the Munising harbor, returned their tanks and regulators, reviewed the equipment they would need to rent, had lunch at the Dog Patch restaurant and headed east again to the quarry.

An hour later, back in the new garage at the quarry, Mrs. Vega joined the eager threesome as George Vega finished cutting the top off the box. Grinding dust and the smell of hot metal formed a cloud around the expectant group as Vega's leather-gloved hands pried back the lid.

The black box opened to expose a white interior. The similarity to a water moccasin occurred to Matt and George Vega, who glanced at each other, but didn't mention anything about snakes to the ladies.

Inside were two ledgers, leather edged, greenish corduroy with a patina of white and green mold, several folders with official seals and fancy printed lettering, a small box of pistol shells that came apart at the touch of Vega's gloved finger—scattering green-coated cartridges— and finally an empty leather pistol holster.

"Let's get these into separate plastic bags," suggested George Vega. "We can work on the mold and reduce their exposure to air."

In minutes, large and small ziplock bags protected each of the box's contents, all arranged on a well-lighted workbench. All four eager treasure hunters were busy over individual bags—each wearing rubber gloves of various types.

Tanya broke the silence. "Har mates, nary a doubloon or a treasure map to be had, looks like these were just plain shipping folks."

Matt held the bag containing the unglued box and loose shells, "This is 7.65 mm ammo, German, and it's half full." He next picked up the larger ziplock holding the holster. "Military, small, round barreled, semi-automatic. From the snug fit of this holster and the shell size we won't have any trouble finding out what used to be in this."

The Vegas worked together on the ship's papers. George finally spoke. "We need to photograph all these pages, and get the material back into bags. We give this mold some air and moisture and it will destroy the paper. I'll get my new Canon digital, and we can go through the whole lot."

For the next two hours they photographed every page of their discovery. They got into a productive rhythm. Matt and Tanya held each page as flat as possible with a plastic ruler and a couple of long bladed chisels from Vega's cornucopia of tools. George Vega set up a tripod, secured his Canon XTi with its Sigma 18-200 lens and added a florescent-light filter. "I'll use a fresh four-gigabit flashcard—it will hold over seven hundred of the high-resolution pictures."

They set up a backboard at an angle convenient for the camera, about 45 degrees from the work bench. Mrs. Vega took notes as names and dates were learned. Very little extraneous discussion took place.

The first ledger went quickly, the second had many pages stuck together. They carefully separated each page, finding to their relief that the latter half of the ledger was empty of writing. The ship's papers were in good condition, opening to show all their information, highlighted with fold lines that showed mold stains.

Photographing each page twice, they checked for quality on the camera's large display every few pages. Allowing the camera's flash to function gave the best results. The autofocus system provided excellent clarity. Twice they stopped for some coffee and cookies, their backs and fingers cramped from working over bench and camera.

They finished.

After some discussion it was decided to leave the bags on the work bench. The refrigerator or freezer had been alternate choices. The camera display was again scrutinized for image quality. The thumbnail displays of the myriad of pictures showed their work was perfectly captured. The notes and camera were taken to the main dining area in the cathedral-ceilinged great room. The sun was setting, and the room filled with the warm colors of wood paneling and the Upper Peninsula September sunset.

Scattered among plates of leftover food, Anita Vega's notes were being reviewed by everyone. Matt finally took a blank page of copy paper and began to summarize:

```
The ship is the Carol K.
Built in 1922. 150x35x12, 500 gt.
Officers and Crew: 12-14.
Owned by K&L Coal & Shipping out of Fort
    William—that's now Thunder Bay.
Cargo: mining equipment and passengers,
Last port noted as Detroit & bound for
    Houghton.
Last date entered: 1933.
```

George Vega added, "It's interesting what's not there: no ship's log, no Master's papers, no itemized bills of lading, and passengers noted without names being listed."

Matt made a note of Vega's comments on his paper. Stacking all the pages together neatly, placing his sheet on top, he rose from the table. "Let's go take a walk down to the beaver pond, get some fresh air in our lungs. We can attack this mystery tomorrow and see if the *Carol K* still has an owner."

4

House Life

The next three days were divided between working on the house, researching the ship and preparing for another dive.

George Vega showed his skills as a finishing carpenter, mitering and installing all the oak trim around doorways, windows and floors. He also supervised the tile work and, finally, the carpet layers. His wife stained and sealed the expensive oak trim as the pieces were cut. They fell into a comfortable rhythm as room after room was completed by their teamwork.

Tanya visited the Great Lakes Shipwreck Museum at Whitefish Point.

Matt spent his time working at a neighbor's computer and arranging rental diving equipment for the next week. Mr. Vega insisted on shipping up some extra tanks, mixed-gas dive computers and several special items he knew were available in his now-sold dive shop. He said cost was no object when the safety of his daughter was concerned.

They shared their progress at each evening meal.

"Here's to the master carpenter and his mate," toasted Matt. "You've got a third career if you want it."

George Vega clinked his beer bottle to the others' wine glasses. "Thirty years in the Air Force and then running a dive and charter business was work, this is pure pleasure. New saws and work benches that hold the trim are worth every penny they cost, nail guns and cordless tools make the work easy. There was a time you needed to drill each nail hole, nail and then countersink the nail. Now, it's one pull of a trigger—and you're done."

He took a long drink of beer before asking, "What did you learn about the ship?"

Matt replied, "It took some work to find her listing. There were hundreds of ships lost in Lake Superior, most undiscovered. Knowing she came from Fort William was a big help as well as the 1933 last date on her papers. She was insured, her owners are still listed in the Thunder Bay business directory. K&L has become Livingston Brothers. They're still in business, and judging by their many phone numbers and addresses, they are a big outfit. The ship is listed as, 'Lost in storm,' which is interesting—because the anchor is out. I couldn't get much more without going to the insurance company directly, and they are Canadian. There was a hearing by the Canadian Department of Transport in 1934 about the sinking—but no information on the computer."

He turned to Tanya. "How did Whitefish Point go?"

Tanya brought out a small note pad. "I didn't do very well, and almost got in trouble. Going in person was a mistake. It's hard to explain your interest without revealing you found a sunken ship. We are in deep doo-doo already for removing anything from a wreck. Divers have faced fines and lost all their equipment for what we've already done. It seems there is no end to the greed and control that governments want over anything that might make them a buck—all in the name of conserving our history. The law of salvage and the good old rules of finders-keepers are all tied up with state, federal and international laws. Even the UN wants to get into the act. We need to contact the original owners.

"I did learn a little about preserving paper, metal and wood artifacts. We're fine with some anti-mold spray, plastic bags and WD-40 on the box." She leaned forward. "When can we dive on her again?"

Matt checked papers the from the Munising Dive Center. "We have four days of rental equipment late next week—weather willing, we should be able to do some good exploring. I have extra equipment for your dad as an emergency backup, and his order from Florida should be here in three or four days."

"I don't think George should do any real deep diving anymore," said Anita Vega. "Besides, it's so cold. The work on the house needs his time, it's almost done. We should be planning a house warming party for you two."

Tanya and Matt looked at each other—Anita was really saying they should be planning their wedding, a theme that she constantly interjected into most conversations.

Matt began clearing the dishes, enjoying the fact that at last they were eating at the table in the great room and using a finished kitchen, and the house was becoming useable after months of the camping feeling of improvised tables and unfinished cupboards and the general dust and clutter of building. "Why don't Tanya and I do the dishes and you two have a walk. September in these woods is the nicest time of the year—no bugs, poplars and maples turning color, perfect temperature and raspberries along the paths."

Tanya and Matt worked at the sink and counter, watching the Vegas walk down the road. There was space for a dish washer, but it was filled with unpacked boxes of kitchen utensils, a large waste basket and various bottles and cleaning supplies that had not yet found a storage area.

"Mother's a one track record about a wedding," said Tanya as she put washed and rinsed plates on the drying rack.

Matt touched a warm dry plate with the towel and placed it in the cupboard. "I think we've come a long way in less than a year."

Tanya, closing the cupboard door, agreeing, "Yes, my folks are finally retired, their home on the Keys is perfect and paid for, they have millions in CD's and investments, they don't have to worry about drug running, gangsters and what trouble their only daughter always seems to be getting into."

Matt put away the dried silverware, "We really have the best of all worlds—this place in the summer, fall and for some snow fun; the Keys in the winter and spring. This is a fine house to start and share a new life. Financially, we're sound. The land contract I took on my Gladstone home more than pays for this house's mortgage, and my retirement and our investments are more than most families live on."

Tanya, wiping the aluminum sink dry and shiny, turning off the overhead kitchen light, leaving the under-counter lighting on for her folks, led Matt into the great room, added, "It would be nice if we could make some money off the ship we found, but so far all we can find are laws and complications that say what we can't do."

They built a fire in the central fireplace, warming the great room that looked out over the clearing and woods to the northwest. The hearth also was shared by the master bedroom on the other side of the floor-to-ceiling stone wall. The house had in-floor heating for use when the weather got colder or when a thermostat and propane would keep it warm without the daily chore of wood burning.

Matt closed the glass fireplace doors, felt the heat coming from the side heatolater slits pushed by nearly silent fans. "Tomorrow, we make some calls to Canada and see if we can spark some interest in the wreck of the *Carol K*. Hopefully, we can make another dive before any more people get interested."

▷▷▷▷

They made cocoa in a two-quart pan, poured two mugs for themselves and left the rest on warm for the Vegas. They took two throw pillows from the couch and made themselves comfortable on the new rug before the fireplace.

Tanya cuddled inside Matt's arms, holding her mug of cocoa with both hands. She leaned back, putting her head against Matt's neck. "I've never been so happy. My whole life I've felt I wanted love and security, and the harder I tried to find them, the worse my life became. My folks did everything they could, but they had problems. Living on air bases—everything was temporary. When dad retired we thought the marina was the answer for stability and roots—but dad got mixed up with drug trafficking—seduced by the money he made by just turning his head from what his charters were doing."

Matt kissed her forehead, "Yeah, he told me all about how he got involved, it's so easy to get on a slippery slope, easy money for just not asking questions or for just keeping his mouth shut, finally shirking his responsibility as a captain and as an honest citizen for a lot of easy money."

Tanya continued, "When Webb got in the picture and he ended up owning dad and later me; mom nearly had a nervous breakdown. Even now, if you say Webb's name she leaves the room. Living here, she is like I remember her when I was a little girl. I heard her on the cell phone talking with one of her Miami girlfriends; they go back to pre-Castro Cuba. Mom was a real Cuban beauty in the wild, expatriate world of Miami in the early '60s. Let me show you what she looked like."

Tanya went upstairs to her folks' room and returned; carrying a small photo album—old and scuffed. Inside were mostly black and white pictures sharing some space with fading color pictures and a few Polaroids, all held in place by black corner mounts.

Matt looked at pictures of happy smiling beautiful, young people, having fun at parties, on boats, beaches and at restaurants. Tanya pointed out her mother. Anita was truly a showstopper, every bit as beautiful as her daughter and maybe even a little more striking—having that indefinable balance of cheek, chin and eyes that brought your focus to her in a group of beautiful girls.

Tanya pointed out several pictures, "Here she is with dad, before they were married—he's in uniform. All the Cuban expatriates were very patriotic, loving their new country with its freedom and opportunities."

Matt noticed a beach scene in color, Anita wore a two piece checkered suit, lots of cleavage. The photo had a corner cut off, and had to be secured with now-yellowed and curled Scotch tape. A very thick, muscular man's body remained in the picture. Even with his head snipped off, Matt thought to himself how it resembled a young Webb. Matt had spent a week on a yacht with Webb; he had seen the formidable frame many times.

Tanya turned the pages, showing more pictures of Anita and George Vega, many with the same set of couples at various locations.

Pointing to a particular picture of several couples, Tanya said, "Her girlfriends seem to have all married doctors and real-estate speculators and are all rich with tons of spoiled kids and grandkids. Most of them have yachts and a second home is Colorado, the Ozarks or Maine. Now mom has her summer getaway home, her daughter with a good man and her husband financially well off."

Matt kissed her hair, "What about grandkids?"

Tanya closed the album, "Mom will focus on that after a wedding. Your grownup son will count, but I bet you'll probably get more oyster and conk dishes than you can ever imagine."

"Sounds good to me," said Matt as he nibbled on Tanya's ear lobe. Slowly working his way to her neck, lost in her hair and yielding warmth. Just as his thoughts and body were becoming very focused on Tanya's charms, he smelled cocoa and opened his eyes to see a sauce pan with an inch of steaming, brown liquid.

"Want to finish this up," intruded George Vega, emptying the last of the cocoa equally into Tanya's and Matt's cups. He continued to the couch across from the fireplace. "I've been thinking about your dive. Mixed gas and over 100 feet isn't for rookies. When the tanks, computers and gauges arrive, I'll work with your friend in Munising to make sure you have what you need. In the meantime, we need to get to the Canadian owners. We've got about a week before we will be ready anyway. I'll have the wood work done and be glad for another project."

Tanya and Matt snapped back from their romantic cuddle and got their minds on the sunken ship, while their bodies quickly returned to the world of parental scrutiny.

Matt reluctantly left the pillow nest and the beauty of the dying fire to retrieve some papers from the kitchen table. "I have the owners' names—the two brothers of Livingston Brothers are alive and still living in Thunder Bay. They are all over the internet—three pages just on Google. Their family is woven into the area's history. The father, Captain Jud of the parallel rule, became sole owner when the K of K&L, his very rich wife, died. As I follow the articles on the web, Ol' Jud started K&L shipping with a few old ships and his to be wife's family bankroll—he bought more ships and rail businesses during the early '30s by smart and hard work, and marrying the boss's only daughter. He ended up one of the richest men in Canada. They had two sons before his wife's death in 1933. Her obituary states she was formally Carol Kaiser and she died in the sinking of the ship her father named after her. I've got their main office number and will contact them tomorrow. They seem to own or have a part of every major business in our northern neighbor—shipping, power, mining, wood products to name just four listed in their corporate directory." Matt passed his notes to George Vega. "I think we'll hit the hay early so I can get right on it tomorrow."

Matt escorted Tanya to the master bedroom, glancing at George Vega who was pretending to study the papers, while watching them leave. Vega moved to the large picture window where he chuckled. Matt knew he had no difficulty reading the pages from the light of the just setting sun, Vega glanced at Matt—with a glint in his eyes that said, "Early to bed—indeed."

5

Can You Hear Me?

Matt spent the morning using his cell phone to call Canada. He cut his way through the corporate jungle surrounding the Livingston Brothers. Finally directed to a person called Jennifer, an executive assistant in the Corporation's HQ, who would be glad to help.

"Mr. Hunter," Jennifer spoke slowly, as to a child, "Carol Kaiser was the mother of the Livingston Brothers. I understand you have information about her?"

"Yes, Jennifer, except it is about THE *Carol K*, a ship, not Carol K. the woman," Matt replied, while he heard three beeps on his cell phone, indicating low battery. The phone charger was unavailable in the SUV, being used by George Vega with trailer in tow getting landscape shrubs. Matt couldn't find the plug-in charger usually kept on the kitchen counter. Rummaging through all the kitchen drawers proved futile, running to the master bedroom—another hiding place of the charger—broke the connection. He didn't have Jennifer's extension or last name. After finding the charger and plugging in the cell phone in the garage with the double doors open—Matt had two signal bars and a charging battery. Eleven more minutes and three phone transfers later, Jennifer was back.

"Can you hear me now?" asked Matt.

"Yes, Mr. Hunter, however, we own no ships named the *Carol K.*"

"Jennifer, can you pass information to the Livingston Brothers, or do they have voice mail?"

"Yes, Mr. Hunter—what is the message? I can get it to them if it is important," Jennifer explained in neutral tones.

"I guess this is the best I can do. Tell them I know the location of the ship, *Carol K*, that sank in 1933." Matt concluded by getting her direct number and giving her his cell phone number.

Just as Matt was putting the cell phone back on the garage work bench to finish its charge, George Vega returned with the load of shrubs and ground cover plants. George was happy to show Matt the great buys during the fall clearance sales. They distributed the plants along the driveway and lower patio, awaiting final approval from the ladies. On the last trip to the trailer Matt heard his cell phone's tune. Answering the phone, Matt noted he had missed two previous calls while in the front of the house.

Matt said hello, but before he could give his name, an anxious male voice broke in, "This is Jared Livingston, what do you know about the *Carol K*?"

The line went quiet, Matt wasn't sure the connection was still made, so, partially in jest, he said, "Can you hear me now?"

"Yes, answer my question!" came the reply, without a please or hint of humor.

"I saw the name, *Carol K*, on the bow of a sunken ship. We traced its ownership to you," Matt replied, keeping it as short and cold as the question, not mentioning any artifacts retrieved.

"Who knows about this discovery?" the cold voice grilled.

Matt replied, "We're having a billboard painted as we speak and the TV crew will be here anytime soon …." Matt thought, *shove that up your tight ass.*

"I'm used to having my questions answered, Mr. Hunter." Livingston said.

"I'm used to civil people and friendly conversations—want to start over?"

"When can we meet and talk about your discovery?" Livingston replied, barely a few degrees more friendly.

Matt felt a primitive fear and mistrust of this person with whom he only had a brief and tenuous electrical contact. He thought for a moment. "How about meeting in Marquette, Michigan at the visitors' center south of town on highway 41. You can't miss it—it's a nice log cabin with a parking lot in front. You name the time." Matt thought about the airport as a convenient meeting place for the Canadian—but felt like screwing with him.

"Where do you live, could we meet there?"

"I think the visitors' center will be fine. And don't worry; we'll keep this a secret. Call me with a time." Matt almost asked for a few hours of warning—but checked himself in time—he didn't want to give Livingston clues to his new home.

"Tomorrow at noon." Came the near instant reply.

"Fine. See you there. How do I recognize you?"

"My brother and I will be obvious. We are tall, wearing suits. There will be people with us. What do you look like?"

"I'm average, driving a green minivan." Matt thought the rental minivan of the Vega's would be more anonymous than his Yukon with his license plate and school stickers. The need for secrecy was primal and not intellectual—Matt went with his instincts.

"We will meet tomorrow. Thank you Mr. Hunter."

Click.

George Vega heard the last parts of the conversation. He read the firm jaw and cold tones of his maybe soon-to-be son-in-law. "Problem? I've heard friendlier phone conversations with the IRS audit folks."

Matt looked thoughtfully at the cell phone. "We need to huddle up and talk this out. The phone call was all strained and wrong. This Livingston is powerful, decisive and cold. I wish we knew more about the ship and the Livingstons. I didn't remember anything personal from the web research: no pictures or family history, just buying and selling businesses, opening a new plywood plant and closing several older ones, legal controversies over railroad issues—which I didn't read. If their mother died in 1933—they must be at least mid or late 70s. He didn't sound that old."

"Well, we'll learn a lot tomorrow at noon," said Vega. "Why are we meeting in town and not at the airport?"

"Just being mean. I should call them back and agree to an airport meeting. It would save time and trouble. They probably have a private plane. Crossing Lake Superior on their own timetable didn't seem to be a problem for them. I'll call Jennifer, change the meeting place and maybe find more info on the brothers Livingston."

Matt looked up and punched in Jennifer's number. The phone rang five times, picked up by a company operator, informing Matt that Jennifer was not available and had no prospects of being available in his lifetime. Matt's attempt to contact either of the Livingstons was rebuffed through a variety of corporate kiss-off procedures. Frustrated, Matt closed the cell phone.

"Shit, so much for our friendly neighbors to the north…"

The minivan honked and slid into the garage.

Tanya moved to the opening back hatch, gathering handfuls of plastic bags of groceries and other shopping booty. "We are going to have a house warming. Lunched with your aunts—they have it all thought out. Pig roast and beer—our contribution, everyone else brings a dish to pass—hors d'oeuvres, salads, beans, desserts. We'll have music, dancing and my mother will make some Cuban dishes and Dad can make some rum drinks. We can get free folding chairs from the town hall—if we invite the township supervisor.

Tanya paused for a quick breath and a peck on Matt's cheek as she passed him on the way to the kitchen. "You have a cousin that has a pickup truck with a portable music system…goes to all the parties and there is an old man that plays the accordion while his wife plays the drums and works a rhythm system…I was assured they do a great garage dance…I can learn to polka."

Matt and George stood amazed at Tanya's ability to enthusiastically impart a whole morning's activities and complex future plans while moving sacks of groceries and only taking three breaths.

Matt noted how quietly happy Tanya's mother seemed, probably grateful for the domestic, if not religious, recognition of their relationship.

Matt and George gathered more bags and followed their women into the kitchen.

As the kitchen counters filled with plastic bags, Matt asked, "When will we have this party?"

"Next Saturday…if that's OK with you."

Matt nodded as he and George helped the women unbag and put away the bounty of the morning's shopping. Lunch, the next order of business, put them at the table, before them were sandwiches and a pasta salad fresh from the supermarket deli. Matt updated them on the Livingston situation, his concerns about their lack of a plan, presenting the subject for their opinions.

Tanya opened, "Let's hear what they have to say before we get defensive. Some top executives just naturally are ill-mannered. What do you plan to say to them? Are we going to show them what we found?"

Matt replied, "I think the parallel rule and a photograph of the strongbox showing the K&L logo should prove we found the ship. We can print four-by-six-inch pictures here or go in early and make an eight-by-ten at Wal-Mart.

"I know it doesn't sound so bad when I tell it, but I wish you could have heard Livingston's voice and attitude. I've got a former student that's a detective on the Marquette Police Department—but he'd want to know why we are meeting. I really don't want to bring any more relatives into this situation either. So I guess we just meet and see where it leads."

"Matt," broke in Tanya, "what about the house warming?"

"Fine with me, if your folks are for it, sounds like it's a done deal," Matt concluded that Tanya had the party as a higher priority than a treasure ship and meetings with billionaires. He noted George Vega just ate his lunch quietly, not fighting the flow of Tanya's enthusiasm or choice of table talk.

"Mom's all for it and Dad loves a party. Oh, this was in today's mail." Tanya passed a letter across the table. "It's a letter from Carla Webb—with her Ann Arbor address. She says she loves the school, all her instructors and the drama group. She loves the football weekends. She says her dad and mom will be staying at their place on Manitoulin Island in October for the color—she will be flying up there for a weekend—would we be interested in meeting her?"

Tanya's mother got up from the table and took her food into the front room; her way of dealing with the slightest mention of Webb or his family. She had voiced her opinion many times that Webb only brought trouble. George Vega just looked discouraged and concentrated on his salad.

Taking a swig of beer to clear his throat and let some time pass to clear the atmosphere, Matt answered, "Other than almost getting us arrested, imprisoned, and nearly killed several times I don't see any reason to not visit him. How many Russian crime bosses do we know? How many people do we know that give away a handful of diamonds as a thank you? I'll go along with any plans you make, Carla needs a big sister and Webb is a fascinating guy."

Anita Vega returned to the kitchen, having heard Matt. She noisily put her remaining lunch down the disposal—letting it run much longer than needed. Turning to the three at the table, hands on her hips, she started to say something but turned and went outside.

George Vega put down his fork. "Webb caused us lots of misery and heart break, we ended up with more money then we ever expected, but still, he's a dangerous person and I don't want to be around him ever again." He stood up. "If you go, be very careful—he draws trouble like dead fish draw flies."

He shrugged and joined his wife outside.

Matt and Tanya cleaned up the lunch dishes; Tanya finally wanting to talk about the Livingston plans.

6

Meet the Livingstons

Matt drove the minivan into the Marquette Visitor's Center parking lot at exactly 12:00. There were four other cars in the parking lot: two in front of the log building with Illinois plates and two at the side that looked like nondescript rentals. As Matt pulled next to the plain sedans, their doors began opening, three men came out of the nearest car, the driver and front passenger of the other vehicle moved to rear doors as Matt, Tanya and George vacated the van. Before anyone said a word the back doors of the sedan opened, and the Livingston brothers appeared.

Tall, thin, in dark suits with white shirts that matched their hair, they came around their car, walking to Matt.

The nearest brother, balding with short hair and a semblance of a smile, began, "You are Mr. Hunter?"

"Yes," Matt replied cautiously. "Call me Matt, and this is Tanya and her father George Vega."

No handshakes were offered or taken.

"I am Jud Livingston and this is my brother Jared." No notice or mention made of the others in their retinue who waited out of ear shot. "We are very interested in your news about the *Carol K*. Do you have some proof of your discovery?"

Matt opened the back of the minivan, the shade of the raised rear hatch formed their meeting area. "Here is a parallel rule we found in the room off the bridge, and here are pictures of a box we found. The name and company are very clear."

Matt passed the materials to the brothers. He noticed they didn't wear glasses and handled the materials with care, even some reverence. The brothers moved into the sunlight, two paces from the van. They studiously looked at the pictures and rule for over a minute. Then, looking at each other in silent agreement, they returned to Matt.

Jud reached into his suit, producing a single, folded sheet of paper. His brother also took an envelope from his suit-coat pocket. Jud unfolded the paper and handed it to Matt, explaining, "This is a nondisclosure agreement, it simply prohibits you and anyone listed from disclosing, except to my brother and me, any information or location of the *Carol K*. And for your knowledge and silence we will pay you $10,000 now and 10 percent of any salvage value realized from the wreck."

He handed the document to Matt and took the fat envelope from his brother, opening it so Matt could see it was full of $100 U.S. bills. "The laws of salvage are very complex, most of the time the persons who actually find the wreck get nothing but the thrill of discovery. Governments, bureaucrats, lawyers and plundering thieves are the only ones that make a dime any more. The *Carol K* is part of our family history, we want it respected and not exploited, and we are willing to pay you for your trouble and for keeping a confidence."

"Who else knows about your find?" added Jared, in the same cold voice Matt had heard over the phone. Jared seemed the older brother, but had more and longer hair. Both brothers were whip thin and moved like men much younger than their ages.

Matt showed the paper to Tanya, George Vega looking over her shoulder. While they read the paper, Matt said, "Just the three of us and Mrs. Vega know about the ship, only Tanya and I know the location."

*And that money would pay for all the carpeting, window coverings and new furniture...*thought Matt.

Jud went on, "If you agree with this we can have a dive boat available yet this season. We have many business groups, one includes a salvage firm."

Matt held the paper for Tanya and George to finish reading, looked at Jud and half listened as Jud went on about Livingston activities involving their fleet of ships, their salvage works, the diving boats they controlled. He noticed the effort Jud was expending to be friendly and chatty. Brother Jared just stood there like a pallbearer.

Matt was amazed at their youthful appearance. He knew they must be over 70—but they looked 10 to 15 years younger. Jud seemed the younger and more animated brother. Jared just continued to study the assemblage like they were so many specimens. Their suits were summer wool, perfectly tailored, shoes thin-soled, cordovan wingtips and their silk ties never saw a sale sign. The temperature was in the high 70s, no wind off the lake only a hundred yards away; Matt was warm in a short-sleeved polo shirt—the Livingston Brothers didn't seem to sweat. They had the look of the very, very rich and powerful.

"We need to talk before we can accept your terms." said Matt. "Would you like to have lunch while we chat? There are several good restaurants in Marquette."

Jared spoke, pushing a little warmth into his voice, "We eat a special diet and have lunch available on our helicopter at the airport. You are welcome to join us. We can get to know each other better and hopefully conclude our business. We..."

George Vega uncharacteristically interrupted, the mention of a helicopter sparking his interest, "What kind of craft do you have? I was in the air force most of my life, responsible for many types of prop and rotary machines."

"It is a new Eurocopter Super Puma—less than 100 hours on it, our pilots would be very happy to show it to you." Jud added, "Let's meet at the airport—we have the only large helicopter there, we're parked among the private planes, and you can talk among yourselves as you drive."

Matt and the Livingstons agreed to lunch in the Livingston helicopter. They all returned to their vehicles and headed south toward the Marquette county airport.

▷▷▷▷

In their van, Matt, Tanya and George studied the paper Jud had given them.

"I don't see anything wrong with this," said Tanya. "We can't take anything from the wreck or even hope to get any fame without years of government complexity. The money comes at a good time."

George added, "Ten thousand dollars is chump change to these men—that helicopter cost millions and hundreds of thousands a year in upkeep. We could hold out for more, or just not agree and see what they do."

Matt suggested, "Let's have lunch with them, tell them we're afraid of legal papers and see what they do. If they get mean, we stonewall them. If they up the ante, we take it and I can pay you back for all the carpentry equipment you bought and the diving equipment you're shipping up. Also, I'd almost like to see what's on the ship before we give away any rights—however tenuous."

Tanya closed the discussion, "Ok, no agreement at first, or if they get mean. If they stay nice, we take an improved second offer, sign the agreement. Oh, doesn't Mom need to sign it, too? How do we do that?"

Matt spoke, "I think up-front money and a percentage of futures is fair from what I've been reading of salvage laws and shipwreck discovery. We'll get at least one more dive on the ship to see if there is any real value aboard. Anyway, this whole experience is certainly interesting and if we can make it profitable so much the better."

They rode in silence for the next ten minutes, coming to the entrance of the huge former SAC air base. They found the private-plane area and the large, cream and blue, twin-turbine helicopter. They drove through a guardless gate and parked near the impressive machine.

7

Eating Their Lunch

The large helicopter made an impressive backdrop for the informal gathering of the Livingston brothers and their minions. As Matt, Tanya and her father approached, the group divided into three sections: four men went to the cars, the Livingstons waited near the opened door of the cream-colored machine, and a man and a small oriental woman stood a few feet away.

Jud stepped forward and made the introductions. "Mr. Vega, this is our pilot, who is also an engineer and will be very happy to show you our Super Puma—we hired him away from the Eurocopter plant in Fort Erie, Ontario. You are welcome to join us for lunch after your tour. And this is our chef and dietitian Lolan, who will have lunch prepared in just a few minutes."

Matt noticed the pilot was introduced without a name, unlike the chef. Perhaps the brothers didn't care enough about their underlings to learn their names if they weren't in daily contact.

The pilot took George into the cockpit; Matt and Tanya were ushered into the luxurious confines of the corporate helicopter. Carpet, leather and chrome all beautifully arranged for the comfort of six with a small kitchen/bar/office at the far end. The only detraction from the ambiance was the fact that it had headroom fit only for a Hobbit. The less than five-foot-high space forced everyone to seek a chair to comfortably fit into the six-foot-wide cabin. The brothers took chairs on both sides of Matt and Tanya. A bench seat was left open for the return of George.

"This is the same model helicopter used by the Emperor of Japan," said Jud. "The Eurocopter has over 30 percent of the market worldwide and their smaller models have 65 percent of the Canadian market, more than Bell and Sikorsky combined. We worked with our government to get the plant located in Canada—we need the jobs and the technology that a domestic helicopter industry brings us."

Matt though, *Jud must get a commission on these birds.*

As Matt felt the first slash of a nationalistic duel, the aroma of cooking filled the cabin. Lolan was kneeling in front of what looked liked an electric wok. There was a built-in refrigerator and microwave in the far, aft bulkhead.

Jared interrupted Matt's inspection. "Have you decided to accept our nondisclosure agreement?"

"We are concerned with a few areas," Matt answered. "What if someone other than us gives the location or information about the *Carol K*? The secretary I talked to originally knows there is a ship that got your attention. Also, why do you insist on such a total gag order?"

Jud leaned forward in his chair, extended then wrung his long thin fingers, finally opening his hands as a sign of surrender to his seated guests. "We will guarantee no leaks from our side, the secretary has been transferred and will be kept too busy and happy to think about one telephone call. Your second question is much more complex." He took a deep breath and sat back in his seat, legs apart, posture open— giving all the signs of an honest disclosure about to be uttered. "Our mother was on that ship. Her death gave all the considerable wealth of her inheritance to our father. It was 1933, times were very hard, many people—mostly encouraged by her relatives the Kaisers—were suspicious of the sinking, the insurance claims and the events that surrounded the transfer of corporate power to the Livingstons—who at that time owned struggling shipping and rail interests. We do not want to rekindle a flame between our relatives that hasn't burned for over sixty years. Publicity and speculation will also hurt or delay many business interests now at delicate stages."

Jared broke in, "If you think there is treasure on the ship you are totally mistaken. Ten thousand dollars is more than fair for your silence, you can have 50 percent of the salvage value if you want—personally, I believe it will be 50 percent of nothing." He made a big zero out of his bony hands, staring at Tanya and Matt through the space.

That might have been almost funny or cute by anyone else, but Jared looking at you through his fingers had all the warmth of a zeroing-in sniper sight, thought Matt.

Jud and Jared exchanged glances, then Jared spoke, "We can give you the cash you were shown and an additional check for 5000 U.S. dollars, 50 percent of any salvage value after expenses and an additional $5000 when we locate the ship. That's doubling our initial offer."

Matt looked at Tanya for a signal of her acceptance.

The moment was broken by Lolan asking if she could serve the lunch. Tanya said not to wait for her father, who could talk engines for hours. Jared nodded approval, and Lolan quickly brought cork-bottomed, oblong china plates to Tanya and Matt, each with a cup, silverware and cloth napkin nestled in divided areas of the plate.

"We are having a stir fry with chilled green tea." reported Jud. "Our diet is very important to us. Through very careful nutrition we have improved our health a great deal."

"Are you vegetarians?" asked Tanya, as she waited for the Livingstons to be served.

Jud continued, "No, but we eat very little red meat, and then it is very lean. Lolan has prepared a lunch of several nutritious vegetables, flax seeds, nuts, soy fiber and, for meat pieces, I believe we are having ostrich—an excellent lean meat."

Matt swallowed a fork full. *It tastes like chicken, or maybe somewhere between a swan and an eagle! These are weird buckaroos, eating ostrich in a leather Hobbit hole.*

After eating for several minutes, Jared spoke conversationally, versus his usual CEO style, "Where are you from, Tanya? I detect a slight Spanish accent."

"I come from Florida, but my parents came from Cuba. We speak Spanish at home and I have been with the Cuban community and with Cuban relatives all my life.

"I understand you own many businesses," Tanya concluded by gesturing right and left toward the brothers.

Jared replied, still in pleasant, if slightly condescending, tones, "Our father ran the company from the thirties through the sixties. He took us from a small shipping and rail company to top positions in coal, plywood, rail and trucking. Jud and I began working in various divisions during and after our college days. Father retired in 1968 and died two years later. We now work through a board of directors, which we chair equally."

Jud handed Tanya a glossy company brochure—almost a magazine—and continued the lecture, "Our company is privately held and we are the majority partners; employing over 50,000 workers, grossing many billion Canadian dollars annually. Right now energy is our largest area of interest—from oil shale to nuclear plants. Frankly, the politics involved with national contracts are the main reason we are dealing with you directly. This would be a very inopportune time for an unfortunate ship sinking to become a feeding frenzy for our ever vigilant fourth estate. We wish to very quietly show the respect due the *Carol K* and let her join the pages of history. We can double the amount we have brought in cash if you would take our check."

Detecting an actual grin from Jared, Matt thought, *the old fart is flirting with Tanya!* He said, "With all the national and international financial troubles, how are your Canadian banks doing these days?"

Jud, the younger, friendlier brother answered, and the conversation became like a tennis match with Jud on one side and Jared on the other side of Matt and Tanya—the brothers finished each other's sentences and quickly pointed out an avalanche of facts about the Canadian banking system. Matt didn't follow all the points shooting by him, but quickly understood that the Canadian banking system was continually the healthiest in the world—as ranked by the World Economic Forum. The Canadians used common sense and good regulations regarding their leveraging system. They followed good rules of banking and the Canadian tax codes didn't provide massive incentives for overconsumption—mortgage interest wasn't deductable. The government had had more than a decade of budget surpluses and their national pension plan is very solid and funded.

Jud then pointed out that the Canadian health-care system statistically put the U.S. to shame, its lower cost being a major reason for many car companies moving to Ontario and not Michigan in the '80s and '90s.

Matt knew he was out of his league in a financial argument with these titans of industry, he didn't want to debate health care, he figured if he couldn't pound on the facts, he should pound on the table! So he put his cup of tasteless cold tea down hard on its circular nest and said, "Enough, I guess your check will be OK then."

Jared, taking Matt's comment as an assumptive close to their negotiations, produced a leather folio from a pocket on the side of his chair, he wrote out a check. "This is for five thousand US dollars, drawn on the Toronto Dominion Bank, where we sit on the board. We will pay you another five thousand dollars when we have located the *Carol K.* We will recover any monies paid if you make public the name or location. We can get your signatures on an agreement we can update now, and Mrs. Vega's signature can be added to an addendum agreement we can also produce here." He handed the check to Matt and spoke to Lolan, who magically worked some machine behind the chairs and produced a revised contract and a second page titled Addendum.

Matt looked over the agreement—differing only in the cash amount and location bonus from the original paper they had read in the car. He looked at Tanya, who nodded agreement.

Seeing this, Jud handed Matt a pen and Jared passed the cash envelope and the leather folio to serve as a signing surface.

As Matt and Tanya printed and signed their names, George Vega entered the helicopter. The opened door brought in dust, fresh air and the noises of the airport.

Mr. Vega quickly saw the state of the negotiation and without a word, took the contract and pen offered by Tanya—he raised an eyebrow when he saw the new monetary figure and added his name. Seeing they had all dated their signatures. Jared handed Vega another paper and envelope.

"This is for your wife, with a return envelope." said Jared. "When can we be shown or given the location?"

Matt looked at Vega and Tanya, "I'd guess as soon as you can get your dive vessel here. The wreck is just north of Granite Island, which is about twelve miles north of Marquette. We can meet you at the island in our boat and save you coming in and taking us back, saving about fifty miles of your travel. The wreck is in 150 feet of water—give or take—so it is not a recreational dive. We will be prepared to guide your divers to the ship. You have my cell phone number, give us about a week to get our equipment ready. The weather gets colder and the storms more out of the north the longer we wait. Why don't we shoot for sometime in the next two weeks?"

The brothers looked at each other; Matt caught a spark of almost sinister intensity. *Could be just thoughts of their mother,* mused Matt. They agreed to try for a two-week timetable—weather and vessel permitting.

Their business done, everyone popped out of the leather comfort of the executive chairs and said their goodbyes on the tarmac.

Matt, Tanya and George stood by their van as the men, who were waiting in the shade of the tail rotor, boarded. The pilot gave a wave to Vega before he pulled the collective to bring the machine into the air. In a little over a minute the turbine-powered craft was out of sight over Lake Superior.

Back in the van, Matt pointed toward Marquette. "Let's cash this check, go shopping for some champagne that costs more than six dollars a bottle, get some fancy food and go home and celebrate."

8

Money in Hand

Driving into Marquette, four stops provided champagne, some expensive bourbon, and deli delicacies. After seeing the price and quality of lobsters, they agreed to get some fresh fish fillets at the harbor's fish market. Shopping at two dive stores and a marine supply outlet produced three new, cold-water, dry suits with hoods and gloves and two compensator vests, all on fall closeout sales. Matt didn't like the rental suits—which were several years old, worn and had hard neck dams that choked like a noose. New anchor rope, rode and anchors filled the back of the van as they went to the harbor to check over the 34-foot Silverton. George Vega inspected the two, 270 horsepower engines, while Matt and Tanya stowed the lines and hardware. Their last stop was the fish market where they bought fresh, lake trout fillets—enough for several meals. The shop threw in a small, ice-filled Styrofoam cooler with the agreement they would return it.

The spending frenzy was so consuming they almost forgot about cashing the check, a major reason for coming to Marquette, a big town by U.P. standards. Matt had done business with the First Bank for many years. He took the check to the head loan officer—one of his former students—who cut through the usual procedure at the teller's station when an out-of-town, out-of-country, check is cashed. Even with inside help, the cashing took over a half hour.

The former student/bank officer came to Matt. "Do you realize who these people are? They own a major hunk of Canada! Your check would have been good for hundreds of millions of dollars. They have a special arrangement with our bank. What are you doing with them?"

Matt hated to lie to a student, or a former student, but said, "It is just a little matter of some boundary rights. Thank you for your help, you saved us time, driving miles, and the usual wait for such a check to clear."

Back on highway 28 driving for home, George talked about the technology he observed on the helicopter. "Those engines are French—built by Makila. The pilot flew CH-53Es—twice as big as the Eurocopter—for the Marines in both Gulf wars. He said the Puma is a fine bird—but he was comparing it to a thirty-year-old military machine. He was very curious what business we were doing with the brothers; I said it was some kind of a land deal. He didn't believe me, but didn't ask more. They had cancelled several appointments and rearranged weeks of careful scheduling to make this trip a priority. He was amazed the brothers are talking to regular people—they work together like twins, either flying or on their ship—all business, no time for their families. Their sons run the day-to-day stuff—the brothers work on new projects, read reports and only really talk to politicians."

"Did he say anything about working for the Livingstons?" asked Tanya.

"Only they pay well, expect perfection, use their words like they are paying for them on a telegraph message and can be very ruthless in business. He was instructing and checking out their previous pilot, who made the error of saying how much time it would take to get as good. The comment got back to the brothers and—voilá—the pilot was gone and the instructor was hired. All the usual Canadian hiring rules were bent or broken. When he's not flying the helicopter, he sits on the right seat of their corporate jet. They have businesses all over Canada. He said he moved his family, but they didn't throw away the wardrobe boxes—meaning he doesn't trust his job to be long term. That's about all I got out of him.

"By the way—didn't you feel it was a little cramped for a machine they probably paid fifteen million dollars for? In the big Sikorskies you can stand up in and not touch both sides at once."

Matt changed the subject to the upcoming dive. They talked about some of the technical issues of mixed gas and how George wanted them to use high oxygen in the decompression stages.

George added, "High percentage of oxygen at depth is toxic, but it is great in a decompression stage—flushing out the nitrogen faster. I've got diving computers coming and special steel tanks—you'll have at least forty-five minutes of bottom time and, using the rule of thirds, over an hour of back up and decom air.

"I'll set up all your stages and help in the water at the main decompression stops. Your mother isn't going to like me getting wet, but I'll show her the nice new suit and she will like the sale price and all the money we are bringing back—as well as the great fillets."

Tanya broke in, "How are we going to deal with the money? What about listing it as a diving contract?"

Matt added, "That could break the Livingston contract if the IRS wants specifics. Any government involvement will also make us divulge the location so they know who has jurisdiction. We need to run this by a good CPA firm—like *Car Talk*'s Dewey, Cheatem and Howe."

Tanya, in the back seat inspecting the new diving suits, commented, "These will be great, we need to do some work before we go on the wreck. We need to check our buoyancy in these new suits as well as the compensators. We'll need the new tanks, too. As soon as the tanks come, maybe we can go down to Naubinway and work off the dock area. I think these cuffs and necks will need some stretching. We can just push them down over the tanks overnight for the necks and use some soup cans for the cuffs."

George was hungry, so they stopped in Christmas where he had a hamburger, and Tanya and Matt drank beer and kept stealing his French fries. Munising was the next town, where they spent time at the dive shop canceling their suit rentals and changing their tank needs, plus researching the compressors and gas mixing abilities.

As they pulled into the garage in late afternoon, Anita Vega greeted them with her party preparations for the next Saturday. Eleven thousand dollars in hundred dollar bills spread across the dining table made her gasp. "That should be in the bank, what are you thinking, carrying so much money around?"

Matt told about the reasons for secrecy and, while George handed her the paper for her signature and explained the agreement, he added, "We think it's best to do cash business with this dive. It leaves no paper trail and for all anyone knows it came from the casinos. We don't know about tax implications right now but we will be careful and fairly honest."

As Anita signed the paper, she thought aloud, "I always worry about agreements, cash deals and keeping a secret. You know I worry when you get easy money. I haven't had any stomach trouble since we sold the dive shop." With furrowed brow, she asked, "You sure this is all on the up and up?"

George took the signed paper, putting it in its envelope. "I'll make a copy before I seal and send it. I think we are dealing with big-business people—this money is nothing to them, they want no publicity and are willing to pay for secrecy. Money in the hand is a lot better than hoping for rewards from a shipwreck. I just read about a guy that spent thirty years searching for the *Griffin*—La Salle's ship from the Seventeenth Century. He thinks he finds it in Lake Michigan, so what happens—courts, court of appeals, state and federal claims, international law brought in by France, multiple expensive lawyers—and it will be years before anything is settled. Salvage laws and the Law of Finds are complicated enough in the open ocean—but Great Lakes shipwrecks have three or four more layers of jurisdiction issues. The Abandoned Shipwreck Act is full of the usual Congressional double-talk, the fact that the *Carol K* went down over fifty years ago and we know the living descendents is one thing, but the fact that it's in Michigan waters and the owners are Canadian is another thing. I say getting money out of the discovery and turning the issues over to the Livingstons is the way to go."

Champagne, pickled herring, various cheeses and crackers took over their attention as they waited for the fish fillets cooking in the oven. Fresh corn was ready to boil at the appropriate time. The salad bowl was filled and chilling in the refrigerator. The conversations jumped between dive talk, some needed new furniture and Anita's party project.

The fillets and the sun both went down simultaneously. The last half of the third bottle of champagne went undrunk. Matt used his jackknife to trim the cork and put it back into the bottle; he replaced the wire harness, wedging the bottle in the very full refrigerator. "There, we can have mimosas for breakfast."

The ladies cleared the table and washed the dishes as Matt and George inspected their diving purchases in the florescent light of the garage work benches.

As George looked over the removable weights on the compensator vest, he said, "Did you see the Livingstons look at each other when you gave the location? There was something between them. The story is the *Carol K* went down in a storm in mid-Lake Superior—a good fifty miles north. The brothers should have been more shocked at the location, maybe even incredulous. They looked like they knew it was nearer a land fall."

"Yeah, I saw the looks, and couldn't read what they were thinking. I sensed something more sinister, like they had outsmarted us or we played into their hand. All this could be imagination, but I'm glad you will be on our boat and watching our backs."

Vega and Matt finished inspecting the diving suits and went into the house. The kitchen was spotless, the money had been sequestered somewhere by the ladies who had gone to their bedrooms.

Matt said good night to Vega and went to the master bedroom. Tanya was in front of the large mirror that dominated the wall over the dresser, modeling white polypropylene long underwear to go under the diving suit, the sight of which and the residual effects of many glasses of champagne immediately turned Matt's mind to matters of advanced home recreation. He started kissing and fondling her lovely body.

Looking into the mirror, they both began moaning and laughing in equal measures.

"Quiet—mother has ears like a bat," whispered Tanya as they made their way to the bed.

9

Busy, Busy, Busy

Six large, heavy boxes arrived in the brown UPS truck; all were the maximum weight the carrier allowed. Matt and George unboxed and stored all the diving equipment in the garage.

Seeing the open boxes and packing material and the tanks, gauges, lamps, regulators and hosing, dive computers—piled with the new suits—Anita Vega said, "This won't do. We need this garage all clean and neat for the party. You need to move it someplace out of sight. I've got chairs coming tomorrow and we'll have thirty people here Saturday afternoon. The pig roaster will be here early. Tanya and I are cooking for the next two days. You need an inside bar and the beer barrel out here. We need another table, too. It can't be messy in here. Get your tools put away or hung up, do something with all the wood scraps, empty the garbage cans, put in new liners, dusting and using the shop vac would help too. You need to figure where people can park. There are some limbs on the road that need cutting back and maybe you could put up a sign out at the paved road."

Matt and George just listened as Anita went on for another five minutes; the Normandy landing was only a little more complex than Anita's preparations.

Matt opened the Yukon's back doors. "Let's take all the diving equipment to the hunting cabin down in the quarry and bring back the table."

Loading gear into the SUV, they went to the hunting camp a mile down a winding, two-rut road located inside a huge, old building on the quarry floor, the only standing structure that remained of the once vast complex for the mining of high quality limestone that had ended in the 1930s. Driving through the main entrance—large enough for steam engines—they parked next to the hunting cabin located inside the structure. In the '70s, a pipeline company gave them a cabin just for removing it from their job site. Matt and his hunting cronies—mostly relatives—initially stored the prefab building inside the old quarry shop building once used to repair the quarry's steam engines, shovels and locomotives. The massive building had a metal roof and a concrete floor. The prefab building soon morphed into a two-floor structure complete with water, bathrooms and sleeping facilities for ten hunters. There was still room to park cars, store canoes, snow mobiles and all-terrain vehicles. The building kept most snow off the hunting cabin, the large empty windows and huge entrance archway let in light and, sometimes, drifts of snow.

After storing the diving equipment in the cabin, Matt and Vega muscled the old kitchen table onto the top of the Yukon and roped it securely. Looking around the now unused cabin, Matt thought about all the changes in his life since he had rescued Tanya from a plane crash almost a year ago. He had taken her out of a downed plane on the nearby lake. The plane had held cocaine and soon linked him to Russian mobsters. The blizzard that had brought the plane down also isolated Tanya and him for many days. He ended up fighting killers, working with the DEA and falling in love with Tanya. Entering her world, his life had filled with adventure and danger. He also had become very close to her parents—living with them for a while in the Florida Keys and bringing everyone back to the Upper Peninsula to help build a new house.

George observed Matt's reverie. "You're thinking about all that happened here. You saved my daughter many times and in many ways. I'll never be able to repay you for all you've done. This is the happiest our family has ever been. I've not seen Anita this happy and bossy for twenty years. She didn't like our life at the marina; she knew both Tanya and I were in over our heads with a bad group of people. I let easy money and fears of reprisal get control of me—you got us out of that world—so you saved Anita and me also."

Matt saw tears welling in Vega's eyes and knew his Latin blood brought powerful emotions to the surface. So Matt changed the subject and mood. "Do you have all the rum and fixings you need for your Cuban drinks? Remember, these folks are used to beer and some brandy—you can get them all knee-walking when they think they are drinking sweet lemonade instead of a deadly rum concoction. I can see them polkaing right into the woods and being lost for days."

George laughed at the thought and got control of himself.

They brought the table back to the garage and quickly cleaned and policed the area. The ladies had filled the inside of the house with a plethora of wonderful smells—the counters held many dishes of party foods—all off limits to Matt and George, who finally agreed to go to town for bar supplies and to fill a short list from the women.

As Matt got into the Yukon, his call cell phone played its tune. It was Jared Livingston.

"Mr. Hunter, we can have our ship at the dive site this coming Monday and Tuesday if that is acceptable with you?"

George heard the message and gave a nod, Matt responded, "Weather permitting, we'll meet you north of Granite Island Monday afternoon. Our boat is called the *Ferr Play*—a 34-foot, white Silverton—we'll monitor VHF channel 19 and our cell phones work most of the time. What is the name of your vessel?"

"We are the *Gull Cry*," said Livingston—who also gave his cell phone number. "Weather looks good for those days. I see you cashed the check. We'll have money aboard for you. Remember, breaking security will be expensive. How many will be on your boat?"

"Tanya, George Vega and me."

"Fine, I just wanted to know for dinner plans. My brother and I will be there with our divers. See you then."

The connection broke.

Matt looked at Vega, "He doesn't chew the fat much. I'm surprised the brothers are coming on the dive ship. I'll be interested in your opinion of them. You didn't get to talk with them much in the helicopter. And you missed the ostrich stir fry."

"I can pass on ostrich, but I'm really curious about the *Carol K.* I wish I was going on it with you. Tanya is good, but I have double her hours over one hundred feet and mixed gas certification. But I don't like cold water. There's a big difference in the Key's water and Lake Superior—I'm used to twenty-five degrees warmer and a lot more light. Oh, and I've got a digital underwater camera coming—I hope it gets here by this weekend. I ordered it when I sent for the tanks. I think it will come UPS." George settled into the passenger seat and latched his seatbelt. "Well, let's get to town and get the party supplies. I think I'll need to practice a few drinks before Saturday—I hope you like rum."

Matt and Vega spent the afternoon shopping and driving. They returned to find a strange vehicle parked in the driveway—a new, metal-gray Mercedes, looking out of place because it wasn't four wheel drive and was free of the ever-present U.P. mud and dust. Matt pulled next to it and almost hit the table filling his parking space in the garage, as a large man surprised him coming out of the house.

Recognizing Al, Matt reeled a bit from the rush of memories and emotions and stopped breathing for a few seconds. Al—the Russian Webb's muscle man. Last November, Al had been at the quarry with the Russian and, later, on an adventure through the Bahamas on a 54-foot Hatteras with Webb, Webb's wife and daughter, Matt and Tanya. Al had been a Detroit detective who slipped over to the dark side. He was big, fast and very tough—totally loyal to crime-boss Webb. Having him in the new house and in Matt's new world made Matt's heart race and activated all his primitive terror responses.

Next out the door came Tanya, holding the hand of a beautiful, young girl—both all smiles and laughing. It was Carla—Webb's daughter—slim, dark hair, perfect face, sparkling eyes. As Matt got out of the car, he remembered Carla had started at the University of

Michigan and had mentioned to Tanya she was going to see her folks on Manitoulin Island in Canada.

Tanya rushed to Matt—dragging Carla, "Darling, look who's found us—isn't she beautiful, all grown up and a college girl!"

Carla gave Matt a hug and a very Russian cheek-kissing. She sparkled in a bulky, silver lamé turtleneck and black slacks.

Carla bubbled over with pleasure and excitement. "We were driving to Canada up I-75 and I made Al drive me here. My parents are expecting me late this evening, but I just had to see you and your beautiful land. I can't believe you can drive all day and still be in the same state. We could have gone through five or six countries in Europe in the same driving time. I love the university, football, and the colors, everyone is so friendly and free in the United States. I'll be happy to see my parents again—it's the longest I've been away from my mother. I love your new home. Everything is forest and so many colors, we saw deer and turkeys on your road. Al was wonderful just to find your house. I know you are very busy getting ready for a party—we will only stay a few minutes." Carla gushed all her thoughts, finishing with enthusiastic praise for her school, classmates and having the freedom of being on her own.

Matt wondered, *How many people keep track of Carla in Ann Arbor?*

Tanya broke in. "We will have supper together in a half hour. I wanted them to stay overnight, but Al said they have a timetable and her folks are expecting her. Doesn't she look all grown up?"

Matt nodded with a smile.

Tanya continued, "Let me walk her down to the beaver pond and we'll be right back."

Tanya and Carla started down the north path. Al started to follow, but Matt told him they would be safe. Matt introduced Al to Mr. Vega. They had met briefly a few times at the marina on Islamorada. But when Webb was around, Al just blended into the background.

Matt asked Al, "How're things in the Dominican Republic for Webb?"

"The DR is good, perfect climate, nice hardworking people, he has a cacao drying plant—all legitimate, we have great security and communication—shipping business as usual with lots of political support, no DEA worry —the postal system sucks and television is mostly Spanish—but we get Atlanta and Miami stations. I'm *hablo*ing pretty good and I have a second house where my wife and kids stay whenever they visit: maids, lawn men, the wife loves it—we couldn't take the kids out of their high school. Later, I could see retiring there."

"What brings you to the States?" Matt asked.

"I'm here to be with my family, getting the kids started in their schools. Webb and Karen left for Canada over a week ago."

Matt remembered Webb's beautiful wife.

Al continued, "Carla wanted to see the country from the road—it's a great time to drive up. Your place is a lot different without four feet of blowing snow—I was lucky to find you again. Carla will fly back, I've got some errands to run for Webb. Wait 'till you see Webb's place on Manitoulin, a combination of log cabin and Swiss chalet—only about six thousand square feet —but they don't mind roughing it. There are a few bedrooms without their own bathroom. I understand you've been invited. I hope you come up. We could do some fishing or bird hunting."

Matt listened in amazement, he had never heard Al utter more than two sentences in a row. Tanya had felt that Al had learned conversation from Jack Webb on *Dragnet*.

Al helped Matt and George carry the liquor boxes and grocery bags into the house. Anita Vega was scurrying around getting the dining table set and checking the oven and pots that would soon provide supper. She had her jaw set—like she did when she wanted to say something but thought it best just to keep her mouth shut. She didn't greet or even look at Al.

Matt got three beers, distributed them to the men and spoke to Al, "I'll bet Carla has some security at school."

Al took a long pull of the cold Corona beer, "Yes, she has to live in a dorm the first year—next year she may get into a sorority house, her roommate is on the payroll. It was a condition of Webb allowing her to come to a U.S. school. The bodyguard girl—really a woman—takes classes for credit. She's a former marine and Black Water employee: looks ten years younger than her age. Webb worries about Carla all the time—but knows she needs to be her own person."

Anita, listening, finished setting the table and began preparing bowls of steaming vegetables, a sheet of biscuits, finally bringing a beef roast from the oven, placing it on a cutting board. She mumbled to no one in particular, "This isn't a very big roast but it will have to do." She cut the roast, putting the slices on a platter, which she covered with the roasting pan cover. "Now all we need is people."

Not sure what to do, Matt took the men back into the garage to watch for the girls to come back. They were about a quarter mile from the house—returning down the narrow dirt road. The leaves of hard maples and oaks, mixed with birch and poplar, formed a colorful frame around the lovely women as they walked happily up the road.

Matt thought how they looked like sisters.

Supper was dominated by Carla's experiences of living on her own, her impressions of a university town, her experience at her first Big Ten football game, and her ambitions for drama and art after she completed her basic freshman classes. Her father wasn't discussed very often because everyone sensed that, whenever his name was mentioned, Anita physically seemed to shrink.

Carla and Al had to leave immediately after supper. Everyone exchanged phone numbers and addresses for Ann Arbor, Canada and the Dominican Republic. Anita didn't say goodbye, working on the dishes instead.

Tanya cried when Carla's vehicle finally became just two red taillights disappearing into a cloud of road dust. She put Matt's arm around her and leaned against him. "Carla is so much like me before the world of reality hit. She hasn't met any thoughtless or cruel men, no life-changing legal or illegal problems. I hope if she does have problems she will be lucky enough to have a man like you to lean on." Tanya leaned hard to make her point, finally turning to give Matt a very thorough kiss.

Matt guided her back to the garage, "We've got a lot to do in the next few days: the party, diving gear to assemble and test, a major wreck dive and dealing with Canadian billionaires. What say we help your mother get her mind back on the party and off Webb?"

10

Pig and Party Crashers

Changing her clothes in the Yukon, Tanya provided the day's best entertainment on the old dock at Naubinway. As the three divers jumped in and out of the water to test their new equipment, a crowd of seagulls and rubber-necking townies formed. All tanks had gone to Munising and now held their appropriate gasses and pressures. Time had to be spent adjusting the buoyancy compensator vests—some weights were sewn in, some were removable in pockets. Even the camera and flash got a test. Matt and Vega changed behind the doors at the back of the Yukon opened toward the lake, only seagulls were interested in them, unlike the kids that, earlier, had tried to see through the dark glass of the Yukon with Tanya changing inside.

Hurrying back to the quarry, the happy divers found Mrs. Vega firmly in control of the pre-party activities. Rotating in its black cooker, Mr. Pig was surrounded by tables soon to be full of food, paper plates and plastic utensils; the half barrel of beer chilled in its plastic garbage can, the double garage was transformed into a stage and dance floor, folding chairs lined all walls. There was no room to store any diving paraphernalia.

While Tanya helped her mother and several ladies with final preparations for that evening, Matt and Vega took the diving equipment to the hunting cabin. Soon damp underwear and the suits hung spaced to dry; suit necks and cuffs stretching over tanks or soup cans. The camera was inspected for leaks and reassembled with new moisture munchers in both the camera housing and the flash unit. "These little babies will keep the moisture off the lens, a must in cold water," said George as he completed the reassembly of the SeaLife DC 800 digital camera. "This is older technology now, but it works well. It's small, and the quality's fine with the 28 to 122 millimeter lens. The flash makes a good handle and is far enough away to reduce silt reflection. It's rated to 200 feet. I really want to see what that ship looks like."

The party started in the late afternoon. Everyone for many miles was there—30 folks, all relatives or should-have-been relatives. They saw each other at every activity in the area: church, voting, town meetings, hunting balls, weddings and funerals—but everyone was always happy to see each other. Everyone knew everything about everyone there except Tanya, Anita and George Vega. With greasy fingers, they alternately ate roasted pork and handled plastic beer cups, all the Vegas' history became part of the northern culture. The loud boom box on the pickup truck finally gave way to the two-person band. George's rum drinks helped get several people dancing who hadn't felt like dancing in years. The accordion and drum, augmented with a rhythm box, played by a man and wife who had already celebrated their 50th wedding anniversary did a fine job. Everyone danced to polka, two-step and waltz, singing some country and western songs when they knew the words. The sounds of music and loud comradery dispersed into the dark, seemingly endless forest. It felt like a wedding reception, without the toasts and kissing: just what Anita had intended.

While searching for a friendly tree to water, out of the lights from the driveway and garage, Matt saw a car slowly moving up the lane. Thinking it might be a late comer, he walked up the dark road. He didn't recognize the car, which had stopped well back from the party lights, alongside the row of cars lining the lane. Coming from the dark, and bending down to the open window, Matt said, "Welcome to the party."

The driver jumped, wide-eyed because Matt came upon him so unnoticed.

"We're looking for Matt Hunter's house. We saw the sign out on the road," said the driver, seemingly fighting to bring calmness to his voice.

Matt knelt down and looked at both men in the reflected glow of their headlights and the car's interior red and blue LEDs. *Strangers... maybe the law.* "This is Hunter's, welcome to the party, come on in, there's a parking space behind the pickup in the driveway. Still lots of beer, but the pig is down to a little crispy skin and some fat. What are your names?"

The passenger responded, "We don't want to barge in. We just wanted to locate where Hunter lives. This is not an easy place to find."

"Well, hell, after all your trouble, you got to have a beer and I'll introduce you to Hunter," said Matt, his danger alarm into the red zone. Thinking, *I'll know your name before you leave!*

Matt pressured them to drive forward and park and then opened the driver's door. The two men got out, dressed in wool slacks, shined shoes and crisp, long-sleeved, button-down shirts—they didn't fit in. Two cousins joined the group, thinking more friends had arrived. Dick and Billy Lamoreaux walked around the vehicle, checking out the men.

"Canadian car and plates, they always put on some different chrome. Where you from?" asked Billy.

The passenger said, "We work out of Thunder Bay, investigating large land holdings for a lumber company."

Dick cut in, "You ain't dressed like timber cruisers. Hard to see trees at night. But have a beer anyway."

Matt thought, *Dick and Billy can feel something isn't right with these two.*

Reluctantly herded into the garage and handed cups of beer, the men looked at Matt in the light. Matt could tell they recognized him. He ushered them back out into the relative privacy of the driveway, Dick and Billy followed out of earshot.

"Ok, gentlemen, what's going on? Why do the Livingston's want to know where I live?" Matt asked. *There, you lying assholes, you broke eye contact and blinked. Next you'll clear your throat...*

The driver cleared his throat and drank some beer; the passenger regained eye contact for a second then studied the foam on his beer.

Matt squared up in front of the two men, moving into right cross range, "Well...you're a long ways from home, in the middle of my woods, with a dozen of my big, strong, beer-filled friends and relatives five seconds away from pounding you into steak tartar. Now tell how you found me and why you wanted to?"

Nothing was said for 20 seconds. Dick and Billy had been joined by several other large, male guests—more interested in a possible confrontation than the nice, old ladies dancing polkas together.

The driver spoke, "We were asked by an unnamed source to locate you. We were given your name, picture, boat name and a bank you used in Marquette. We went to dive shops, the harbors and scuba-filling facilities, we also looked in a land atlas and plat books listing your name. We were calling it a night when we saw your sign. We're just doing our job—we usually work for lawyers, but this is an anonymous contract. We know who the Livingstons are, but like I said, we don't know who is paying. The contract and cashier's check came in the mail and we respond to a PO Box in Montréal."

Matt backed away to a comfortable distance, relaxing the mood and the two men. Gesturing toward the food table Matt said, "Better fix a plate, it's a long drive to any restaurant. You're welcome to stay or go."

Matt got their names, but Tom and Joe, followed by Anderson and Harris, sounded phony. Matt decided the party wouldn't be improved by having them pinned down and searched for identification. So, like a good host he led them to the food table.

Filling paper plates from a dozen choices of great party food, under the scrutiny of a dozen people, the two Canadians thanked Matt, returning to their car and, showing great relief, carefully turned around, leaving the way they came.

"What was that all about?" was the question from many people. Matt explained it had to do with land speculation. Then he found Tanya and got back into the spirit and spirits of the gathering. He vowed to learn more about the Livingstons—they now knew where he lived and he didn't know as much about them. It was really a small thing, he would have told them where he lived under the right circumstances, but now the Livingstons had located Matt's sanctuary—whose remoteness had always offered a sense of security.

He wondered if the two party crashers would report they had been busted. Matt guessed—yes. How and where they got a picture—another interesting question.

Matt danced with Tanya, her beauty and happiness consuming his attention and charming all the guests.

Tanya did her first polka with Matt, a dance to be repeated with many partners. The oldest partner past 80, the youngest a teenage boy, totally in puppy love with her.

The party wound down with the final groups gathering inside by the warmth of the fireplace. Carrying away or putting away dishes, eventually everyone safely departed. Announcing the whole evening a success, Anita finally turned off the lights.

11

Dangerous Depths

Making love on a 34-foot boat with the girl's father 15 feet away in the next cabin took skill and cooperation. Nevertheless, Matt and Tanya were able to enjoy Monday morning in the bow bunks of the *Ferr Play* in Marquette harbor.

Moving onto the boat Sunday night had given Matt, Tanya and George morning dive time on the *Carol K* before meeting the Livingstons Monday afternoon. All the gear had been stored and ready before they went to the bunks. Anita Vega stayed at the new home at the quarry property—with some neighbor help, cleaning up after the very successful house warming and Vega introduction party.

Lake Superior provided a perfect, early October morning: cold, clear and calm. A low carpet of fog parted for the Silverton's wake as she headed north toward Granite Island, proving the water was warmer than the air—and the surface water was 55 degrees. Breakfast was steak, eggs and reheated biscuits using the shore electricity. The only damper on the day was Tanya's sneezes, sniffles and clogged sinuses. Using a spray decongestant didn't help, she wasn't in shape for the dive.

George was more than happy and willing to be Matt's buddy. Tanya didn't fight the change for all the right reasons—she knew her dad was a more experienced diver, and the dive would be Matt's deepest and most challenging. The 12-mile run gave them time to prepare and muster the equipment onto the aft deck area. George arranged the tanks in their proper order, testing each for pressure and proper regulators, inspecting the connecting manifolds and valves between the twin tanks that would be on their backs. The dive computers were all calibrated, lights checked, safety lines unspooled and respooled, note tablets and pens checked and a score of other items noted and inspected.

North of the island, the submerged plastic float was easily found in the flat, bright morning—mists still formed in the shade and rocky shore of the nearby island. The anchor was set while the warm sun rose less than halfway to vertical. The three divers, running around in heavy, long underwear and light, polar fleece sweaters, carefully arraigned their gear and reviewed their new dive plans.

Matt looked at the four tanks that would be his. "I've made most of my dives with one or two tanks—now I've got four to think about. You ever thought about rebreathers?"

George Vega had a yellow legal pad and a magic marker, "Let's diagram our dive today—but I'll answer your rebreathers question first. I have used several rebreathers for shallow dives—they're great for photographic work, no bubbles to scare fish and great bottom time from a compact back pack. But for deeper work—over thirty feet—I was always afraid of the oxygen going toxic. The label on the scrubber I had said, 'Danger: This device is capable of killing you without warning.' The same could be said about many devices we work with— but when I see professional salvage divers with three oxygen gauges on their wrist I want the technology to mature a little more. I'm sure rebreathers will be the future of diving, but I'd rather use multiple tanks, multiple mixes and a good dive computer for now."

George showed Matt the stages they would be using, where they would leave their DECO—decompression tank—on D rings located at 35 feet on the diving line that connected the boat to the old anchor. These tanks were high oxygen and low nitrogen to get the nitrogen out of their systems faster than by using regular compressed air. The mixtures lowered their decompression times by nearly half. They would continue—each with three tri-mix tanks—one under their arm, two on their back. The underarm tank was their travel gas—used to get to the wreck. It would be left on the bottom to be retrieved when they came up. This left two big tanks on their backs, plenty of gas for penetration and a whole tank as a reserve. The tri-mix had oxygen, nitrogen and helium: oxygen not high enough to risk oxygen poisoning, low nitrogen to lessen absorption into the blood and helium, which would make them talk like Donald Duck, with its large molecules that wouldn't dissolve into the blood like nitrogen.

Vega continued, "Let's plan on forty-five minutes on the bottom, more due to water temperature than our tank capacities—with a thirty-foot decom, a twenty-foot stop and a ten-foot final stop. The dive computer will give us exact times. The computer knows our depths, times and gas mixes. We both have one, so we have redundancy—we'll use the longest numbers if they differ. These are steel hundreds, not aluminum tanks—they hold more gas, under higher pressure. We have excellent redundancy and back up capability. Tanya can be ready if we get into problems at a decompression stage, but anything deep is out for her."

Tanya put up the dive flag while the men suited up. Tanya did the final inspections on both divers, zipping the back that all men find difficult. With tanks and equipment attached and dangling from almost every part of their suits the men eased into the clear, cold, calm water. After letting out excess air from their dry suits and hoods the men headed down.

They attached their DECO tanks at the 35 foot level. With one tank under their arm, swimming down the yellow nylon rope was easier. Both breathed slowly and evenly, checking their dive computer for depth and finding all numbers changing correctly. Matt paused to pressurize and, looking up as he passed 60 feet, could see their boat's bottom clearly but couldn't see the *Carol K* until another 40 feet of descent. The white of the cabin and part of the side as well as some of the lifeboats were visible in the ambient light at over 100 feet. The general hull and form of the ship were not visible until they were within 20 feet of the wheel house—located above what could be the salons and cabins that made up the main deck.

Matt and George Vega had agreed to do a complete exterior inspection using the travel tank, before they decided to do any internal exploration. Visibility was 20 feet and decreased as they went down the slope of the ship toward the stern. A mast stuck up 20 feet above the wheel house, lifeboats were scattered along the upper deck, mixed with their respective davits, the block and tackle lines disintegrating and broken wove around the boats. Matt noted two davits void of lifeboats on the port side. There was one other lifeboat in place as they worked their way aft. The ship's funnel was broken and bent. The stern was in good shape, the propeller was visible. The depth at the three-bladed screw was 160 feet. As Matt noted his depth—an individual record, flashes came from the camera in Vega's control. Vega got Matt to pose by the name—after wiping it clean of algae. Moving up the starboard side they turned on their underwater lights, the looming basaltic monolith that formed the shelf along the ship made that side of the ship appear much more sinister. Vega shot pictures as they moved along—documenting the three starboard lifeboats in a row, scattered on the top deck with their associated davits. Vega pointed out double doors located at amidships; pantomiming that it probably went from beam to beam. The intact cabin windows lined the main deck—large house-like windows, not portholes. Matt kept a count as they worked forward—13 if you didn't count the double doors. Matt liked the fact they were large enough to get through if he had to break in or out. In 20 minutes, they had explored the exterior of the ship and assembled outside the wheelhouse. They secured their travel tanks on the small deck outside the wheelhouse. Matt lead Vega into the cabin—Vega documented the binnacle and wheel, cleaning the brass to see the numbers and builder's identification. The telegraph was set at all-stop. Matt took him into the cabin behind the wheelhouse, they explored the little cabin, taking pictures of the locker containing the small boots and slicker—probably owned by the Livingstons' mother.

Returning to the space and better light of the deck below the wheelhouse they noted another large door that had a mate across from it on the other side. Vega motioned Matt closer and under the bright cone of the diving light made a diagram of the ship on the slate—showing the two hallways that bisected the upper deck and indicating what had to be the cabins that had to open to a central hall, running the length of the ship. They could see six large windows forming a semicircle on what had to be a large common room or salon facing the bow. Vega wrote on the slate: *Let's go in here*, and indicated they should begin their internal work where they had the most visibility and means of escape.

Matt checked the dive computers—they had used 25 minutes so far. *It seemed like five minutes*, thought Matt.

Vega secured their diving lines to the rail. They easily pulled open the wooden door, metal fastenings either weak or rusted away. Diving lights swept the large salon that went from rail to rail in the bow. It must have been a pleasant area. Matt noted a coal furnace centered in the middle. The wooden furniture was neat and still secured. What looked like it was once wicker had disintegrated.

Vega touched Matt and indicated they should keep moving—pointing at his dive computer. They went into the main corridor, light probes showing it ran the length of the ship. The first cabin on their right was labeled, Master's Cabin—they pushed the door open. The cabin was actually a suite, with a setting room, small head and a windowed bedroom. The windows were lighter than the walls, but they could only see where their beams illuminated. Vega, behind Matt, paused to secure a small chemical glow stick to the safety line, motioning Matt to move ahead.

The cabin was a mess, drawers were scattered and clothes cabinets were open. A safe next to a desk was open. Vega started taking pictures while Matt went into the bedroom. The room was neat by comparison to the previous area, the bed was a depression around a rotting wooden structure. Shining the light into the dark hole framed by rotten bedding material Matt choked as his eyes focused and his brain comprehended he was looking at a skeleton. Not all the bones were visible but Matt could see it was a small skull, he could identify the pelvic bones and parts of a small hand and wrist. It was female. Vega's flash surprised Matt, causing him to turn quickly, kicking up a cloud of algae. While they waited for the swirl of turbidity to settle, Matt moved close to the skull—checking teeth for possible age information. He saw well developed teeth and, just above the bridge of the nose, a small hole in the forehead. Matt pointed to the hole, Vega nodded and took several pictures. Matt placed his diving knife next to the skull as a scale—the knife was really called a diver's tool with a pry bar as a tip, serrated on one side and knife-edged on the other. The blade was scaled in inches.

Turning it so its stainless steel blade didn't reflect the flash into the camera, Vega took six more pictures. Matt finally turned the skull to get a side shot—noticing a dark protuberance in the occipital area, the cold and thick dive gloves made feeling nearly impossible, but with the knife edge and some effort, Matt pried out the lead from a small caliber bullet. Vega recorded the whole procedure. Matt put the lead in his collection bag.

They both heard the sound of big propellers and diesel engines at the same time. The beat was an addition to their hearts—it was felt as well as heard. Holding their breath to silence the noise of the regulators and the streams of bubbles, they heard the engine noise clearly and they heard the propellers stop.

Vega made a sign to get out of there and go outside. Carefully retracing their way to the deck rail and locating their travel tanks they were winding up their dive lines when they heard splashes, the sound traveling through the cold still water, reflected by the rock wall behind them. Outlined by the light 130 feet above them, Matt and Vega saw three figures descending toward them from the surface, one touching the dive rope and two following. The three divers came slowly. Matt and Vega, watching in the obscurity of the dark water, observed two facts—no bubbles, therefore rebreathers—and two had spear guns!

Matt understood a few seconds faster than George—you don't need spear guns in the Great Lakes. All their fears and distrust of the Livingstons gave them a common emotion and conclusion: time to run.

Vega pointed at their rising bubbles and drew a finger across his throat. Matt understood and stopped breathing. They went around and down to the door they had just left. Retrieving their travel tanks, Vega retied his dive line, motioning Matt to do likewise. Tying the lines they went into the vessel, breathing again. Vega wrote on his slate: *They follow line...we hide.*

The two let out lines down the long corridor, using only one light close to the floor. They came to the aft end of the hall, a large metal door at the T. The door wouldn't open, they beat on all the levers and handles—rusted tight, so they pulled the lines into what was probably a crew's quarters area on the aft starboard side. Cutting the lines, they swam back up the corridor the way they had come, entering a cabin halfway up the port side. Careful to disturb very little slime on the door, they swam in, quickly pushing the door closed. With their lights out they could see lights and shapes against the ambient light outside the ship. Their bubbles sounded like an avalanche of boulders rolling with each breath. The slant of the ship collected their expelled air on the ceiling, not leaking out the door. In the dark, cold world of a dead ship the two men floated in a large cabin, worrying about their fate and that of Tanya.

Matt and Vega moved to the ceiling—lessening the regulator sounds. In a few minutes enough of an air pocket formed to stick their heads into. They used a chemical light held in Vega's glove for illumination. They didn't speak, minimizing their regulator noise and, with drawn knives, they watched the door.

Metallic banging came from the hall. From the disturbed rust and slime, the men must have thought they had gone through the engine room door and redogged it. Matt and Vega heard the men working and even talking through their full face masks. The hunters must have made a disturbance going down the hallway obscuring Matt and Vega's back trail.

The false trail had done its job.

Matt and Vega had their travel tanks and two more each—literally hours of air, but the longer they were at depth—the faster they used their air and the longer they would have to decompress. Vega had built in double safety factors—but he never figured spear guns.

They heard the men moving up and down the hall, more banging and sounds at the stern and bow. Holding his breath, Matt moved to the window, scraping away algae slime, he could see light from above and not much more. He then gave his extra tank to Vega and began to explore the large room using a light stick, hoping to find a way out. He found skeletons piled on the deck, falling from what had once been triple bunk beds. One set still held bones in the clutches of rusted, metal springs. Matt couldn't see more than a few inches of the room at a time, but a terrible mosaic took form, a room holding nearly four triple bunks of what were human bones.

Matt wanted to communicate with Vega. He returned to the air bubble—which now formed a pocket of nearly eight inches from the ceiling. Now they could talk.

Vega whispered, his voice distorted by the helium, "Need to go up—help Tanya, cold."

Matt noted his dark lips in the yellow light—the older man was cold. Matt knew that to have any chance of helping Tanya he had to first stay alive. He nodded understanding and duck talked, "There are a lot of bones by those bunk beds—wish we could risk a picture. Let's make a bigger air pocket—if they start listening for us they'll hear our regulators. I'll bleed my travel tank."

Matt detached the regulator and opened the valve on his travel tank. The bubbles made a noise and the hissing made a noise, but by moving it up and down and masking the O-ring with a glove, the air pocket quickly and quietly grew to over two feet of air space.

Vega took out his mouth piece, "Remember CO_2 toxic if it builds up— we're at a hundred thirty feet. Headache, convulsions—be careful."

Matt nodded again, whispering, "I don't hear anything—maybe they are listening for us. Be quiet."

Matt and Vega floated in the growing air bubble, breathing from their regulators and from the air bubble—anything to minimize sound. The dive computer had them at depth for over an hour and fifteen minutes when they heard the diesels start again. Matt went to the window, he couldn't see anything but a glow of surface light. He could hear the diesel engines clearly, and then he heard the two 270 horsepower engines of the *Ferr Play* come to life. Vega joined him in an attempt see through the window. They listened as both boats moved some distance.

Vega turned on his diving light and swept the room, illuminating the bones and bunk beds. He wrote on Matt's slate: *Stay in front of window.* After quickly taking pictures of the bones, he motioned Matt to the air pocket. In the pocket, with light on their faces, he said, "We have to go up, now."

Matt nodded his agreement and they started to replace mouthpieces into numbed lips.

The explosions came in three blasts, seconds between them.

Their heads in the air pocket probably saved their lives. A liquid doesn't compress—a gas does—so the air pocket absorbed some of the shock. The crushing power of the explosions knocked out their wind, mouthpieces and equilibrium. Vega's dive light broke, debris and algae made the room totally black. Vega was knocked against the ceiling, Matt was knocked against Vega, the door and windows were blown open. Both men concussed.

They tumbled around the room as shocks and movement resonated thorough the ship. There was no up or down—everything was black and painful.

Matt got his mouthpiece in, hit the purge button, having no air to blow it dry. After two breaths he remembered where he was. His diving light cut through the floating slime. He found Vega sinking against the port wall, his body limp and his mouthpiece out. Matt got to him, inserted the mouthpiece, pushed the purge valve and saw Vega's chest expand. Matt shook him and got him to the much-reduced air pocket. In a few moments, under Matt's diving light, Vega's eyes came open and he was back among the living.

Matt took both travel tanks and pulled Vega through the now gapping window, into open water. Vega wasn't fully conscious, but didn't fight being towed.

The *Carol K* was torn into several pieces—the stern was not in sight, the wheelhouse was totally gone and the bow was scrambled. They had been in about the only part of the ship that hadn't had a charge set.

Matt moved toward where the dive line should have been. It wasn't there. Matt was disoriented and fought the urge to go to the surface.

Find the old anchor, Matt told himself. He needed a point of reference. After several minutes of slow swimming Matt, pulling Vega and the now buoyant travel tanks, located the chain which he followed to the old anchor. The yellow nylon line was where he had tied it—the nylon line held the DECO tanks. Or so he hoped.

Working down the nylon line, Matt came to the two DECO tanks, full and on the bottom. At 75 feet, his diving computer thought it was dealing with an idiot, he couldn't tell any direction except up. By dropping some weights and putting some air into the buoyancy vests, Matt worked them up the nylon rope to 35 feet, where the extra tanks had been initially secured. Matt worked to organize the tanks, free line that should have been tied to the boat and the nearly unresponsive Vega. Matt worried that Vega would fatally sink or float upward, so he looped the yellow line around him. Vega's eyes were starting to look around and he was breathing regularly, but he wasn't OK.

Matt secured himself to the dive line, got them onto the high-oxygen DECO tanks and checked their diving computers. After working with the computer for a minute—careful to not screw it up—Matt finally felt the instrument was happy and doing its thing—they had 11 minutes at this stage which was 30 feet and another 18 minutes at 20 feet and a 20-minute stop at ten feet, using the always-conservative PADI tables. The dive computer showed a chart with a depth and time-line for the gas mixes they were using. It also showed an easy-to-read countdown display.

Vega finally came around. Worrying about the decompression stages, he went over everything; urging Matt to move his arms and legs, and doing likewise himself, to minimize trapped gas bubbles and build some body heat.

Matt noted Vega's eyes were glassy. But the higher oxygen seemed to be helping him. He looked as beat-up as Matt felt. As diving buddies, they kept watching each other to see who was the most screwed up.

Matt felt lost. He didn't have a compass, he had no idea where he was until he got to the surface—he would have liked to be moving toward the island but couldn't establish a direction. The light was early afternoon and coming down too directly to read anything into it. His gut hurt, his neck hurt, his kidneys ached, and his body felt very, very cold. The cold oxygen didn't help his internal temperature either. He was sure Tanya was in danger.

He floated like a party balloon on a nylon rope, 30 feet underwater in Lake Superior with no boat above him. Holding the end of the line in his glove, he noted it had been untied, not cut. It was the add-on line he had used to tie the float to the rail cleat of the *Ferr Play* to pull themselves up as they decompressed. He knew Tanya had untied it. She must have known the deadly consequence if the DECO tanks were found by the Livingston divers. She knew Matt could find them if they were on the bottom. Without the high-oxygen mixture, their ascent would have been much more complicated and dangerous. He knew he should be more hateful and mad, but he just felt physically spent and getting increasingly mentally numb with each cold minute.

And he had to pee.

12

Cold and Ghosts

Floating in a gray-green world with no sounds, Matt found sensory deprivation accompanied hypothermia. Watching Vega's movements, Matt knew the man could be in trouble. Finishing their last decompression stage, just ten feet below the shiny surface, the water was noticeably warmer on cheeks and lips, but still in the 50s.

The dive computer finally counted down to zero, marking the end of their subsurface time. Matt brought them up. Drawing in fresh, warm surface air helped both men. The sun's heat felt wonderful. Matt removed the short rope that had tied the marker float to the boat. The float, without the tanks, returned to its subsurface vigil. Matt assembled the four extra air tanks—which were either now buoyant or at least neutral. He saw Vega wasn't much more alert than the bobbing tanks, so he tied himself, the tanks and Vega loosely together. Vega was moving but his eyes and face showed no emotion. Matt talked, yelled and shook him, finally getting some recognition, but Vega's reality state didn't seem to last more than a few seconds.

Granite Island loomed a half mile south of them, a light northern breeze gave them a little help and made the surface water warmer. Matt thought about ditching all the tanks but didn't, for several nonprioritized reasons that floated in and out of his cold brain: did he trust the hunk of plastic computer that looked like an third grader's Etch-a-Sketch when it said, "OK, go to the surface," —their decompression was very short compared to other dives, on regular air, Matt had experienced and if cramps came they might need to go down again. Maybe he could vent the gases, make a raft and put Vega up on it—getting him further out of the cold water. And a final reason: he didn't like abandoning good equipment. Back to task: swimming to the island and getting out of the water would help Vega the most. They used their snorkels and began kicking toward the rocky island. Vega responded well to the mission. The tanks bobbed along and chimed like friendly musical dolphins. Vega kicked well and did a weak breaststroke with his arms. He looked over at Matt several times and seemed to understand their goal of making a land fall. Neither talked.

The rocky cliffs that made up the island offered no shore, no easy climbing access. Rising eight to ten feet above a barrier of broken rocks and massive boulders the cliff face became more formidable as the swimmers approached. Gentle waves and winds kept the shore from being a death trap. Matt and Vega swam along the cliffs toward the west end where the island gradually sloped toward lake level. Matt saw Vega rise up and point at a break between two large, rounded boulders—the size of cars.

Vega yelled, "I see two men climbing up the rocks."

Matt looked and only saw waves breaking into a small opening and on to a flat shelf. Energized, Vega swam strongly toward the opening—his burst of speed pulled Matt by his nylon tether, the tanks clanked behind. Matt began to swim hard. In five minutes they were between the boulders and helping each other up onto the flat, rock shelf.

Pulling the tanks up and securing them above wave action, Vega had his swim fins off and was looking up the cliff. "I saw two men climbing right up there," he said, pointing to a series of rocks and outcroppings that stepped their way to the cliff top.

Vega yelled "Hello" several times while he shed his diving gear. Matt did likewise, including the yelling. They helped each other up the cliff and were soon warm inside and out from the exertion in the sun and warm air. Matt looked west and saw the *Ferr Play* floating over the shoals that were frequent diving areas along the island. He longed to see Tanya waving at him, but just looked into the bright sunlight bouncing off calm water around an empty boat. Matt felt thankfulness and loneliness in equal measures as he watched the white boat swinging at anchor.

Checking on Vega, Matt decided he was stable, even if he was seeing ghosts. The visions galvanized Vega, warming his skin and bringing a sparkle to his eyes. Responding to questions, he insisted he saw men on the cliff.

They agreed upon a plan—Matt would walk as far as he could and swim the rest of the way to the anchored Silverton. Vega would wait with the gear, stay in the sun and warm up.

Matt took flippers, mask and snorkel. The dry suit, buoyant as a life vest, would make swimming easy. The walk along the cliff went well, but working his way out into the water was slow, difficult and potentially dangerous. Matt could break a leg or arm on the sharp, slippery rocks, his rubber booties giving poor footing. Matt was actually sweating when he got into the water and kicked toward the boat.

Boarding the boat and yelling for Tanya, Matt quickly checked the bunks, engines, bilges and batteries and sucked down a beer. He had the VHF mike in his hand to call the coast guard—but hung it up again. *What do we know, except Tanya is missing and a wreck we didn't report has blown up?* Matt thought.

It took over a half hour to bring the boat back to the spot where they had climbed the cliff. Matt secured an anchor and very carefully let it out to bring the stern within a few feet of the rock ledge. The wave action, slight in the afternoon calm, and the crystal clean water, showing all the rocks and boulders to avoid allowed Matt to use bumpers and a spring line to secure the boat stern toward the shore. Matt could step from the dive platform to the rock ledge. He called for Vega and began to load the tanks and gear, getting very warm in his dry suit. After the gear was stored with still no Vega, Matt peeled off his dry suit, replaced it with a hooded sweatshirt and went in search of Vega. Matt was not comfortable with the boat's vulnerable position—the anchorage was open to the waves, with rocks at every side.

Matt found Vega in an excited state; Vega pulled Matt along a flat pathway that lead to an inland cliff, guarded by several large, granite outcroppings. The rocks formed a cave-like structure.

Vega went to a ring of stones that once formed a fire pit with a wind break. The stones were darkened, but no ashes remained. This area was clearly a camp site at one time. Vega lead Matt deeper into the overhanging rock wall, he pointed at what looked like random white scratches on the ancient, black, basaltic rock surface. He pointed to and ran his finger over several scratches, talking as he moved over the wall, "These are words—that could be Carol and that clearly is a K. There is—something, something – then 33. Here—something, something, something, L L and that is clearly POX. Here is a whole group of letters that the lichen has destroyed or covered. This is a J and an L—as in Jud Livingston—and more scratches covered with lichens. I need to get the camera."

Matt looked around, "Whatever happened here isn't going to change much for sometime—we need to get off this island and get our asses to shore—all the time we swam I tried to think of what is going on, I've got a feeling the Livingstons will be moving on Anita—they left us for dead and are covering their tracks and destroying their history. I think Tanya is a hostage to control your wife. *I hope so anyway.* I made a mistake believing that they were only weird, but basically decent, people. I dismissed my primitive instincts: stupid. They will pay for what they've done today."

Boarding the boat, Matt and Vega quickly headed for Marquette. Dry clothes, hot coffee, a couple of brandies restored their strength and spirit, and they unsuccessfully tried to contact Anita Vega. They discussed calling the police and decided against it. Vega didn't trust legal authorities. Matt felt that an all-out confrontation with the Livingstons would prove futile and would likely jeopardize Tanya. Vega's pictures provided some leverage over the Livingstons and—if all else failed— Matt wanted the opportunity for rough justice without the law as a buffer or witness.

Vega talked about the men he had seen on the rocks. Matt told the tale of the misty figures he also had seen there. Vega mentioned his Cuban childhood when ghosts and spirits were readily a part of their traditions and folk tales. He summarized, "We need to find out how two men ended up on that rock in 1933. There is a lot we don't know about this world, and who knows about the next?"

On the run back, they packed away the diving gear aboard the *Ferr Play*, leaving the tanks on board. Their priorities—get to Anita at home and find Tanya.

The drive east was strained. Mat and Vega reviewed all they had seen and experienced. Spear guns—in themselves—are not death threats, trying to free trapped divers could explain the explosions, taking a grieving woman on board might be an act of kindness, leaving a boat in a less exposed position could be good boatmanship. Matt squeezed the wheel and kept the speedometer at 80 mph, slowing for a few approaching vehicles but never seeing a car coming up behind them. Deer had to worry about themselves.

Matt observed Vega repeating himself but then, finally, the tired man nodded off when they were on the long, straight road between Shingleton and Seney. Matt was tired too, but kept the GMC's pedal to the metal until they hit McLeod's Corner, leaving highway 28 and shooting down toward Garnet, Rexton and then the quarry.

Two hours and a few minutes after leaving the hills of Marquette, with Matt breaking every speed law, the sun was setting as they pulled into the driveway.

13

Anita

The car lights illuminated the open garage, overcoming the dark shadows of twilight as Matt and George Vega swung into the driveway, showing a clutter of boxes and materials previously on the walls or various workbenches. The screen stood closed but its accompanying door was open into the kitchen area. Matt rushed into the kitchen, shouting for Mrs. Vega, George Vega searching outside the house yelling, "Anita," over and over. Silence answered their cries.

The house had been searched, the metal box from the wreck was gone, the Canon digital camera lay on the table, its CompactFlash chip slot open and empty. The file of pictures gone from its storage box; the plastic bags of ship's documents also gone. Matt found a hand-printed note on the kitchen counter reading simply:

YOU WILL BE CALLED ON THIS PHONE.

No phone could be found by sight or search. Anita's purse was sitting at its usual daytime position, a table by the door, her cell phone gone. Matt tried her number with no result.

George ran in. "Call her again—I could hear the tune."

The men went outside, Matt continuously calling Anita's number. The faint sound of a Bach tune came to them on the wind from the north. Quickly walking north, 50 feet apart, they converged on a stand of hard maples with thick brush forming a forest wall. The notes got louder. Diving into the brush Vega came upon his wife. She was curled into a fetal ball, clutching two cell phones, nested in forest dirt and leaves. Her eyes were open but she showed no recognition when Vega picked her up and backed through the brush to return her to the house.

Matt followed; George Vega wouldn't let him help carry Anita. Vega, breathing hard and making raspy whimpering sounds, carried her into the great room, putting her on a sofa. Anita immediately resumed her ball-like posture. Matt wet a cloth and began cleaning her dirt- and leaf-covered face and hair. George Vega knelt beside his wife and held her hands. His breathing was fast and shallow, his color white. Matt had two suffering people in his charge. He got water for Anita and a splash of brandy for George.

George didn't touch the brandy, but Anita took a sip of the water and seemed to realize someone held the glass for her. Matt saw her eyes clear, then focus and then move over the two men in front of her. She took another sip and spoke. "Are you really here?"

Dropping the cell phones, Anita began touching both men, color filling her cheeks. "Tanya said you drowned. Men have her. She called from a ship. I'm not to talk about her, the ship or the wreck. Two men came—took all the boat things—masked—mean—whispering, gave me a note and phone. Tanya called me. If I didn't do what they said they would come back and I'd never see my daughter again."

Matt heard a groan; turning, with Anita's water in his hands, watching helplessly as George fell face first to the floor. He never put out his arms and the hollow sound of a head striking a hard surface filled the quiet room.

Matt rolled him over—blood streamed from one nostril, a neck artery gave a thready pulse. He was breathing, skin wet and color white. Matt moved him to a sitting position against the sofa. For lack of other ideas, gave him a sip of water. George, eyes unfocused, started to slump forward. Matt held him and ordered Anita to get some aspirin. Anita, moving from the sofa, quickly returned with an aspirin bottle. Matt got two 325 mg pills into George, then helping him up, got him into the back seat of the Yukon. Anita followed, pillowing his head on her lap.

They headed for St. Ignace, using the cell phone and 911—an ambulance met them half way. An hour later, they sat in the emergency room waiting area while a medical team examined and got medications and fluids into George. Anita surprised Matt by showing strength and resiliency.

A doctor finally came into the room. George had had a heart attack. The blood work and various other tests would tell them the extent of the damage and aid their diagnosis and prognosis. The doctor questioned them about Vega's preattack activities. Matt told about their dive—holding nothing back about its depth or length, gas mixtures, or their exertion and head bumps. He omitted the explosions, hyperthermia, ghosts, spear guns, kidnapping, concussions, hiding in a black room 150 feet under Lake Superior, robbery, carrying his near-catatonic wife a hundred yards and the ongoing threats of two crazy, Canadian billionaire brothers. Halfway through the list of the day's activities that Matt described, the doctor diagnosed the cause of the attack as brought on by overexertion. He waited impatiently for Matt to finish, proclaiming the patient stable and needing a night in their hospital for observation. Because they had no cardiologist Vega would be transferred to Marquette in the morning. For now his EKG, BP, blood oxygen levels were all good. The Air Force and Medicare insurance programs allowed for a complete battery of heart-related tests and procedures in Marquette and for the several thousand dollars of ambulance transportation.

Matt and Anita visited George—conscious and comfortable, in the care of mature floor nurses. The gathering of nurses, Matt, George and Anita all agreed that a good night's rest was best for all concerned. After a tender goodnight kiss and an agreement to table all problems and activities until tomorrow in Marquette, Anita walked out to the vehicle with Matt.

During the ride back to the quarry Matt, hoping Anita would remain as strong as she had been in the hospital, told her about the real underwater conflict—not the abbreviated account he gave the doctor—emphasizing the coolheaded action of Tanya untying the diving rope and giving them the DECO air. He omitted the skull and bullet discovery. He reminded her they had a diving camera record of most of what they saw. Matt had Anita review her actions and the specific words and movements of the house robbers.

She gave a general description and clear chronology, but nothing new or useful. She didn't remember the type of vehicle they had. She was sure they were white, English speakers and in their 30s. Their face masks looked military issue. She remembered Tanya's call—after consideration, she felt Tanya might have been reading the message. Anita verbalized the feeling of her world coming down on her. She remembered closing the new cell phone, taking the phone from her purse and walking outside to call someone—but she couldn't think who to call and just kept walking into the woods.

Matt couldn't read Anita, her voice and attitude stronger than he expected. As she talked she was thinking and mentally coming to some conclusion. No one spoke for almost 15 minutes, then Anita suddenly broke the silence. "We need to call *Georgiy*."

Matt responded, "We just left your husband, and he's probably asleep by now."

"No, not George—*Georgiy*—you know him as Webb. He's the only man powerful enough, mean enough for this situation. He will get Tanya back and anyone involved or anyone harming her he will crush." Anita emphasized the final word by bring her fist down on the dashboard.

Matt couldn't see Anita's face in the darkened vehicle as they drove through the black night, the strength in her words seem to come from a different Anita.

Matt asked, "Don't you hate Webb?"

"Yes, like I might hate a gun, but sometimes you need a gun. A big nasty gun."

14

Get Webb

Studying the cell phone, the last link to Tanya, Matt and Anita drank coffee at their kitchen table. Matt used call-back and the number that showed on incoming calls—no phone available, no answer. Matt noticed the charging port filled with some plastic-like material—maybe hot glue or some type of epoxy. The instrument was a better grade of TracFone; but still throwaway technology.

Matt talked—as much to himself as to Anita. "All their moves thought out ahead. This was bought days before they headed out on their boat—they figured to take someone hostage, they knew they had to get the wreck material we had here. Every move was coordinated ahead of time, both on the water and land. They needed to control you while escaping back to Canada or someplace on the lake. We have to let them know George and I live—it should make sure they keep Tanya healthy." Matt looked at Anita—she was tracking with his logic, she hadn't pulled back into any world of denial or fantasy. Matt continued, "What makes you think Webb will help us?"

Anita took the phone, holding it tightly in her hand, "Just call him—he'll help—I knew him from before I married—we met in Miami in the late '60s. George Vega was in boot camp, and we got married on his first leave. The Russians were all over Miami back then—lots of fun and money—a wild time. I ran with my Cuban girlfriends, too young to drink in the bars—we still always found a party someplace. Anyway—call him—he watched Tanya grow up— he'll help us."

Using his personal cell phone, Matt punched in Carla's number. Her phone was not available. Matt then tried Al's number—on the same note Carla had left when she and Al visited—no answer, but a "Please leave your message after the beep" instruction came up. Matt left an urgent plea for a call back or, better yet, for Webb to call—it was regarding Tanya's being missing, actually taken. Kidnapped.

Closing his phone, Matt took a sip of coffee and looked at Anita— she was crying.

They agreed to get some sleep, calling early in the morning to coordinate their travels with the transfer of George to Marquette. Matt left his cell phone with Anita while he showered, afraid to miss any calls. Matt had made the coffee machine ready for the morning and was just turning off the kitchen light when his cell phone chimed.

Matt answered and waited for a response, there was a pause of several seconds before a familiar voice said, "You know who this is?"

"Yes," answered Matt—it was Webb.

"Do not say my name or any names. Can you get to Sault Ste. Marie in two hours?"

Matt automatically looked at his watch, turned on the coffee pot and said, "Yes."

"Good, the main entrance of the U.S. side casino." Webb confirmed they were on the same time and hung up.

Looking up, Matt saw Anita in the doorway.

'Webb wants to meet at the Sault in two hours—do you want to come?"

Anita looked tired and uncertain; she thought for a few seconds. "No, I'm needed in Marquette in the morning. You have all the information—my description of the two men I saw isn't much help. We can talk by cell phone if something comes up you need from me. I'll be alright—I'll lock up the house and load George's shotgun—don't come in quiet."

Matt put on clean clothes, poured his vacuum cup full of coffee, grabbed an apple. "I'll call you in the morning—keep your phone on and charged. I'll take the phone they left with you—maybe Tanya will call again or maybe Webb can get some information from it. Try to get some sleep. I'm glad you're being so strong."

Matt gave Anita a hug and left.

The drive to the Sault went quickly, no near misses with ever-present deer. The easy-to-find casino was actually in the suburbs of the city—down several regular streets that all funneled into 40 acres of parking lot. The clearly marked main entrance welcomed Matt 15 minutes before the two-hour rendezvous time. The midnight hour on a school night didn't seem to lessen the hundreds of gambling guests, the constant jingle of slot machines providing pervasive noise. Walking by a guard standing at the main security desk, Matt easily scanned the huge room from steps leading down into the main floor of machines and tables. No one of interest looked at him, no Webb.

Carla came up behind Matt. "Hi, we're outside."

She hugged Matt, took his hand, leading him several rows into the parking area. Al joined them as they moved away from the bright lights of the entrance. Webb stood by a large, dark sedan and opened a door for Matt to get into the back seat. Al and Carla got into the front seats.

Webb looked tanned and fit in a light-colored shirt and sweater worn with Dockers and Sperry loafers. His hair was still in a crew cut, his massive arms and shoulders took up his half of the backseat. His eyes looked tired but very concerned.

"Tell me everything—Carla and Al want to hear too."

Matt went through the whole experience from the initial dive to the last moment when he heard the engines moving away. The situation with Anita made Webb's jaw knot and he gripped his coffee mug like he wanted it to be someone's neck. He only interrupted Matt's story a few times for points of clarification. Carla broke in twice to offer sympathy and concern. Al asked two questions about spelling and company names—he was taking notes on a very cop-like pad.

"How is Anita taking this?" asked Webb.

"She was literally a basket case when we found her after she talked to Tanya, thinking everyone she loved was gone. She came back strong—especially when George had his attack. She'll take care of George in Marquette tomorrow." Matt glanced at the luminous hands of his watch and added, "Actually, today."

Hunger and a few yawns forced them to adjourn to the casino's restaurant. Matt got his Canon digital and the CompactFlash card he had taken from the underwater camera. In a booth of the nearly empty eating area, they reviewed the excellent pictures of the dive. Matt tried to spare Carla the pictures of skulls and bones—but she insisted on seeing everything. Al recorded the names and numbers from the wheelhouse's brass plates. He recorded the name and as much of a description of the Livingston boat as Matt could provide and the license number of the car that came during the party. Al looked at the cell phone Tanya had called. Webb said to take it—it might provide some information. Webb and Al asked a dozen questions about the Livingston's that Matt couldn't answer or could only answer partially: family, children, homes, education, sources of income, who are their enemies, why do they really care about a 60-year-old shipwreck, who does their dirty work?

Carla asked if Tanya's clothes were gone off the Silverton—Matt said he thought they were gone. At least they weren't on the bunk where she put them in the morning when she changed into diving underwear. Carla optimistically pointed out that was a good sign they would be keeping her.

Webb took the bill from the table, got up and looked at everyone. Speaking in a low voice, he said, "We will find her and get her back. Matt, there's a phone in the car for you. You can't believe what the NSA and DEA can do with cell phone traffic. Don't ever say my name or anything incriminating. I've heard about these brothers—through friends of friends. By this time tomorrow they need to know you are alive and have those pictures. Guard yourself and your home—I know you can be smart and mean." Webb looked around the empty room again, "I'll have some communication with the brothers Livingston, too—I don't use lawyers or courts."

At the sedan, with a space-age cell phone and a list of numbers in his hand, Matt said his thanks and goodbyes. Webb hugged Matt,

Carla kissed him on both cheeks, Al shook his hand, mentioning they needed to drop the rental off at the airport on the Canadian side where they had a Cessna Skymaster parked. Matt looked puzzled until Al told him Webb was an accomplished pilot. The plane explained how they got from Manitoulin Island so quickly.

Matt, wired with caffeine and making only one pit stop, got back to the quarry as pink hues lightened the eastern sky behind him. He made a lot of noise: the garage door rumbling, key rattling in the locked kitchen door and finally announcing his presence before he entered the house. Anita met him in the kitchen showing him she didn't have a shotgun. She had him repeat all the activities with Webb. After Matt finished, she smiled and got up, announcing she was going to lie down for another two hours.

15

Finding Livingstons

Failing to sleep, Matt put the CF card from the underwater camera into the Canon MP970 printer/copier, making prints of various underwater pictures of the *Carol K*. Running out of photo-quality paper, he printed on regular paper. He made two sets of prints, saving one set in a file folder and the other went into a manila mailing envelope. Addressing the envelope to a friend in Gladstone, he planned to mail it at the first post office on the way to Marquette. Sealed with the prints in its own envelope, labeled "DO NOT open until October 31," was a signed note giving the location of the wreck and naming the Livingston's as murderers and kidnappers. A cover page included an instruction asking his friend to take it to the State Police post if Matt didn't get back to him by the end of the month. Matt felt his actions must be duplicating some B movie he had seen, but at least it was action, making him feel less powerless.

Anita made a big breakfast; she hadn't slept enough to matter, either. She also had packed a bag with her husband's clothes and toilet articles.

A shower and clean clothes made them feel better. They headed for Marquette at 7:30, lists of all the phone numbers they might need lying on the dashboard.

Matt mailed the package at Seney, having no luck contacting Thunder Bay—the Livingstons' office not opening until 9:00—but with a hospital call they learned George Vega was doing fine and in transit, scheduled to arrive in Marquette by 10:30. Intermittent cell phone coverage put drama into every call as they drove west on highway 28. Nearing Munising, Webb's phone rang,

Anita answered it, speaking directly to Webb for the first time in many years. Matt only could hear one side of the conversation, but Anita's tone was anxious, not rude, some of her comments grateful, some with low conspiratorial tones. Stopping the vehicle, Matt took the phone, switching its speaker on so Anita could hear, and said, "Hello, Webb, what's happening?"

"I have people working as we speak. The ship named *Gull Cry* doesn't exist, but the Livingstons own an eighty-two-foot, converted Coast Guard vessel, they both have master's papers and the ship left its dock two days ago, the regular crew on shore. It is called *Sleeping Giant*—after the hills behind Thunder Bay. Al and I are in Thunder Bay now, Al's being an investigator again. We flew Carla back to her mother on Manitoulin, gassed up and flew here. I'll be at the Livingston's office when it opens—we know they're gone but we'll pump their staff for information. They both have families and enemies. Keep trying to contact them. Don't call me unless you have some new information. Good luck."

Webb ended the call.

Starting the Yukon, heading it west, Matt felt tired. No one had mentioned Tanya. Matt felt blind hate flooding his soul. He wanted to hurt the Livingstons, make them feel helpless and scared like he felt now.

The hills of Marquette and an answer at the Livingstons' office came at the same time. Matt stopped the SUV to talk to the answering secretary. She was polite but couldn't help Matt contact the CEOs, not even offering phone mail. She blocked every tack Matt took. He hung up in disgust.

They drove to the ambulance entrance of the hospital. From a parking lot across the street, they could see the driveway. In the parking lot, they made a new plan. Matt wrote out names, numbers and a cover story, then rehearsed Anita for a new attempt to get to the Livingstons. They had over an hour before George Vega was expected to arrive and now they had a plan.

Anita called the Livingston headquarters, asking for Lolan, the private chef of the Livingstons. She said she was calling for her boss—Mr. Dawson—who ran *Specialty Meats*, the supplier of the ostrich meat they had shipped to the Livingston Brothers. It was very important, even urgent they talk with Lolan before any of the last shipment was consumed. After several responses of "Please hold" and two more explanations, Lolan came on the line. In broken, hesitant English she explained the Livingstons were on a trip in their boat while she remained on shore. She had made and frozen several meals for them, ostrich being used in two of them. Anita said to hold for Mr. Dawson, passing the phone to Matt, her eyes sparkling with the progress they were making.

Matt took the phone, trying to talk in a deeper voice than Lolan had heard on the helicopter. "Lolan, it is imperative no one consumes the ostrich meat from the last shipment we made. We are shipping you, free, another order of frozen breasts and thighs. How may we contact the Livingstons?"

Lolan nervously replying, "They go their boat, it had radios, they have phones too. I get their phone numbers—please wait."

Matt pumped the air with his fist in triumph.

Lolan, after a minute's delay, gave both men's personal cell phone numbers. Matt thanked her and said he would call them immediately, but she should also leave a message to not eat the ostrich—winking at Anita as he said it.

Matt next called Webb's number—giving him the new information. Webb said for Matt to call them, adding, "Ask them if their granddaughters still use the white playhouse."

Matt said he didn't understand, Webb said, "Just do it, I'll call them in a few hours, when I do they will know they are not playing with amateurs." Then he hung up.

Steeling himself for the phone call, Matt thought of what he wanted to say and how he would issue a demand to talk to Tanya. As he was putting in the phone numbers, a red Rampart ambulance pulled into the emergency entrance. Anita got out of the vehicle and crossed the street, returning quickly to the SUV to announce, "Not him."

Matt pressed the Send button.

"Yes?" was Jud Livingston's answer.

"Jud, this is Matt Hunter—I want to speak to Tanya."

There was no sound for several seconds, then Jud answered, "What makes you think we know where she is? This is a private number, how did you get it?"

"Mr. Vega and I are very much alive, we have pictures of the wreck with skeletons, and very clear ship identification. Let me talk to Tanya."

Jud, sounding less authoritative, replied, "I repeat I don't, I can't, help you."

"Know this Livingston, if Tanya doesn't call me on this number, we will take you and your family apart—totally. Oh, and do your grand-daughters still use the white playhouse?" Then Matt closed the phone.

He felt totally drained, Anita was crying.

Matt put the phone on the console between the seats, his hands ice cold, his stomach tight and shaky. *Adrenaline reaction, if I could choke someone I'd feel better...*he thought. Grabbing the steering wheel, Matt tested its tensile strength—it didn't break, but bent a little. *Breaking the wheel would really be a dumb move—asshole.*

Another ambulance pulled in across the street—St. Ignace on its side. Matt and Anita crossed the street and entered the emergency area. Matt checked the cell phone and, seeing only one reception bar, stopped like he had hit an invisible barrier.

"I can't come in here," he told Anita, holding up the phone.

"It's OK, I've been in hospitals before and the best medicine for George will be getting Tanya back. I'll come to the car when I know something." Carrying a bag, Anita followed the gurney.

Matt returned to the vehicle. Pushing the button to recline the leather seat and closing his eyes, he tried to relax.

Anita's tapping on the window woke Matt several hours later. Matt checked the phone in case he had slept through a call—there were no new calls.

Anita gave her report on her husband. "George is fine, tests, and two doctors say so—they will wheel him out to the main lobby in a few minutes. We need to drive around and pick him up. He's hungry and wants to get home."

Collecting a very tired but healthy George Vega, they ate fast food in the Yukon while driving east, watching the reception bars fluctuate between five and one all the way to the quarry. No calls, no communication. Anita and George were both sleeping when Matt drove into the garage.

Later, in the house at the table, they all watched a nonresponsive cell phone.

Matt finally broke the silent vigil. "The Livingstons will call, but it's our bluff. We need to get ahead of them. They always have plans, they attack when threatened. They will come after us. Webb will go after them. We don't know about Tanya."

He nervously tapped his fingers on the tabletop. With a sigh, he said, "OK, Let's call them again and record the call—it's doubtful, but they may say something we can use. I've got a tape machine and a plug-in microphone—it will record a cell phone with the speaker phone on. Also, we should close up the house and get some firearms ready."

Matt unplugged the speakers from his Aiwa stereo system in the front room and brought the unit into the kitchen, an old Sony mic plugged into it. Adding a new tape made it a good recording device. They also locked the house, turning on outside lights against the approach of evening, and loaded a Marlin 30-30 and a Remington 700 deer rifle. Matt felt better being active. He even made a scouting tour around the house and down the road, taking an old 20 gauge shotgun, a roll of twenty pound fish line and some duct tape.

Half an hour later, they were around the table again. Matt spoke, "I put a line across the road, about fifty yards away—it will fire the shotgun if someone drives in. I taped the gun to a limb so it will just shoot out into the woods."

Fortified with caffeine from strong coffee, the trio made their call to the Livingstons—with agonizing finality neither phone answered or even acknowledged the call with an offer of voice mail. Frustrated, staring at the phone, they waited.

Unable to stand the inaction any longer, Matt left the table, returning dressed in camouflaged hunting clothes and boots. He took the loaded Remington, pocketing several more of the large shells. "I'm going outside. You know how to work the cell phone, turn on its speaker and just push the record lever with the orange dot on the Aiwa. Don't get the Sony mic too close—stay about three feet away so you don't get feedback. I've been thinking—the shotgun is a crude warning. It lets the enemy know we know they are here. Also, if I wanted to get us, I'd call—keep us focused and attack us while we were talking. I'd come in the dark—which is soon. While I'm out, lock the door and close the blinds."

Matt left through a side door, not opening the garage doors; edging around the house, he quietly worked through the brush toward the road using a game trail paralleling the road. It wasn't really dark yet, the lights inside just made it look darker outside.

He came to the tree he had tied the monofilament line to—the line was slack. Picking up the line, Matt melted into the thicker brush and pulled the line slowly. Retrieving over 20 feet of it, Matt knew it was cut or broken close to the shotgun. The end looked cut. Working slowly and quietly to the road Matt saw a car 50 yards down the road. Matt picked a spot with trees and shrubs close to two-track road and, crawling across the road, quietly cut free the shotgun; the line had been sliced two feet from the gun.

Game on.

Good hunters get into position when they can see—knowing it's dumb to stumble around in unfamiliar woods in the dark. So they had probably come up the edge of the road and spotted the line silhouetted against the setting sun.

Matt took the line and gun to the car, the same one used by the two men he met at the party. Pushing the shotgun under the vehicle from the passenger side, stock in the ground, barrel jammed into the undercarriage and touching the gas tank, Matt reattached the line running to the trigger. Passing the line under the car, tightly over the right front tire, working it into the tread, finally Matt secured it to the valve stem. Any forward motion would pull the line. He also put a strong stick against the trigger, braced into the dirt and mud of the road. When he cocked the hammer, Matt knew the shotgun would go off; its one-ounce slug going into the tank, regardless of which way the car moved. If the men lived through the stalk Matt planned to put on them, he hoped they would cook in their own car.

I hope I don't burn down the woods, Matt thought.

Matt checked his watch—20 minutes before full dark and about 25 minutes to the hour. Given the Livingstons' skill for organization, Matt bet the phone call and attack would happen on the hour. Visualizing what the men had seen as they stalked to the house, he could guess where they would be hiding. Matt checked his rifle, putting another shell in the magazine to make up for the one he had chambered.

Brushing out his tracks, his stalk began on the far side of the road.

16

Bolt Action

Unsnapping the rifle sling to reduce noise, Matt started up the road toward the house. He hung the sling on a roadside branch, hoping he could find it later. The boot tracks of two people showing clearly in the last of the low-angle twilight, Matt had to decide between finding the men or cutting right, getting off the road and warning the Vegas in the house. If their positions now covered the house, he would be giving up the tactical advantage of being behind them. Matt was tired of being the victim, he really wanted to inflict some pain.

The tracks cut into the woods about the place that the driveway and house lights could be seen from the road. Matt cut in too, going deeper through the woods, all the way to a trail that was a road in the 1930s. Clear of noisy leaves and underbrush, the trail allowed Matt quickly to circle to another path that had been the walkway from the old boarding house to the crusher plant. Leading directly to the house, the path provided quiet, fast travel. Stopping 20 yards from the main road and 40 yards from the house, Matt edged off the path and blended into some chokecherry bushes.

Whispers travel for many yards in the woods, sounding as unnatural as opening a foil bag of potato chips; they identified the location of both men. Matt went back on the path, moving to the far right side, concealed from line of sight by a natural curve. The path allowed quiet travel for another dozen yards, putting Matt close to and behind the unseen men. Matt knelt in the high weeds and listened, panning his eyes back and forth to pick up any movement in the now totally dark woods.

The lights from the house scattered and glowed through the trees and brush. Matt avoided looking into their brightness. Seeing a movement, Matt thought he could see one man's shape and then a second. Duck walking through the grass, Matt got closer, his knees protesting this exercise. Stopping 40 feet from the men, he clearly distinguished two silhouettes against the lights of the house. They had rifles.

Matt's Remington model 700 7mm Magnum was not a weapon made to capture men with rifles. It was a bolt-action rifle, made to put one shot very accurately on a target. Working the bolt action meant taking his eye from the scope. One shot, one man wasn't good enough. The other would roll into the brush and have the advantage of the ambient light behind him, exposing any move Matt might make. Matt framed the men in his scope—cranking it to its maximum 10 power, so close the focus was blurred. He could only locate the cross hair by sliding the sight off target into a light area, finding the center and then bringing it back to where he hoped it aligned with the target. The men were close together, the same two who had come to the house. Their rifles were AR-15 or M-16 military—with 30-shot magazines, lots of semi-automatic firepower—they had on vests that held extra magazines but didn't seem to be body armor.

Weighing his alternatives, Matt rejected all but one.

With a thumb and finger, Matt silently took his rifle off safety. Rising up, taking a shooting stance, Matt had both men in the sight picture. When they leaned together to whisper Matt clearly saw the left shoulder of one, overlapping the right arm and shoulder of the other. With five ounces of trigger pressure, Matt fired a 150 grain nosiler partitioned bullet through both men.

Matt couldn't tell where the bullet hit. Both men went down. Matt worked his bolt, ejecting the spent shell and chambering another, as he sprinted to the sprawling men. Standing over them he saw one rifle thrown to the side, but couldn't see the other.

Both men thrashing in the leaves looked up to see Matt holding the rifle six feet from their heads.

"Move away from your rifles. Get on the path," barked Matt.

One crawled toward the cleared ground and increased light of the path. The other just sank onto the ground and stopped moving. Matt moved to the rifle he could see and picked it up. It had a sling, so Matt put it over his shoulder. The other weapon was still not visible, but neither man now had a rifle.

Matt had no intention of getting closer to either downed man. He couldn't see wounds or blood and really didn't know where or how badly they had been hit. Just as Matt started to plan his next action, a bright beam of light shined down the path.

George Vega came up the path with a five-cell flashlight held against the stock of a 30-30 rifle. He called out, "Matt? Are you OK? I heard a gunshot."

"Yes, I've got two men with rifles. Come on, I need your help." Matt answered.

With the light they found the other rifle. Vega put the 30-30 with its sling over his shoulder and aimed the black rifle he'd picked up at the men. He studied the selector lever on the left of the rifle above the pistol grip, noting, "These are M-16s, military—safe, semi and burst selections."

Helping the man in the path to his feet, Matt noted his left shoulder and arm appeared as one bloody stain, the arm hanging uselessly. The other man was dead. Rolling him over, the flashlight beam exposed a massive, upper chest wound, a shiny black pool of blood and a haunting death stare.

Matt checked his watch—four minutes before the hour. He went to the wounded man. "When will they call us?"

The man looked blankly at Matt. Taking the man's rag-like left wrist, lifting the arm, Matt exposed the man's watch. Matt turned the watch up so Vega could put the light beam on it. The man yelled in pain, Matt rotated the wrist back and forth, the man fell to his knees and said, "Three minutes, on the hour."

In the glare of the five-cell Matt removed the wounded man's vest, causing him more pain as the material touched his arm. Matt also searched him for more weapons, finding a wallet and a jackknife. The vest was heavy and contained more magazines in its many pockets. Vega checked the dead man once more, almost hoping their original assessment could have been wrong.

"Let's move to the house and get the call," said Matt, helping the wounded man up the path.

17

Exchange

The chiming cell phone greeted Matt as he entered the kitchen. George had the wounded man in the garage, sitting on a chair. Anita brought the phone to Matt and peeked into the garage at the wounded man.

Matt opened the phone, a number showing with no area code Matt recognized.

Tanya's voice came from the phone, "Matt? Matt?"

"Yes, thank God, how are you?"

Matt took the phone over to the table, clicking on the recorder and positioning the microphone toward the phone, keeping a two-foot distance.

Tanya answered, "I'm fine, haven't been harmed in any way. I have to read a note." She began reading a statement about how this was all a mistake and an overreaction. Apologies went on for several sentences, very sincere, very redundant. Never mentioning the Livingstons, kidnapping, the diving or the ship, the statement included the rescuing of a distraught Tanya from a stalled boat and several attempts to contact

Matt via radio and cell phones. All a litany of lies, half truths and just filler bullshit.

Matt noted both Vegas listening closely, George just inside the door, a rifle in his hands aimed at the wounded man. Matt noted a tapping noise as Tanya was reading—Morse code? He couldn't follow the taps, but he knew the recording would give them more information. Matt wanted to break in and tell them to shove this crap, but it would interrupt the tapping. The cell phone only allowed one-way conversation, if Matt spoke, Tanya's words and taps would be lost.

The message finally ended with Tanya's own words, "And that's all I can say."

Matt waited a few seconds to make sure Tanya's message was over.

Speaking slowly, Matt said, "I love you honey. Please tell the Livingstons we met the two men they sent. One is in the garage ready to tell us everything he knows and the other is beyond earthly cares. We will trade a wounded man for a healthy you. If the man doesn't have medical attention he will loose his arm, then his life, depending upon how long this exchange takes. Also remind them we are not the only ones concerned about your health, there are others—far meaner than us— who will punish the Livingstons worse than any of their nightmares."

"Just a minute," Tanya said. Then there was silence for over a minute.

"We'll call you back." Then the call ended.

Matt put the phone down, stopped the recorder and went into the garage, muttering, "Let's see if we can help him."

An hour of medical efforts left the man with a bandaged left arm, resting on the guest bed, comfortable thanks to some pain pills. His arm bone was not broken, but his left bicep would never be the same again. The wound, now clean with the bleeding stopped and some of the muscle badly traumatized and looking like hamburger could easily become gangrenous without expert medical treatment and drugs.

His name was Lester Anderson, not Tom as he had told them before, he had several hitches of Canadian military service but never saw combat. He would not admit their mission was any more than to scare, not kill, anyone. Matt tied the man's ankles to the bed, leaving Anita to watch him and to sound an alarm if he tried to get up.

Matt and George listened to the tape several times. The tapping seemed to be random at first, a nervous hand with a ring holding the cell phone. Then the taps became regular and structured. Nine letters in groups of three were repeated several times. The letters and groups, Matt and George finally agreed—after working out all the variants of groups and Morse letters, discussing what a long dot or a short dash might do to the group— spelled BOT CAN ISL.

"She's on a boat at a Canadian Island," Matt concluded. "That limits her location to about a thousand places, but it's more that we knew before."

"And she's alive and has her wits about her," added George.

Collecting the note papers and closing a book of Morse code, Matt said, "We're looking for an 82-foot boat in the Canadian Islands of Lake Superior that's a specific shoreline with a finite amount of islands. Webb can get us the ship description, and he has a plane. We need to call him."

Vega ran the tape to a new spot and turned the machine off, then said, "We need to do something about Lester upstairs and the guy outside. I don't think we'll get any more out of Lester—he didn't admit to anything while I probed his arm and pulled out chunks of muscle, he didn't even pass out. He's tough."

"Yes, and I shot him from behind, without warning. Watching a house at night with automatic weapons shouldn't be punishable by death or dismemberment, if he gets a good lawyer. I read about a person getting prison time for just wounding an intruder in their house at night, the guy said he just needed to use the telephone. We need more evidence about their mission."

Matt pointed at the rifle beside George. "Can you make the M-16 not fire—but leave the bullets in?"

Picking up the M-16 leaning against the table, Vega nodded. "Nothing to it, we just file down the firing pin—wrecks the rifle, but he wouldn't know anything's wrong 'til he pulls the trigger."

"Do it, we need to protect ourselves and stay ahead of these people. You get the rifle rigged and I'll try to think up a way to get Lester to get the drop on us."

George held the M-16, pushing a little pin located just a little behind the trigger on the right side through the action, the pin's exposed head came out the other side. When George pulled it out to its limit, the rifle broke open like a shotgun, he pulled out the tubular bolt assembly and took it to the work shop. Using needle-nose pliers, he pulled out a cotter pin and shook the bolt. The firing pin dropped into his hands.

Matt watched. "That took you almost twenty seconds."

Laying the shiny pin on the workbench, George took a pencil and marked its length on the wood. Flicking on an electric grinder he made sparks for a few seconds, then compared the pin for length with the pencil marks, then more sparks, another comparison. He let it cool for a moment, sprayed on some WD-40 and put it back into the bolt assembly. He maneuvered the bolt and cocking handle back into the breech, closed the upper assembly back into the lower trigger and stock unit and reset the locking pin.

Taking the rifle outside, George said, "Let's see if it will fire."

He pulled the loading lever, letting it slam forward to chamber a shell from the magazine. Aiming it into the woods, he pulled the trigger.

Click.

Four more reloads just produced four ejected shells, four metallic clicks and no bangs. Picking up the shells and snapping them back into the 30-shot magazine, George handed the rifle back to Matt and said, "I had to qualify with this weapon every year, the Air Force was the first service to use the M-16."

Matt put the rifle on the work bench. "Let's make a plan, then have you take over guard duty with Lester. I'll explain what we're doing to your wife when she comes down."

After some plotting and rehearsing some choreography around the kitchen, George went upstairs and Anita came down. Explaining their plot to Anita out in the garage, they returned to the kitchen and waited. Matt turned on the recorder and put it and its microphone on a side shelf, with a box of cereal in front of the recording light.

Matt and George went up to the bedroom where Les lay on a bed. Matt stood just out of eye sight in the hall way, ready to help George if their plan got out of hand. He could see and hear most of the action in the room. Les couldn't see him.

George checked for a chambered round and that the lever was on safe, before propping the rifle against the door jamb He crossed the bedroom to check on the wounded prisoner who watched his every move. He asked, "How do you feel?"

Lester looked tired and had a voice to match. "I hurt, you asshole. What are you going to do with me? I need a doctor."

"We just had a short phone call with the Livingstons—we told them you would loose your arm or even die without help. They didn't seem too concerned—said they'd call us back. They're very cool customers. Have you worked for them long?"

"A couple of years…" Lester said, knowing he had said too much. Then he just glared. Moving around on the bed, he jerked a leg against the rope. "How about taking this off so I can move my leg? It's cramping."

George slowly untied the rope from the foot of the bed. "Don't get out of bed or I'll pull your arm off and beat the shit out of you with it." Then he went to a chair across the room by the door. Watching Vega settling into the overstuffed chair, Lester laid back onto his pillow, exercising he newly freed leg.

Twenty minutes went by. A scream preceding a crash came from downstairs. A few seconds of silence, then Matt, who had moved downstairs, called, "George, get down here, Anita fell."

Racing down the stairs, George left the rifle, yelling, "Anita, Anita, *Madre de Dios!*"

George, Matt and Anita shuffled chairs and the table around to make some noise. The talked in somewhat hushed tones, just loud enough to be heard upstairs.

Then they waited by the sink, Anita on the floor, propped up by George who knelt beside her. Matt was applying a cloth filled with ice cubes to Anita's forehead while they all kept their backs to the stairs. They could just hear Lester slowly coming down the stairs.

"Turn around, but don't move fast." Lester's sounded firm.

They all turned slowly to see Lester standing there with the rifle sling over his head and across his chest, supporting the M-16 which he held aimed and level in his good right hand and arm. His words were accompanied by a grin, and his eyes sparkled with pain, power and control.

Matt stood and moved in front of Anita and George, who remained on the floor. "Easy, no need to get excited, we can work out a deal. The Livingstons will be calling any time." Matt motioned to the cell phone on the kitchen table.

Lester moved into the room, "When they call, I'm going to be the only one to answer."

George Vega pleaded, "We saved your life, took care of you, we aren't any problem to you."

Lester moved to cover them with the smallest angle in the room. "My orders were to get rid of all of you, after I had the pictures of the boat. Where are they?"

Matt took a large envelope from the kitchen counter, spreading the pictures and dumping the CF chip on top of them. "Here's everything, just take these and it's our word against yours. You don't need to shoot us—it would be hard to explain."

"Yah, like my buddy with a hole in his chest out in the woods. Put all that back in the envelope."

Matt did as he was told. "Why don't you wait for the phone call, maybe your orders will change?"

"The Livingstons don't change their orders—this is for my arm and my friend." Lester pulled the trigger, the click and rattle of a spring in the stock the only sounds. He dexterously, with one arm, pulled and released the charging handle, the rifle was pointed at Matt's chest when the click came again.

Matt approached with an aluminum ball bat he had hidden against the table leg. Moving into an imaginary batter's box, turning sideways, Matt said. "Put the rifle down slowly, touching just the sling, move any other way and I'll hit a triple with your head."

Lester put the rifle on the floor, sinking to his knees, his face void of color. "Look, I was just doing a job, you shot at us first."

Matt moved the rifle away from Lester with his foot, the bat still cocked.

George now had his shotgun trained on the kneeling killer. He said, "Tell us the whole story and your involvement with the Livingstons, and we'll take you to a doctor."

The totally defeated gunman told of his contact system, how they got orders and money. His words started to slur as he came off the adrenaline high associated with the commitment to shoot three people from ten feet away with an automatic rifle.

Matt asked, "How do you know you're working for the Livingstons?"

"Any assignments always have something to do with their business or interests, and there aren't many people in Thunder Bay that pay what we ask. That boat was their dad's. Some bad shit happened back then; they don't want it getting out."

Matt helped Lester up and got him back into bed. Anita brought him some vodka on the rocks. Also, stringing the microphone as far up the stairs as its cord would reach, the interrogation continued, led by Matt.

"Do you know Livingston's boat?"

"Yes, it's the biggest in the port, old navy ship."

"Where do they go when they aren't in port?"

Lester took a sip of vodka, looking very tired. "They have a big place on an island in Lake Huron, I've never been there, but there was a story in the paper once. I'm hurting, can I have another pill?"

"You get a pill when we know where the Livingston boat is docked," whispered Matt as he shook Lester, one hand grabbing a fist full of hair, the other squeezing his neck.

Lester gasped, "I don't know, you can see all the ships going toward the locks from their front porch—it was in the article. Please."

Anita brought a glass of water and a Vicodin. Lester took the pill and sank into the pillow, turning away from Matt and George.

The cell phone rang down stairs.

Matt, pulling Lester's face toward him, said, "If you move from this bed, it will be your last move."

Matt and the Vegas gathered around the table. Matt opened the phone.

"Matt, Mom, Dad, can you hear me?" Tanya's voice filled the quiet room.

"Yes, dear," answered Mrs. Vega. "Are you all right?"

"I'm fine, I have to read again. I'm wearing gloves."

Tanya read from a script that never mentioned the Livingstons, her kidnapping or any illegal actions. The killers were called "visitors." The visitors were to be released taking all documents and photographic negatives or a flash drive covering recent diving activities in exchange for the care Tanya was being given. There were no taps this time.

Matt took the phone, "No deal, we have Lester's confession on tape. We have enough for the FBI and the Mounties—"

Tanya's voice broke in, "I've got another note—the authorities would ruin my vacation."

The three around the table, plainly hearing a slap and a scuffle, heard the phone go dead.

18

More of Les

George Vega slammed his hands on the table. His wife jumped and looked helplessly at Matt, who stared at the phone—the last link with his lovely Tanya.

Matt took out his own cell phone. "We need Webb. He can get doctors to work without records, bodies to vanish, and he's the most frightening man I know. I'm playing checkers, making one move after I see a move; he's a chess master, thinking of his moves and the other guy's, four or five possible actions ahead.

"The Livingstons rejected an exchange, they are playing for time, it must mean something: another attempt at us, covering their tracks, some deal they don't want messed up or something we can't imagine. Let's talk to Lester some more. He follows the business deals the Livingstons are into, maybe we can get a clue."

Matt went upstairs. The lump under the covers was the pillow. The window was open. Looking out the window, Matt saw marks in the newly seeded grass.

Running downstairs, Matt grabbed the working M-16 he had put in the clothes closet. The Vegas looked up questioningly. Turning at the garage door, Matt said, "Lester is gone! Call the fire department, Anita—I rigged his car to blow up. The number's on the first page of the phone book. Just tell them a car is on fire on Quarry Road."

As Matt rushed out, he yelled, "George, put the big garage extinguishers in the van and follow me! I'll try to catch him."

Matt sprinted down the middle of the road, rifle at port arms, selector lever on SEMI, ready for an attack from either side. He was prepared for a shotgun bang, followed by the boom of a gasoline explosion, neither happened. He reached the car, wishing he had taken a flashlight. The car was locked, line and shotgun as he had left it. Matt scouted slowly around the vehicle, listening for noise of movement in the brush. He slid under the car, cut the fishing line and carefully removed the shotgun.

It was a dumb booby trap anyway.

It occurred to Matt that they had searched Lester and found no keys. They had not done anything with the other man. He must have had the keys—or—Matt went to each wheel well and felt for keys. The front left one had the key and door opener. Matt felt the cold chill of realization that Lester wasn't going for the vehicle—he was going back to his partner. Pocketing the keys, shotgun and rifle in hands, he sprinted back toward the house. The van almost ran over him. Matt jumped into the brush, barely missing the front bumper.

Stopping the van, George jumped out. "Where's the fire?"

Matt jumped into the van. "Back up fast as you can, get to the house."

A scream and flash cut through the dark night as George backed up the narrow road with only the backup lights to guide him. Matt jumped from the van with the black rifle as they approached the driveway entrance. Flames shot from the kitchen windows, dark smoke came rolling out of the garage. Running to the house, he saw Lester in the driveway outside the garage with right hand working the pin out of a red incendiary grenade he held between his legs, his other arm flopping uselessly. Matt fired from his hip as he rushed by Lester, multiple bullets struck and twisted the crippled killer, blowing him out of the garage lighting and Matt's interest.

Trying to enter the kitchen, Matt met a wall of flames, the garage funneling air into the house. He backed away from the blistering heat. George came into the garage dragging two 30-pound CO_2 fire extinguishers.

Matt yelled, "Fight it here! I'll go around and come in from the front room."

Throwing the M-16 onto the lawn, he grabbed one heavy extinguisher and headed for the side door that led to the great room off the patio. He found Anita standing in the great room with a wet towel and a bucket of water. She tried to talk, but just coughed. The smoke roiled above them into the vaulted ceiling, the top half of the kitchen door looked like a huge blowtorch. Matt moved to the side of the door and shot the CO_2 gas below the wall of flames. Anita stood pitifully looking at the flames.

Matt pointed out the door. "Go outside! Turn the hose on and take it to George in the garage—this gas won't last long."

They fought the fire. Both extinguishers ran out in a few minutes. With the flames decreasing, black smoke increasing, water seemed more effective than the CO_2. The success of their initial attack allowed them to get the hose through the kitchen door, all the custom-built cupboards, so lovingly varnished, were engulfed in flame. The carpeting billowed black, noxious smoke, the wallboard scorched but not burning, the structural insulated panels forming the outer walls failing to catch fire. All other combustible materials within the kitchen area and up the stairs flamed. The hose would not reach more than a few feet into the house. Matt worked the only hose, and George ran to the propane tank to turn it off, before returning with a garden rake to pull down burning material. Both coughing, totally focused on the fire, glad the lights still worked, they didn't notice the arrival of the local fire department volunteers in two pickup trucks.

Anita directed them to the garage, across the patio, and into the great room. Within ten minutes of their arrival, using foam and practiced skills they had the fire out.

The fire team leader stood beside Matt in the blackened kitchen. "Wasn't the call for a burning car? We had lots of foam—good thing, too. We've got some big fans you can use. I canceled the fire trucks, but an inspector and the police will be in on this. It could have been at lot worse if it had gotten out of the kitchen."

Matt thanked every volunteer, getting each a beer from the garage refrigerator. As he went to the patio, he kicked the rifle under the newly placed hedge plantings to hide it under their cover and shadows. Thinking—*now I just have to hide a shot-up body, holding another fire bomb. This will be bigger gossip than that lady who shot her husband while he slept, and got off with self defense.*

Matt eased his way to the other side of the garage, glancing into the darkness on the far side of the driveway.

George came up to him and said, "I covered him up with stuff I dragged out of the garage, let's put some plastic tarps over everything so no one tries to help us put stuff back."

Two plastic tarps were sufficient to cover the tools, chairs, camping items and building materials that hid Lester.

Surveying the kitchen, Matt and the Vegas found the diving evidence and the tape recordings all turned to ashes or plastic goo.

The State Police and Mackinac County Sheriff cars arrived an hour after the volunteers had had their second beers and departed. The noise of two large fans made communication a challenge as Matt described how the tape recorder had just seemed to explode and spread burning plastic all over. The actual fire damage was confined to the kitchen, with smoke damage through the house in varying degrees.

The officers filled in their little notebooks by the garage lights, standing in the driveway. Matt noted the shoe of the State Police officer was less than a foot away from the plastic tarp pile that covered Les. No blood seeped out from under it. The patrol cars' exit was a moment of great relief for Matt and George.

Matt called his insurance man: yes, everyone was fine; no, he didn't need a motel, they would stay in the hunting cabin; yes, he would like an inspection tomorrow; yes, there was smoke damage—how much would wait for a few days.

Alone at last, they took some food from the refrigerator and garage, packing up the van with what they would need for a few days of living in the hunting cabin located in the quarry and drove Anita down there carrying the food and materials. She would get the cabin's beds made. Matt and George returned to deal with the two bodies. Vega drove the van, Matt drove back on a Honda ATV pulling a trailer used to retrieve deer and haul wood.

The men dragged the well-ventilated Lester under the garage driveway light, counting four entry holes, Matt was surprised he had shot him so many times, remembering just a couple trigger pulls. Next to Lester they found a military incendiary grenade with a label saying it was made by Haley and Weller, with a bunch of numbers on its waxy red sides. Matt worked the safety pin fully back in, a matter of a mere quarter inch, its spring loaded metal lever over an inch away from the bomb's body pushing to be free. Matt found another in Lester's pocket. So, the two men had come prepared to kill them and burn the house to the ground. Matt considered the grenade.

Fire is a good evidence remover—again, this level of military ordnance means planning ahead and playing for keeps.

Loading Lester on the trailer and taking the five-cell, another powerful lantern, a shovel and a pry bar, they set out to find the other man.

He hadn't gone anywhere. Lester had rolled him and opened various pockets on his vest. Loading him on the trailer next to his partner, Matt, riding double with Vega, drove the macabre load down onto the quarry floor. The far side of the quarry had multiple sinks in the ancient karst limestone. In the light of a quarter moon, the quarry walls took on a pale white color, the various blocks they passed looking like tombstones.

Matt found a sink hole on the far north side—dry, 15 feet deep with an opening just wide enough to take a body. The men had no IDs, valuables or useful materials except the .223 Remington shells in 30-shell magazines, which Matt kept. The vests too shot up and bloody for use.

Down they went. Rocks, gravel and a few hunks of limestone went down on top of them. Knowing Webb wouldn't think this was a very good piece of body work, Matt felt too tired to care, he just didn't want to explain dead people in the morning.

They left the ATV and trailer in the smoky garage, driving Lester's car back into the quarry to the far side of the huge shop building that covered the cabin. While Anita slept, they quietly sipped brandies, deciding Webb could wait until the morning.

19

Smoke and Neighbors

Dawn brought friends, casseroles, the insurance man, a cleaning and repair service and a phone call to Webb. Matt assumed split personalities: one the fire victim and the other the worried target of Canadian billionaires who held his Tanya prisoner. Playing their roles equally well, the Vegas dealt with the fire situation and their worries about Tanya.

While a dozen people worked on the kitchen, Matt and the Vegas sequestered themselves in an upper bedroom. The cell phone cut out twice, but they were able to communicate with Webb, still in Thunder Bay. Webb listened to all the new happenings and the fire story, stopping Matt when he got to the two men, changing the story to wild turkey hunting.

Webb said, "I don't blame you for popping those turkeys, but getting rid of the feathers wasn't very neat. With that and the fire, we don't have proof of the hunting trip."

'Not so," interrupted Matt, "we have a whole packet of pictures I sent off to a friend in Gladstone. We have a wallet, special weapons, special firecrackers…and I just thought of it—a slug in the pouch of my diving suit."

Webb continued, "Canadian law doesn't have a statute of limitations on most crimes—unlike US law. We've been talking to the Kaisers—the Livingstons took over everything when Old Jud came back without his wife. Claiming foul play would lead to massive court action. The Livingstons have lots of enemies in the political system and within power groups in Canada, all of whom would love a scandal. Jud returned from the sinking in a life boat with two other seamen. Their families, off the record, admit a payoff to keep a big secret, but it's only speculation and hearsay. Al just found the Livingstons have Lake Huron property, it was in a Sunday newspaper pictorial along with an interview. I already hired six planes with observers to cover the Lake Superior Canadian shore line—no 82-foot Coast Guard-type boats spotted. Never thought they would go to Lake Huron, but it makes some sense—better anchorages, more islands to hide among, and the water is a lot warmer for beach activity and swimming, better for a summer house. I'll have planes over the Canadian islands along the shipping channel by noon. Take care of your house, and I'll get back to you. Get the hunting trip pictures into your possession—don't trust the mail—make copies and get them to me. We'll talk tomorrow. I'll send someone to get that car, you should have put the turkeys in it. He'll have a code word. Tell Anita to be brave. Again, you did OK. Keep people around you, and good luck when the turkey guts start to smell."

Webb broke the connection.

Crying again, Anita walked out of the room, going back to supervise the cleanup activities. Matt and George followed. Knowing search activities filled the sky made Matt feel better about returning to the burnt kitchen.

The insurance, minus a $500 deductible, would pay for everything. The kitchen floor had several braided rugs over 16 by 16 inch Italian tile on a concrete slab—no structural floor damage. The room was soon gutted to the walls—the studs and internal drywall would be removed and replaced, appliances ordered and installed, new solid-oak cupboards would replace the custom cabinets. The stone-topped kitchen counters would take the longest to replace. The materials and the labor were all covered. George agreed to supervise and try to stay out of the way. Upstairs, the smoke damage wasn't so bad. Bed spreads, rugs and window coverings needed replacing, some clothes needed dry cleaning but most had to be trashed and exchanged for money.

Matt had several questions to answer about .223 Remington shell casings found in the driveway, blood stains in the new grass growth got some looks, too—could have been from cleaning George's wood-work stain brushes, mentioned Matt. He spotted the top of the incendiary grenade, but no one else paid any notice and it became just more charred crap to shovel up and put in the dumpster that the cleanup crew positioned outside the garage.

Friends and neighbors streamed through all day, offering condolences and offers of help. Anita set up in the great room, using multiple donated coolers inside and on the patio for kitchen storage. They decided to sleep in the house that night—the cell phones didn't work down in the quarry and they preferred separate bathrooms. The weather cooperated: cool but not cold, light breezes and cloudless skies. The constant noise of the giant fans finally ended at sunset when the volunteer firefighters took them away.

Sitting in the great room, third bourbon and club soda in hand, Matt was exhausted. No word from Webb, nothing from Tanya. "I called my friend Augie in Gladstone. He has the envelope. I'll drive there tomorrow morning—meet him at the golf club—he wants me to play golf with the men's scramble, about the last one of the year. He insists it's a good way to see lots of friends all at once; I haven't swung a club for months, now they smell like smoke. Golf is about the last thing I want to do right now, but just picking up a package and not saying anything to long time friends would raise a lot of eyebrows.

George added, "There's nothing you can do here but sit around and look miserable, Webb needs those pictures, and you could make a loop and check on the boat in Marquette."

Matt inspected his bourbon, "I've got to leave early then. After golf, I'll go up to Marquette and I'll get the slug too."

Anita said, "All we have is cereal and donuts for breakfast—I can make coffee in the old electric percolator you have in the garage."

Matt took another sip, "You know, we need to get the boat back to Munising sometime—it's a lot easier to take out a boat when it's not freezing and snowing. But you need to keep alert here—I know the Livingstons aren't done with us." He tossed down the last of the drink and considered the glass with a deep sigh. "I miss Tanya so much—it's… like nothing is important…or beautiful or funny without her."

George sipped his red wine, nodding morosely. Anita drank orange juice and just looked miserable. George said, "Better pick up a firing pin—I think the AR-15 and M-16 use the same pin."

Finally, Matt got the coffee and old electric pot ready out on the workbench in the garage. Then he went into the master bedroom, setting the alarm for 5:45. Stretching out on the bed, in the dark bedroom built for, and shared with, Tanya, he buried his face in her pillow, smelling a faint scent of her perfume and soap—along with the acrid smell of burning rugs and cupboards. He had killed for her and killed again when assassins came for him. He didn't feel guilt. Shooting a perfect deer always gave him a moment of pause: appreciation, sadness, a little regret, a sense of accomplishment, plus a link to every hunter in the history of the earth ran through him as he pulled out his Marble knife to field dress the downed animal. But shooting a man that was fire bombing his house or stalking his loved ones felt different. They made a decision for money. Matt had been the better animal. They died. They weren't food, deserving no respect, Lester and his partner had no honor, no real significance, just taking money to hurt or kill another person. Somehow, to Matt they were lower than a bird or a deer.

Matt had his first good sleep in several days.

20

Sand Wedge to Snorkel Tube

Matt made good time from the quarry, turning into the Gladstone Golf Club driveway at 8:45 am. The fall colors highlighted the golf course's beautiful undulating, emerald expanse. The sun sparkled off the Days River as he crossed the single-lane bridge leading to the clubhouse. Inside, 50 men were being teamed for the last scramble of the season. Matt's name had been added because he had called ahead. Teamed with his friend Augie, he put his smoky-smelling clubs on the cart labeled "Damn Right I'm A Wolverine." Augie had played end as a freshman at the University of Michigan, taking a break in '44-'45 to fly 38 missions over Europe as a B-17 navigator, returning for a pharmacy degree.

After they had each hit the ball twice on the par five first hole, Augie pointed out the file in the basket of the golf cart. He mentioned he had mistakenly cut both large envelopes open when he initially got the package. He commented, "Some gruesome pictures, but I didn't read the inside letter. What are you into?"

Matt took his sand wedge for their third shot. "Nothing I can talk about right now, and you don't want to talk or know about it either."

That was throwing gasoline on a curiosity fire—for six more holes Matt evaded questions. When he saw it was useless, he explained he had evidence of a crime and had to be very careful because it dealt with some very powerful Canadians. Matt said he would make several sets of copies at the local library and replace Augie's set to go with the unopened inside letter. Augie should keep the package unless something happened to Matt. Two more holes of questions and evasive answers later, Augie figured out Matt wasn't going to say any more about the pictures.

Their scramble team was five under par as they teed it up on the par four ninth hole. Looking down from the highest point on the course to a sloping fairway, crossed by a river, that led to the huge ninth green, Matt regretted that he hadn't been playing it more often. They got on the green in two, but had a 50-foot impossible downhill slider—lucky to get par, they headed in with a mediocre scramble score that still brought them third-place money.

After some clubhouse chats followed by making copies at the library, Matt dropped off a set at Augie's house and headed for Marquette.

On the road he called the Vegas. They were fine. The carpenters were working like bees, coming and going. A fire inspector had come, upset that they were cleaning everything up before he could inspect the scene. He wondered if they should put all the burnt material back but just shrugged, filled out some papers and left. Matt suggested they could use some guards, but the consensus held that guards would raise more questions than they wanted to answer. Besides, the workers would be there about twelve hours a day anyway.

In Marquette, Matt found a gun store with firing pins and bought two—one regular shiny steel and another made of titanium, which the gunsmith said was special. At the marina, the Silverton appeared secure, but the hasp had been pried off and reseated—Matt could see where the glue had run while replacing the screws. Matt thought, *Must have been a night job or they would have wiped up the glue...*

Inside, they had made no pretense of hiding evidence of their search—all the diving equipment had been moved, drawers rummaged and even the food boxes obviously inspected. Moving slowly, imagining a wire pulling the last quarter-inch of a fire grenade pin or lifting an object that freed the fuse lever, Matt spent a half hour inspecting the cabin. He found the bullet in the small pouch of his dry suit, too small and black to be seen or felt by the nighttime searchers. The engine area outside took only a few minutes, opening the hatches would have been too noisy and noticeable—even at night. He visited the harbormaster—really not a master at all, just a skinny college kid, who was sorry the boat had been vandalized and promised to give it special scrutiny in the future, then he returned to his calculus book.

Matt returned the Styrofoam cooler he had taken the fish fillets home in only a few days earlier—days that now seemed a lifetime—only to refill it with ice and more fish with a vow to return it again. He thought of the fine meal they all had had, how happy and beautiful Tanya had been.

The phone tune played as he secured the cooler in the back of the Yukon. It was Webb.

After inquiring if Matt was in Marquette, Webb said, "We found the boat—not at their island cabin, but in a bay on the north side of Manitoulin. They didn't fly too close, we've already scoped it from shore—it's *Sleeping Giant*. You and Al could board her tonight—you got gear and some air in the tanks?"

Matt couldn't breathe—now he could do something for Tanya. "Yes, I've got gear and several tanks with enough gas to get to a boat. No suit big enough for Al, though. How do I get there?"

"I'll send the plane across to the Marquette airport. It will be there inside of an hour: a white Skymaster. The pilot is also a diver—smaller build—bring what gear you have and two tanks. He'll fly you here, and we'll plan as we fly over to Manitoulin's east airstrip…Oh, and I already talked to Anita. See you soon."

Matt took the fillets and cooler back to the fish store. He was almost laughing as he backed the Yukon into the parking slot nearest the *Ferr Play*. The harbormaster, true to his word, came down as Matt unloaded the diving gear. Matt had two regular air tanks full and the backup tanks. He offloaded two dry suits with accessory hoods and gloves, plus his regular wet suit—Lake Huron was ten to fifteen degrees warmer than Superior in October and the wet suit was a lot easier to move in. The college kid helped Matt load the pile from the dock into the Yukon.

He packed a small canvas traveling bag with extra clothes and toilet articles then, as an after thought, went to the anchor locker and got a foldout, rubberized grappling hook with its coil of nylon rope. Never used, it still had the plastic ties and price tags. Matt didn't think he was strong enough to pull himself up a rope—but visions of pirates boarding a ship persisted.

The Skymaster arrived 15 minutes after Matt parked in the special area used for international small planes and passengers. The vast airport was built for SAC B-52 bombers and had a long runway that seemed to curve out of sight. After a quick Customs check, the pilot checked the diving gear, seemingly familiar with all the masks, snorkels, vests, tanks and regulators. He only took what they needed for a short, shallow dive, conscious of the weight of four men and diving gear in the small plane.

Matt took a jacket from his vehicle as he left the airport's parking area. The little plane had two engines each driving its own propeller—one in front pulling like most single-engine planes and one in back, framed by double vertical stabilizers, pushing. They left the runway at 70 knots. The cabin noise and vibration surprised Matt—they had on earphones, but the sound seemed to come in through his bones. The pilot didn't talk except to use the radio as they crossed Lake Superior—soon Isle Royale was to port and Thunder Bay appeared straight ahead. Matt could see the two towns that took on one name in the '70s; they flew over the town and greased a smooth landing on the shorter of the two runways, taxiing to the private plane area.

Matt saw Webb standing by a car as the plane's engines made cooling sounds. They went to lunch while the plane was refueled. Matt handed the copies of the underwater pictures to Al, who examined them and looked at the bullet, before saying, "Be good if we had the gun, but these pictures are real good. We can't prove this is Carol Kaiser Livingston—though clearly someone shot in the head. The bullet might be discredited by a good lawyer—but your testimony should still make it evidence."

Matt added, "We had the holster and some green moldy shells—Vega and I figure it was an old Walther, issued to German officers in World War I. Thousands were made, real common in the '20s. They took everything we brought up and the box they came in."

Al put another of the pictures on the table. "Why do you suppose there is a whole bunkhouse of bones—a lot of bodies, all in their beds at one time? Bad shit happened on that ship. Was everyone killed except the three that got off? If they were carrying CCC workers to Houghton, around that time there were whole camps down with smallpox. The CCC started vaccinations in 1933 just because of the spread of the disease."

Webb gathered up the pictures. "Let's get in the air, we can't talk very well in the plane, but we'll fly by the bay—high as we can—so they won't see the plane. We've got binoculars so you will be able to spot the boat, the bay and the beaches near the boat—I guess it's really a ship. We will also have boats to use, but I'd like to have Tanya safe before the cavalry arrives. These men are rich and very powerful, but they really piss me off."

The plane ride was rough and noisy. The noise made talking difficult and planning impossible. As the loaded plane slowly climbed, Webb, in the left seat, motioned the pilot to put the ship on the right side of the plane. Passing the binoculars back and forth, the three passengers checked out the trim, white ship surrounded by the green forests and the sparkling blue-green water. Matt couldn't see anyone on deck, but they were a long way up. If the ship was 82 feet, Matt estimated it was no more than 300 feet from a southwest point of wooded land with a rock and sand beach. They kept a constant west to east course—even slowing to 100 miles per hour—the reconnaissance went quickly.

At the east-west island airport the plane made a smooth crosswind landing. They were met by two vehicles—a van and a pickup. The bags and diving gear were quickly transferred, and the caravan headed for Webb's log cabin estate.

Leaving the main road, an unmarked gravel driveway ran north, crossing a harvested alfalfa field and winding through an unharvested cornfield. The huge, log cabin faced north, commanding a bluff, looking down upon a beautiful bay and large boulders, looking like beached whales, dotted the shore. They drove into a multicar garage, more like a four-star hotel than a garage adjoining a cabin on a Canadian island.

Webb gave Matt a bear hug. "Welcome to my dacha: my little cabin in the woods. This is where Tanya was supposed to come when the plane hit that storm last year. Come on in. We'll look over the maps, make plans and wait for darkness."

21

Har, Them That Dies are the Lucky Ones

Matt decided Webb should have been a pirate. Excited and flamboyant described Webb talking about boarding the 82-footer. They worked out the moon rising time and direction, the winds, currents and boarding methods. On a topographic map, they drew in the ship, Webb's men and the roads and trails. He even had a ship's diagram of a Coast Guard 82WPB—Point Class, understanding it would be modified for pleasure craft use. After 30 minutes with charts and maps, Webb took them into a trophy room, walls festooned with dead beasts from around the world, glass eyes staring down at a table Webb covered with knives and small arms. Choosing a British commando knife and a silenced Colt Woodsman .22, Matt figured he would make up a waterproofed bag of some kind. The pilot, whose name was Nick, took a 10 mm SIG Sauer, no silencer, no knife—"I don't slice when I can dice." was his comment. Matt didn't understand it, but figured the guy meant business.

The two swimmers would get on the ship, find Tanya, and send a light signal, then Webb and Al would show up in the boat—or in 30 minutes in any case. The orders were to take prisoners, using force only to save Tanya or themselves. Nick took long plastic cable ties to secure anyone they found. Matt asked for an aluminum ball bat, but Webb was fresh out.

They would enter the water at 10:30 pm, it was still light over the water until after 10:00. Webb had a 22-foot Ranger with a 200 horsepower outboard motor waiting around the point, able to reach Livingston's ship within 30 seconds. Boarding would be via the davit ladder that was deployed over the starboard side. Nick said he could get up the anchor chain. Matt doubted his ability, he would have to have the muscles and the agility of a gymnast.

Webb had men watching the boat from the shore. The watchers, using 20-power lenses from 200 yards, had observed a shore trip by an outboard manned by one person who came back with grocery bags after a two-mile run to a marina. One man, possibly the same that made the food run, had smoked on the fan tail every few hours. Another person—maybe a Livingston—had taken the outboard boat in the morning and hadn't returned. No one had been in the wheelhouse, although there had been people in the salon area. Lights went on and off below deck amidships and the bow area. They couldn't see the port side. With one anchor out, and a light wind, the ship moved very little.

Webb took the time to show Matt around the palatial log cabin. He apologized for his wife Karen and his daughter Carla not being there—they were in New York shopping before heading back to Ann Arbor for Carla's classes and so her mother could see a Big Ten football game. Webb finally guided him to a guest room, and Matt considered a few hours of rest. Webb said he would contact the Vegas to check on any contacts by the Livingstons. Matt opted to join Webb for the call and take a nap later.

Anita answered the call. On speaker, her tone with Webb again seemed softer than Matt expected, more gratitude than her usual critical, short comments. She said George was with the men Webb had sent to get Lester's car, they had been gone for some time. The kitchen had new drywall, and it was taped and sprayed. She told Webb to tell Matt to be careful and wished them luck. They had had no other calls that day.

Matt rested two hours on a fine bed, the bay shining below his double window. He was coming down to the kitchen as Nick was coming up to get him. They had coffee and donuts. Matt went onto the large deck off the kitchen and fired four quiet shots into one of the huge cedar posts that supported the master bedroom deck. He and Nick were going over their weapons when Webb brought in a box of gallon sized Ziploc bags for their handguns, Matt's pistol wouldn't fit with the silencer, with difficulty he unscrewed the four-inch tube, he also elected not to carry the large knife. He would dice instead of slice like Nick, thinking it made no sense but was fun to say. They next checked their diving equipment and got into their diving suits. They opened the grappling hook—decided it was too hard to throw from the water—and put it aside. Webb, ever the pirate, said he'd keep it in the boat.

As they painted their faces with hunting makeup, Matt remarked, "Har, them that dies will be the lucky ones!"

Webb repeated it and laughed.

Matt thought, *He must have missed Treasure Island in his Russian upbringing.*

An hour later, Matt and Nick waded into the cold, calm water of the little bay. The white ship looked like it was close enough to touch. Anyone on board with binoculars might have seen them, although the western sky was much lighter than the tree-lined shore from which they had emerged. The divers had been met and expertly guided through the woods by the two watchers. Webb had trailered the Ranger several miles to a boat launch on the north shore to avoid passing the anchored ship.

Matt was excited, his stomach jumped nervously, and he fought for breath as he stepped onto the gravel and sand bottom. His third step put him over his head, he came back to shore to clear his mask, put on his flippers and regain his composure. Nick knew the beach, setting down on a shore rock to fit flippers and mask, then slipping silently into the dark water. The water was so clear Mat could see the white side of the ship from ten feet below the surface. Their dark suits and faces would be invisible, the exhaled bubbles hard to see in the light chop coming from the north. Large rocks rising within ten feet of the surface gave Matt a sense of movement. He couldn't see Nick, but could hear his regulator sounds off to the left. The ship loomed over them in just a few minutes. They didn't break the surface until under the deployed boarding ladder. It had been pulled up three feet above the water surface. A small complexity for the divers—ditching their tanks and inflating the dive vests to float them against the hull; their flipper-powered kicks brought them within reach of the ladder. As they silently drew themselves onto the platform of the raised ladder, their drips sounded like kettle drums. They removed their flippers, readied their weapons.

Matt went first—having studied the layout of the Coast Guard 82-footer, he knew the door in the salon led to stairs leading below deck. Nothing locked, no one in the deck-wide salon, faint music coming from below deck—a movie, *The Edge*. Matt recognized the theme song.

Nick touched him and motioned him below.

The stairs led to a galley and small dining area with a narrow, dimly lit passageway continuing forward past several doors that ended with several steps and a fourth door, at the end of the passageway. This door was slightly cracked open, the only door along the starboard side of the hallway had a padlock and across from it another door was shut, but light and music escaped from under its several-inch clearance from the deck. Next to it another door was open—revealing a sink and lavatory illuminated by a nightlight. Aft of the galley was the engine room. Nick emphatically signaled Matt to stay by the padlocked door and, moving by him, went to the door from which light spilled, quickly and quietly entering.

"Don't move," Nick's order escaped from the closed room.

Matt wanted to see what was happening but fortunately stayed at his station.

"On the deck." Nick's second command brought some chair noise and scuffling sounds. With the noise from the room came a movement from forward. Matt turned to see a sleep-tousled Jud Livingston step down the steps and into the hallway. Matt brought up the Sportsman and aimed between Jud's surprised eyes.

"Open that door." Matt words were loud but a little high and shaky.

"Matt, Matt," came from the locked room.

Livingston looked sick, Matt wanted to kill him where he stood. Nick came out of his room with a key on a metal-bead necklace. Tanya was beating on the door. Matt took the key, keeping the .22 leveled at Jud. After some lost seconds finding the key slot, the lock and door opened and Tanya stood in the doorway.

Tanya, wearing a t-shirt, washed Levis and no shoes or socks, presented a beautiful sight. Her black hair, flat and unwashed, framed a happy, lovely face.

Matt's killing hate drained from him as he hugged her with his gun arm. Livingston used the distraction to duck into his cabin. Rushing past Matt and Tanya, Nick kicked the door open. Judd had his hand in the center drawer of a small desk. He froze when Nick pushed the SIG against his ear.

Nick snapped on an overhead light and hissed, "If there's a gun in your hand, I'll put a bullet in your ear."

Matt kissed Tanya, who was crying, and asked, "How are you?"

"I'm fine—a shower and clean clothes and I'm 100% again."

"How many people are on the ship?"

"Usually there's three, the brothers and another man, originally just the two brothers. We picked up the other guy at their cabin. They never hurt me—the slap was staged. They were using me to keep everyone quiet about the *Carol K*, they never talked about their plans and they wouldn't talk to me, except to make phone calls."

Matt hugged her again. "Any idea what weapons they have?"

"All I've seen are a pistol and a taser. They really don't know what they're doing. One minute I thought they would throw me overboard, the next minute they wanted to know if I liked the food and was warm enough. I knew you would get Webb and the two of you would eat them for lunch."

Nick, after tying Jud with plastic cords face down on one of two beds in a very nice master cabin that filled the vessel's bow, came into the hallway. "I'll signal Webb. You watch the guy in the room and have her watch Livingston—any trouble put one in the knee."

Nick made sure his orders were loud enough for both bound men to hear. He turned and ran up the stairs.

Tanya moved into the stateroom of the converted military ship to watch Livingston, who lay on his side saying nothing. Matt checked the crewman—who had moved to a sitting position. No fight vibes came from him.

In a few minutes, Webb and Al came down the main ladder—sinister figures dressed in watch caps and dark leather jackets. Matt watched Webb descend the steps and noted his mixture of genetics:

high cheekbones from the Mongols of Asia, blue eyes from Viking or northern European stock, dark hair from the Mediterranean, maybe Roman, genes and a thick neck and broad chest. Even without displaying a pistol butt like Al, the more frightening of the two. They checked the ship bow to stern. Returning after a few minutes, Webb hugged Tanya and assured himself she wasn't hurt. Al came out of Jud's main cabin carrying a small pistol by a pencil through its trigger guard.

Webb took a look at it. "It's an old Walther...Har." He kissed Tanya's cheek, laughing, pounding Matt's shoulder, and ordering, "Nick, get on the bridge, no lights—you're lookout. Let's get Livingston to the salon, we need room and we have a lot to talk about."

22

Ship Board

After carefully securing both the crewman and Jud Livingston, Webb, Matt and Tanya moved up to the salon area—polished woods, roomy, a boardroom and office. They kept all main lights off. In the glow of stair and door lights, Webb called Anita and handed the cell phone to Tanya—who still clutched Matt's arm. Mrs. Vega's joyous exclamations could be heard from the little speaker. She asked when they would be home—Webb was uncertain but said to plan on a few days, that they had some business to discuss with some important people. Just as Tanya was beginning to repeat her story for the second time, Nick came into the darkened salon to announce the approach of a small motorboat.

Webb left the salon with Al and Nick. Tanya ended the phone call and joined Matt at the salon windows to watch the three men efficiently surround and capture the motorboat operator at gunpoint.

In a few minutes, a thoroughly defeated Jared Livingston sat at the main salon table, hands bound behind him. His brother soon joined him, also with hands plastic-tied behind him. Webb turned on two lights, one at the table and another over the ladder to below decks—leaving the room shadowed and the mood sinister.

Webb took Al's black semiautomatic pistol and slammed it on the table.

After ten seconds of silence he said in a low voice, almost a whisper—as if talking to himself, "Any reason why we don't just put two bullets into each of your ugly heads, and take this ship out and sink it."

Jared glanced at his brother, their eyes locked for a few seconds. Webb put one muscular finger on the butt of the large pistol, resting on the shiny wooden table, slowly rotating its barrel to point at one brother then at the other.

Jared cleared his throat and spoke. "Billions of U.S. dollars—honest money, more power than you can imagine and we'd all be in history books as heroes."

Picking up the black semiautomatic, Webb moved slowly behind the brothers, lost in the darkness away from the table. His voice came ominously from the back of the room. "If you've ever made a good sales pitch you better do it now."

Jud, the younger brother, spoke, "We are businessmen. We didn't want to hurt anyone. Tanya wasn't harmed, we were just trying to frighten and intimidate you folks to buy time. We have the biggest deal, a business opportunity of global proportions, that can be destroyed by bad, or for that manner any, personal publicity. The discovery of the *Carol K* couldn't have come at a worse time."

Matt broke in, "What about divers with spear guns and men with automatic weapons and incendiary grenades?"

"There were no spear guns, you saw rolled up metal mesh to retrieve a body. We brought back the remains of our mother and then destroyed the ship—no one was to be harmed. The divers had instructions to warn you and get you out of the ship. They honestly thought you were off the ship. They got back aboard with the fuses burning and couldn't do anything, they couldn't go back down. It was all a mistake. We had to keep Tanya to control her mother. We were actually relieved when we learned you and Mr. Vega were alive. The men at your house were to scare you and get any evidence of the shipwreck. The weapons and firebombs were their doing."

Webb returned to the table and sat across from the brothers. "We are going to separate you two. Al, Tanya and Matt will talk to Jud here,

Nick and I will take Jared below deck. We want to know what your big deal is all about. If you don't have the same story—you won't see the sun rise. Let's take a break, get some coffee and find some food—this could take some time. Matt and Nick, your dry clothes are in the Ranger—you must be hot in those wetsuits."

Bringing Tanya with them, Nick and Matt went to the deck area, searched for and found their floating tanks and dive vests. Using a boat-hook, they maneuvered them toward the Ranger, tied at the boarding ladder. Changing into dry Levis, sweatshirts, running shoes and socks, they rejoined Al in the salon where the ex-cop scribbled on a notepad a reiteration of the points Jud had just covered. Al then read his notes aloud, asked for any changes or additions to the benign intentions of the brothers. Jud pleaded with Tanya to admit she was treated well. Tanya added the charge of kidnapping, brandishing a firearm and an electrical stun gun and forcing her to read statements at the threat of her life or limbs. She mentioned having to wear gloves everywhere on the ship except her room—which made her believe they planned to kill her and didn't want finger prints all over the ship.

Matt got very close to Jud. "I'd like to really hurt you. You think you aren't responsible for the actions you set in motion? Men are dead, a home is burned, and days of worry and misery are now part of our lives. Tanya's folks will never be the same. I killed men and will always carry the burden of that guilt....all for a business deal. It better be one mother of a deal!"

Nick broke the tension and the monologue with a large tray containing an insulated coffee carafe, cups and a messy pile of uncut sandwiches. "This is the best I can do, most everything is frozen in the galley, so it's cheese or peanut butter."

As he headed back below deck, he winked at Matt and Tanya who had seated themselves across from Livingston and said, "Now the boss wants me to find some anchors or chain."

Jud's already pasty white skin turned more pale.

Al finished noting Tanya's charges, poured himself a cup of coffee, took a large bite of a sandwich, mumbled "peanut butter," took a gulp of coffee and turned his tablet to a blank page. "I'm ready Mr. Livingston."

Jud leaned forward on his chair, his balding head catching the light from the table lamp—he looked all his 70-plus years. Taking a deep breath, he began, "We have a method for nuclear waste disposal. We have just completed testing and documentation, working with a major Japanese company. We have strong ties with several influential groups at the UN. The results must be perfectly presented, perfectly timed, or environmental factions will kill the whole process. The secrecy of our system is key, until we have an undeniable body of facts and scientific reports. We can provide a solution to the energy challenges of the next century. Right now, most countries have limited or even stopped their nuclear programs because they can't deal with nuclear waste storage. Now, most nuclear facilities have their waste material stored at their sites—totally unacceptable, dangerous and expensive. No one planned for this type of storage—the movement and disposal of nuclear waste is stopping the best source of energy we have at this time."

Tanya interrupted, "What about wind and solar?"

"Wind's too mechanical, it's expensive, you can't count on it—most large wind farms just feed a grid or need a back-up steam generating system using coal or oil. The wind farms are really a pyramid system—you make money if you sell the machinery or the system and get out before it starts to break down. Solar offers several fine systems—but too expensive, have storage issues and are constrained by the amount of sunlight available. You need the electricity most during the night or cold, cloudy days. The solar farms need space but the environmentalists even stop construction on desert wastelands—some useless lizard might get stepped on.

"Nuclear is our best system for the next fifty or hundred years. We own forty percent of Canada's uranium production—which is the world's largest exporter. We used to ship the majority of the world's medical isotopes until our brainless government leaders figured Canada needed to get out of the nuclear business. They are forcing privatization on a system that should be government controlled. Their timing and intelligence couldn't be more wrong. Cancer medical groups are going to Africa to get medical isotopes that were cheap and available right here in North America.

"The government waste disposal group—the Nuclear Waste Management Organization or NWMO—wants to bury waste in the rock layers of the Canadian Shield. Our system used some of the same logic but is much safer and is a truly long-term solution. It can be used by the whole world, it is a one hundred percent safe and final way to dispose of nuclear waste."

Matt broke in, "What is your solution?"

Jud looked down at the table, then searched the eyes of those seated around it. "I can't tell you without talking to my brother. This whole situation is so very complicated. We are waiting for international credentials and agreements. We can change the whole structure of nuclear energy production by removing its biggest problem. Even with recycling technology that will reduce a great deal of radioactive waste, there are still huge piles of unsafe and unwanted nuclear material all over the world.

"Please, untie my hands. I can't breathe well like this. I need some water. I won't be any problem."

Matt found his Swiss army knife in his Levis, moved behind Jud and sliced the plastic bands.

Jud brought his hands in front, rubbing his wrists, and took a sip of coffee from a cup Tanya placed before him. He continued, "Our plan is more than just a way to make money, it will allow nuclear power to become the cleanest, cheapest and most convenient source of power— at least until more advanced technologies can take its place. You could wreck years of very delicate and secret activities."

Sounds of movement filtered up the steps, and then Jared appeared with Webb pushing him. Webb turned on the salon lights, removing the dramatic shadows.

Webb moved Jared to the table and into a chair. "We need to go into executive session. I think Tanya and Matt can go back to our cabin in the Ranger, Nick can run them down and come back—we will bring this ship in at first light. I think we can get it to the dock."

Matt looked at Tanya—they were being dismissed, Webb was taking over. Matt started to disagree when Tanya took his arm, gave him a smile that usually preceded a delicious kiss or better. She broke the silence between the two men. "I think that's a great idea, I'd love a bath and a bed. Your daughter Karen said your cabin is beautiful, and I'd like to see it."

Nick, Matt and Tanya left the executive session. Handling the boat as smoothly as he did a plane, Nick brought them to the massive dock area that fronted the large, impressive log structure—much too large and complex to be called a cabin.

Standing on the log, rock and cement dock, Matt and Tanya watched the Ranger plane on its way back to the Livingston ship. Matt leaned over and kissed her. Tanya moaned and rubbed against him. They had missed each other, and the kiss emphasized their longing and the need they had for each other.

Taking Matt's hand, Tanya led him off the dock and up the steps to the large glass and log main room. In the palatial room—with high ceilings, large stone fireplace, glass panorama of the darkened bay—Tanya commented, "This will do!"

23

At Webb's Cabin

The cabin held many delights for Matt, the greatest being Tanya, who was singing in the shower. Matt had been visited by the man who kept the property maintained and his Dominican wife who did the cooking, both making sure that Matt and Tanya had everything they needed. Matt really only wanted solitude and a freshly steamed Tanya, but the couple insisted on some late-night food and drink. Matt ordered champagne and strawberries—more as a joke and challenge— seeing how they were on a Canadian Island in October. The fruit tray and an ice bucket containing a 2005 Pommery Brute Royal arrived in ten minutes. Matt accepted the offering.

As Matt closed the thick guestroom door, Tanya appeared from the steam-filled bathroom, wrapped in a large, brown bath towel and holding another out to Matt. Turning her back to Matt and allowing the damp towel to slide to her waist, she said, "Please dry my back, I've made so much steam I'd never dry in there."

Matt happily accepted the role of back drier, beginning with Tanya's neck as she held her hair up with one hand and kept the low-draped towel in place with the other. She struck a pose that would have any of the great painting masters grabbing their palettes, among other things. Focusing on his task, Matt began at the nape of the perfect neck and worked down her backbone and out to the shoulders. He knelt, making sure he didn't miss a curve or crevice. Tanya dropped her towel so Matt could continue unrestricted. As he completed the left leg and decided to work up from the right ankle, he noticed a bruise. He touched the red and blue ring on her perfect ankle.

Tanya said, "That's from a handcuff. They locked me to an old metal smoking stand when I was on deck. They didn't want me jumping overboard and swimming to shore. We were very close to land in most of the channels. The stand was like a figure eight, heavy bottomed and there was no way you could swim with it on your leg. I tried to break it in half, but only got bruised for the trouble."

Matt's sexual foray became temporarily sidelined by dark thoughts of revenge. But just as hate began to build, Tanya turned.

"How about doing my front, too?"

In all the annals of time, no woman was more thoroughly pat-dried than Tanya. Matt detected a ringing in his ears and decided he had been holding his breath too long. After a long lungful of air and Tanya's fragrance, he began checking for any lingering drops with his cheeks and lips. Tanya, appreciating his workmanlike thoroughness, made several hums and sighs, finally coaxing Matt up into an embrace. They found the bed just in time.

Sometime during the rest of the night and early morning, the lights were turned off, some champagne drunk, a few sugar-dusted strawberries eaten. Matt and Tanya, happily back in each other's arms, enjoyed the queen-size bed that became their world, which they only begrudgingly left for the shortest of times.

Sounds from the dock, directly below their room, woke Matt and Tanya. It was 10 o'clock, the morning was gray and it had rained during the night. Tanya went to the double window. Matt thought, *Whatever she's looking at isn't as good as my view.*

"They're docking the 82-footer," Tanya said as she found the fresh clothes the staff had provided, probably belonging to Webb's daughter Carla. Matt's travel bag provided his needs. Dressed, they made their way down to the dock.

Floating plastic bottles marked the channel and two more approximated the length of the large ship. Matt remarked to Tanya, "What did they do in Canada for channel buoys before plastic gallon jugs?"

Nick, out in the Ranger, finished with marking, supervised the docking process, ready to help with lines or perform tug boat duties. Livingstons' ship floated in the channel, 50 feet off the dock. Only about half of the 82 feet could be moored to the dock. The stern stuck out, secured with spring lines and an anchor Nick moved into position. Four men on the dock pulling lines worked with Webb and the two Livingstons to secure the trim ship after almost a half hour of effort. They were in the lee of the island and the water was dead calm—neither helping nor hindering the docking.

Matt and Tanya, fortified by steaming mugs of fresh coffee, watched the procedure. Tanya commented on their organization and how everyone seemed to be working together. The Livingston brothers were in their late 70s, but they knew their lines and how to dock a ship. Matt also noticed no guns were present and the atmosphere didn't seem tense. Some agreements must have been made, some plan constructed and agreed upon.

Setting on a wooden bench at the dock, Tanya crossed her ankles and Matt saw the bruise again. He made an internal pact with himself— there would be payback.

The sight of Webb and the Livingstons walking up the dock was accompanied by a bacon aroma wafting from the cabin. Webb looked happy, in control. The Livingstons seemed glad to be alive, looking up at the large log home.

As Webb got close to Matt and Tanya he put his hands on the Livingston brothers shoulders, "We decided not to kill them, instead we'll all get rich disposing of nuclear waste, let's have breakfast and a lecture by our new partners."

The brothers looked shocked by Webb's directness, but didn't say anything. They looked tired. Matt wondered if they would eat bacon and eggs—they seemed to have swallowed a lot from Webb so far.

Tanya and Matt followed the three men up the dock and into the great room of the massive log cabin. Nick and the Livingston's crewman brought luggage and a leather briefcase.

Following a brief tour of the main floor rooms, Webb brought the Livingstons to the dining wing, off the kitchen area. The table was set for six: Webb, the brothers, Al, Tanya and Matt. Webb sat at one end and Matt at the other. Matt noticed the table's construction: large anchor chain links made the legs, the four- or five-inch-thick wood the tabletop—made from distressed boards probably from a shipwreck. A hatch cover, perhaps. The boards all showed age and weathering, thick coats of marine varnish giving a silky gloss. Each place setting included woven grass placemats on which silver utensils with bone handles bracketed silver-edged china plates. In front of each plate were two 12-ounce stemmed glasses one with ice water and the other with orange juice. Large coffee mugs being filled with steaming coffee by the Dominican cook announced the beginning of the breakfast service.

Bacon, eggs cooked to order, toast, croissants, jellies and jams, fried and hash brown potatoes filling steaming platters came from the kitchen. Finally, various fruit platters came, filling the few remaining spaces on the table, bringing more color to the breakfast cornucopia.

Everyone filled their plates and kept their thoughts to themselves until their initial hunger was satisfied. Matt commented to Tanya on the thickness and quality of the bacon. Tanya said she never had a better cheese omelet and would have to talk to the cook. The Livingston brothers said nothing, but did eat eggs and some fruit, they each drank two glasses of water and a few sips of the juice. Matt fought the urge to ask if they wanted some ostrich, but they didn't seem like they needed any further harassment.

Finally, Webb called for his plate to be cleared, the brothers followed his lead, and one end of the cleared table showed only shiny, dark wood. Jared Livingston put his briefcase on the table. Opening it, he took out a thin file. From the folder, he took out several papers, which he arranged in front of him.

Not waiting for Matt, Tanya or Al to finish their plates, Jared began his lecture, "We have a method of disposing of nuclear waste. We put it in our patented, tested, and internationally approved containers, take them to sea, add some fins and a nose cone—also patented—and using a GPS guiding system—like a smart bomb—send the container to a particular area of the sea floor called a subduction zone. The container buries itself in the soft-sediment of the trench, and over time is folded into the mantle of the earth by subduction ocean plates. Our solution is permanent, maintenance free, terrorist-proof. Not only is it a perfect answer to nuclear waste storage—it is overall cheaper than any system imaginable.

"We have tested this method, documented and witnessed by multiple scientific groups plus UN, IAEA and Nuclear Regulation Agency representatives. We are waiting for several governing bodies to bless our system—not with a patent but just a stamp of approval for going through all the testing and certification. Perfect dump sites are found at many Pacific and Indian Ocean subduction zones and we have researched one zone near Puerto Rico: all deep-sea trenches and basins."

Jared pulled two pages of closely typed data and multicolored graphs from his folder. "These reports show Pacific subduction zones—we've marked the Aleutian Trench, close to western North America. Other excellent zones are located at the Juan De Fuca Trench, the Peru-Chile Trench, the Kurile Trench, the Mariana Trench—deepest in the world— and so on—at least five more acceptable sites. We also have located and researched the only subduction zone in the Atlantic."

Jared fumbled with more papers and produced another folder, from which he unfolded a large chart showing ocean topography. He rose and leaned over the map and pointed with a long, narrow finger, "Here is the Puerto Rico Trench—nearly 500 miles long, the deepest point in the Atlantic Basin—28,232 feet of ocean depth. Most importantly it is closest to the major producers of nuclear waste on the East coast. This point right here is called the Milwaukee Deep..."

Webb broke in, "Tell us how we can make money."

Jared continued as if he hadn't heard Webb, "The certification is the key part of all this work. No country would allow just anyone to move nuclear material around, no international authority would allow wholesale, random dumping of materials into the sea—although this has been going on. By having imposed stringent testing on ourselves, while working with the UN—who is always looking for legitimate authority— we are years ahead of any other group that might try to duplicate our techniques. We wouldn't have a monopoly, but a three or four year head start on any competition is an overwhelming advantage. We'd be riding the crest of the wave, while all competitors would be trying to catch up. We would become the de facto standard and provider of nuclear waste disposal for the US, Canada and perhaps most of Europe."

Webb put his hands over Jared's papers. "How will we make money?"

Jud spoke up, "We will issue you stock certificates in our corporation. They will have face value and also pay dividends. They should be worth many millions of dollars over the next five years. The industry itself will gross in the billions."

Pulling another paper from under Webb's thick paw, Jared continued, "This is our prospectus of North American nuclear waste—even accounting for recycling and more efficient liquid sodium reactors—it estimates over 100,000 metric tons of nuclear waste by 2020 in just the zones we could easily service. We haven't included the contaminated earth caused by the temporary storage sites which could add millions of tons more. Again, this is just North America's numbers, we could find or subcontract a huge European business. Japan has been partnering with us in our efforts and will cover the Asian and Pacific areas."

Matt took the four-page paper and scanned it. "What about Yucca Mountain in the US?"

Jared scoffed, "The only waste it will hold is political. Your President Obama has canceled it. Your government has worked on it for over twenty-two years, and thirteen and a half billion dollars have literally gone down the hole—it was always a poor political decision and it's geologically flawed. Your DOE has collected monies for every kilowatt-hour of energy produced by all the nuclear power plants since 1982— over twenty-one billion dollars and hasn't delivered a waste site. The environmentalists and the U.S. Congress have stupidly determined a massive waste disposal site has to demonstrate that the waste could be stored safely for one million years. Because the Yucca project is so useless, the government-administered Nuclear Waste Trust Fund is liable to the nuclear community for over seven billion dollars in damages and five hundred million for each additional year of delay. Your government will jump at a means of getting off the nuclear waste hook. So will all the other nuclear powers of the world."

"Let's get back to our agreement," said Webb. "You will issue us stock in exchange for keeping secret all the crimes you and your father have committed. The terms will be irrevocable and will be issued to Tanya, Matt and to me. The minimum face value will be five hundred thousand each, there will be no liability associated with the stock ownership and you will buy it back at its issuing or market value."

Jared nodded. "We agree, the papers are being finalized as we speak. Our ship is also an office. You understand, by holding the stock you will have an interest in the success of the venture. Actually, you three join several very influential people at the UN, in the U.S. Congress, two influential Senators and Justices on U.S. and Canadian court systems whose relatives or offshore accounts will benefit from the project's success. We have anticipated the environmentalist strategy of making the technology prove it produces no harm—stopping all progress during a many-year study. We have done the study, they will have to prove their precious whales or zooplankton are harmed, because we have shown no radiation or biological issues are associated with our method. The environmentalists use laws like a sword—we are just showing them it's a two edged sword. We have deep ocean radiation tests and on-going monitoring showing zero effects for our methods, run and documented by highly respected independent laboratories. As important as our tests is the money and power that various government groups, including the UN can achieve with the adoption and administration of our methods.

"It seems no matter the benefit to the planet or to mankind—the politicians are all governed by money or power and quid pro quo— rich trumps right."

Jud broke in, "We have everything thought out, but a scandal about our father, and the problems mother's family could bring to bear could upset all our plans. Politicos can take money, but not bad publicity.

"We are sorry for all the trouble you've had, but we hope you understand there is greater good involved—not just rich people getting richer."

Matt gave the paper he was holding to Tanya. "How long before you have the approvals you need?"

Jared answered, "Weeks—by the new year at most."

Webb stood up, stretching his massive arms and shoulders, "I think we are done here. I'm sure Tanya and Matt want to get back to their home. I'm also sure they can send the bills for their fire to you."

Jared said, "Just a phone call with a number will do, we don't need any paperwork."

Webb went on, moving to Tanya and touching her shoulder, "Nick will fly you back to Marquette. I think the Livingstons will find our guest bedroom more comfortable than their ship while we finalize the paperwork." It was an order, not an invitation. The brothers understood who was in charge. They could see two guards on the dock.

The breakfast broke up with the Livingstons being guided by Al to a seating area in front of the great fireplace.

Webb took Matt and Tanya into the kitchen area.

Matt refilled his coffee mug from a large commercial coffee maker. "How can we trust these people? All they've done is lie and try to kill us. Is there any honor among thieves?"

Webb got a fresh cup from a group hanging on hooks, pouring half a cup. After a sip, he placed it on the butcher-block counter in the center of the kitchen. "There is no honor among thieves—just fear and a balance of power. Winning is the only measure of success. These are very powerful, very smart people. I fear them more than a drug lord from Columbia or an ass-covering politician in Congress. I'm going to make nice to them for a few days, but I'd expect some push back or another attack at some point—we need to be prepared. There is a lot of danger here—a secret is only good when everyone who knows never talks. Like in dead."

Webb leaned over the counter, Matt and Tanya leaned toward him. In a low voice, he said, "Go home, take care of business there, be aware of everyone around you, we'll keep in close touch. I'm sending my wife and daughter back to the Dominican Republic—I've got a fort there. Carla is going to be very upset leaving school, and my wife probably won't talk to me for a week.

"Oh, another thought—remember that rock on the island that had writing on it about the wreck? Go there and take pictures, literally dig around and quietly try to get more information. I'm fairly good at playing the secrets game—the more cards we hold, the better hand we can produce if we have to. I'll let the brothers go in a few days. When they're back in their world we lose control and have to live on a balance of mutual fear and greed. Al is supervising the planting of bugs and some computer software that may help us. Let's watch our backs, keep in touch and strengthen our list of secrets."

Tanya and Matt spent several hours enjoying the large estate. While avoiding the Livingstons, Tanya gave Matt a tour of the ship. She showed him a folio of before and after pictures, and Matt could see the customization the brothers done. Tanya and Matt couldn't help comparing it with the Hatteras they had spent many weeks on cruising the Bahamas. Both craft over 17 feet wide, but the military ship, even with a fortune spent on customization, wasn't as quiet or comfortable. It had classic warship rakish lines, and on the relatively small bridge, a captain felt like an admiral. From the wheelhouse, the helmsman controlled the engines, variable pitch propellers and dual rudders and didn't need an engine room crew, a plus for the brothers who could run the ship by themselves or with just one other crewman. A full third of the ship's 82 feet contained the engine room and hold—diesels, pumps, generators, electrical panels – very military. At 77 tons, it had twice the displacement, half the speed of the 54-foot Hatteras. Below deck, there were three staterooms—the master stateroom with added portholes – partially divided by a luxurious bathroom, giving each brother his own space. The other births were smaller and more Spartan. A watertight door had been removed to make more space and an easier-to-travel hallway. The most impressive area was the thickly carpeted main salon—above deck. The Coast Guard had had a second door, the officers' cabin and the communication area dividing the space—now all open with a boardroom table surrounded by very impressive office and communication equipment. A small lavatory was tucked under the inside ladder leading to the bridge, artfully hidden by dark, wood paneling. A sitting area facing a picture window that had been the service locker hatch seemed to be the only really comfortable space on the ship. The overall mix of materials and placement reflected the hard, functional lines of its owners. The engine room and hold had access hatches from the deck area but were only given short peeks by Tanya and Matt.

After the ship tour and return to Webb's beautiful cabin, they needed to wait out a storm front before Nick and the noisy Skymaster could get them back to Marquette and the good soil of the U.S.of A.

24

Home Again

The Yukon's lights bored a colorful hole in the reds and golds of leaves forming a canopy over the gravel road leading to their home. The garage door was up and all the lights on. They had not driven all the way into the garage before the Vegas came out. They had been in the kitchen waiting for the crunch of Michelins on gravel.

Matt, whose parents had died before he was ten, became a spectator to the love and warmth showered upon a daughter by George and Anita Vega. Spanish was their language for special times, private times, loving times; it flowed with tears of greeting and relief. Tanya hadn't wanted to stop for food, knowing her parents were counting every second until they could see her.

The drive from Marquette had gone quickly—reviewing all the events while they were apart, Matt didn't sugar coat the attacks or the responses of her father and mother. Tanya had not thought deeply about the effect of her kidnapping on her parents—the scene of her mother in the bushes and her father's collapse, the fire and even body removal all were absorbed in minutes of silence in the speeding vehicle.

Matt waited for questions—which came, but always after several minutes of thought.

Concluding the narratives while turning off the paved county highway, Tanya's only comment on the straight quarry gravel road was, "What beautiful colors."

Matt followed the three Vegas into the still work-in-progress kitchen. Paint and new carpet smells, work lights and various large boxes greeted Matt and Tanya as they were led to the great room table, set for a late dinner. Eating was perfunctory, taking second place to the stories being told. Matt and Tanya told their stories from the kidnapping and rescue to the ship being tied to the dock. They included the breakfast meeting—but not the evening before.

George described his efforts. "Webb's guys took care of body and car problems. One went into the limestone sink, we pulled'em up and into their car. The another guy came and took the Canadian vehicle away. He cleaned blood stains in the woods and driveway with spray chemicals. He spoke Spanish, not Cuban and wouldn't talk about himself—just kept saying, 'We were never here.'

"Lucky we had foam and firefighters—that incendiary grenade could have burned the house down. If the other one would have got thrown in, we'd have burned down for sure." George got up and brought back two small, red grenades, showing them to Matt and Tanya. "The tiles actually melted and the concrete under it cratered. It didn't get any of the heating tubes in the floor. We had most of the mess cleaned up and the concrete patched before the fire inspector got here, otherwise our story about the tape recorder would have been challenged. Those boxes are cupboards, we bought them—I didn't feel like making them again. I've got carpenters to put them up in the next few days—once they have your business, they kinda show up when they feel like it."

Anita cleared the dishes, looking older and tired, and returned with a tray holding four flan deserts, each topped with a hot rum sauce and accompanied by black Cuban coffee. When everyone had "oohed or aahed" with the first taste of the custard, she spoke for the first time, looking directly at Matt. "Why didn't Webb kill the Livingstons?"

Tanya intercepted the challenge, answering, "Webb felt there was profit and influence, even power, to be gained by keeping their secrets.

We were also surprised when the Livingstons got off on the dock arm in arm with Webb."

Matt added, "Webb isn't afraid of playing at the game of blackmail for power and profit. He is out of the mainstream in the Dominican Republic—he gave up most of his U.S. influence to buy his freedom when they got him with drugs in his car." Matt thought, *Because Tanya had planted them while she was forced to work for the DEA...a fact Webb hopefully would never know.* "Now he has major Canadian businessmen, possibly U.S. Congressmen and Senators, judges in two countries and even UN personnel in his dirty little file of influence peddling. We didn't have anything to say about it."

Anita forked her flan, not eating it. "But he's kept us in danger for his gain. The Livingstons tried to kill us twice—each time after making promises. Now we have a third promise. Doesn't Webb think there is danger?"

Tanya replied, "Yes, he is sending his wife and daughter back to their villa on the north coast of the Dominican Republic. He told us to be careful. The Livingstons know Webb isn't a man to be taken lightly. They know they were close to death for taking me, and for their underwater explosions and attack on this house."

Anita picked up her messy but uneaten plate, saying as she went to the kitchen, "Even when he does something good and noble, he turns it into a scheme and a worry."

Matt added, "Well, killing two billionaires, a crew man and sinking an 82-foot ship isn't a simple or legal thing either. We would have been a part of that. Lots to worry about either way. We didn't make a secret of our interest in the Livingstons. Many people could connect the dots of our inquiries and Webb's airplane. It may be the best deal we had. I could have killed them when I came aboard and saw Tanya locked up, but after talking to them for hours, hearing their thoughts, even the nuclear waste project—it would have been hard to shoot them in cold blood. I couldn't have done it—maybe wale on them with a ball bat for a while, but not kill them. They are cold, powerful people, and very persuasive.

"We just need to be alert, get on with our lives, and maybe make some money from the stock we are getting for keeping quiet." *I'm not going to talk about going back to the island or building more of a case about the shipwreck.*

The coffee and the tension of discussing the threat hanging over them made sleep impossible. Matt and Tanya excused themselves and took a walk. The sky had cleared, the rain front had gone through. The stars were brilliant, the night cool to cold, the air sweet with the smells of fall. Hand in hand, in down jackets, Matt and Tanya walked to the quarry edge, a thin moon casting a silver light on the vast quarry floor. The huge shop shed made an easy marker, the old concrete crusher base looking like Roman ruins. Coyotes yipped and howled to the north. There was no human light to intrude into the lovely night, except several sparkling satellites—looking like fast-moving stars. Matt's arms circled Tanya from behind, giving her his warmth and support. They didn't talk, just loving the touch of each other and appreciating their position in an endless universe, glad to be alive and together.

Walking back in silence, they found only the garage's small, side door light on, George understood night walks.

25

Fall Activity

A week of normalcy dulled the bad memories, threats and worries for everyone in Matt's house. The carpenters woke them up the third morning they were back and had the cupboards all hung by noon, the kitchen counters completed by sunset. Tanya and Anita worked on the kitchen, stocking the pantry with all the zeal of winter preparation shown by the forest critters with which they shared the quarry area. When the nearest store is more than a 50-mile round trip, you need to stock up. They all took walks together each evening. Twice Matt and George hunted partridge in the sunny, cool morning trails and field edges. The rather dumb, but tasty, birds hid in sunny patches and on poplar branches. Each morning the hunters returned with several of the plump grouse. Cleaning most of them at the shooting sight allowed Matt to gain information on their feeding habits: blue wild grapes, carefully cut green clover leaves, red berries of wintergreen swelled their crops—giving evidence of where to hunt.

Matt and George also laid up wood: cutting, splitting and stacking daily. Driving to Detour and taking the ferry to Drummond

Island—to see the magnificent colors that the flat vista and channel sides provided—offered a break for a restful afternoon. Matt's cousins and special friends came and went on the 360-acre property—constructing or repairing deer blinds, opening shooting lanes, checking tracks and trails.

Matt and the Vegas worked from sunrise to after dark. The house was totally repaired, but winter's breath kept coming from the northwest—a brief sleety-snow and the ever shorter, cooler days brought near-frantic activities of preparing for winter, hunting and finally doing the jobs put off all summer.

A second week of normalcy and completing fall checklists kept everyone busy. They finally were able to enjoy several long afternoon leaf tours to both the Lake Michigan and Lake Superior shores to show the Florida folk colors and scenes unique to the Upper Peninsula. Small ponds that had ice on them in the morning a week ago, now had ice on their edges all day. Winter was coming.

The boat was still at Marquette's dock. Its return to Munising and winter storage already on Matt's to-do list, but weather and other activities had put the responsibility off. It would be a two-day job, including a trip to Granite Island for more investigation of the rock writing. It meant bringing the Livingstons back into their thoughts—another reason they had put off the chore.

Webb called twice during this time. His plans to ship Carla and his wife out of the country were crushed by female wisdom and stubbornness. Carla wasn't going to miss her classes, his wife Karen wasn't going to be run off by two skinny old Canadians. She actually had met them—they stayed together at the cabin for almost a week before taking their ship back to Thunder Bay, Ontario. Neither she nor her daughter saw anything to fear, and the Livingstons actually seemed very well mannered and even friendly at times. Webb even seemed to have modified his position—he felt he could control the situation, the Livingstons were totally consumed with the nuclear waste project, working at their various communications systems all hours of the day. They stayed on their ship, but took meals with the Webbs, where they quite openly discussed the progress of their certification and international dealings. Webb felt they had reached a businesslike understanding, perhaps his initial fears and instincts had been exaggerated. He still felt the added research on Granite Island would be a wise effort. Carla, back in school, had two extra guards—much to her displeasure. Webb already had a secure area in and around his Manitoulin Island cabin. He counseled Matt to be alert and keep in contact.

Before finishing his second phone call, Webb asked to speak to Matt alone, no speakerphone. "Matt, remember when we were on the boat in the Dominican Republic, I gave you a reward for saving my family and me?"

Matt thought, *Yeah, a palm full of cut diamonds*

"I also gave you some advice—live your life so you don't need bodyguards—well, I'm sorry but now you're in the secrets business, with powerful and ruthless people. You need to be careful, don't be predictable, watch for people watching you, arm yourself. Also, I'm sending you two satellite phones. It will make our conversations more secure. Divide them up as you see fit, don't lose them. If one breaks you'll have a spare—don't bother trying to get them fixed—they aren't sold in the States yet. Good luck."

▷▷▷▷

Finally, a warm front from the south brought a high pressure area. The forecasting gave them several days. It was time to move the *Ferr Play*.

Matt called the dock facilities in Munising and the local Ferr brothers—who always liked to help bring their boat out of the water. Completing plans that allowed a trip to Granite Island, Matt and Tanya and the Vegas left before dawn, heading for Marquette.

George and Anita would stay overnight in Marquette—eating out, seeing a movie and doing some shopping. The Red Lobster in Marquette was Anita's favorite in the area—she could get the seafood she had missed since leaving the Keys. They would pick up Matt and Tanya late the next afternoon in Munising.

At the Marquette marina, the damaged door on the boat brought home the dangers they had faced and refreshed their flagging fears. Adding to their worries, the student harbormaster came over to the boat, "Some guys were walking around your boat two days ago. I watched them, then came over and asked what they wanted—I remembered someone had broken in before. They said they just liked old, well kept Silvertons. They walked around the marina a little and left."

Matt asked what they looked like.

"Average, older—maybe 40s, good shape, in sweaters and jackets, slacks, boating shoes."

Matt nodded.

"Here's your dock bill, you owe an extra ten days from what you paid ahead. You can pay me or mail in a check." Giving the paper to Matt, the harbormaster returned to his books in the little, brick office.

George and Matt carefully inspected the 34-foot Silverton—from bow anchor locker to stuffing boxes where the propeller shafts went through the hall—they found no fire bombs or signs of any foul play. The four of them moved most of their personal items off the boat, leaving just what Matt and Tanya might need for a single overnight. They checked the charge on the cordless spotlight and made sure the digital camera had enough battery and plenty of space on its flash card. Rolling the M-16 in a blanket, Matt put it in the storage area under the rear helm seat.

While topping the tank and paying the dock fee, Matt and Tanya watched the Vegas drive off for their two days in the biggest city in the Upper Peninsula. Backing the boat away from the dock, happy to have a deck under him, Matt smiled as the girl he loved climbed up the ladder to sit beside him at the helm.

The day was perfect, the fall colors blanketed their southern view from the distant west Huron Mountains to as far as they could see to the east. The two-foot swells were gentle and well spaced. They had a 12-mile run to Granite Island. The southwest wind would make their approach on the north side in smooth water.

Carefully setting the chain anchor rode around a refrigerator-size rock and linking it over itself, in ten feet of water, gave Matt a secure bow line. Backing the boat close to the only real ledge on the whole north side of the island, he cut the engines, and jumped to the ledge with a stern line. Tanya finally adjusted and then secured the bow line, making *Ferr Play* safe for the present wave and wind conditions. They knew enough to never trust Lake Superior—a weather or water change always could mean disaster for any boat so close to a mountain of granite walls. Tanya added another spring line to the shore configuration—the boat could swing many degrees and still be brought back to the ledge for reboarding.

The path to the rock shelter—really more like a cave with a partially open roof—led Matt and Tanya to the wall with its mysterious scratches. The last time Matt was here, he was tired, cold, hungry, frightened, and worried about Tanya—all of which at the time made the scratches less interesting or important. Now he could see they were an attempt by someone to pass on important information—when scratching on stone to leave a message, one would choose words carefully.

Using a soft scrubbing brush from the boat, and angling the light to shine across the scratches, Tanya and Matt began investigating each scratch and line on the rock face. When they agreed upon the form and intent of a line, they filled in the scratch with a felt tipped Sharpie marker pen. They skipped what wasn't clear—then went back to fill in what made the most sense. CAROL K 1933 SMALLPOX became very plain. The next lines were more difficult. As they picked off and brushed away lichen, it became obvious the scratching instrument and the person using it were becoming duller. After nearly an hour the letters and words began to form themselves:

```
CAP J L KILD CREW—WIFE   SANK SHIP
```

Then there was an arrow pointing toward the inside of the rock structure, then another arrow—unnoticeable without study and a strong light. Brushing and viewing from several angles, Tanya finally, using her finger tips and spit, could trace the faint scratches—but they revealed manmade effort and every foot or so an arrow could be detected. Six in all went into the cave-like protection of the rocks and up the rock wall.

In the small enclosure, Tanya commented on a coldness that filled the space. Matt could see her breath in the weak beams that spread the sun's light onto the dark rock.

Matt commented, "Its ten degrees colder in here."

As he maneuvered the spotlight, Matt thought about the figures he had seen when he first anchored off this forbidding hunk of rocks, thrusting themselves up at a steep angle from the depths of Lake Superior. He also thought of George Vega in the water—almost delirious with fatigue and cold—seeing men on the rocky ledge that had lead them through the nearly vertical walls of rock.

Spirits, ghosts helping them? What would Rod Serling have to say? I know what I saw, and Vega was positive he saw men. It does feel spooky in here!

He watched Tanya totally concentrating on moving from one almost invisible scratch to another—her attention drawn along the forbidding, cold, rock surface. Her fingers finally touched a crevice, invisible without the powerful spotlight. The crack was of no note—just two inches wide at its base—running nearly vertically for two feet and ending in solid rock. Lodged near the top of the crack was a brown object. Touching it, Matt felt rusted metal, which he pried out of the crack: a belt buckle. Probably the tool so laboriously used to carve words and arrows into stone. There was a small ledge at the crack's base—also slanted. Animal droppings—white—probably from birds and black with little shiny flecks of insect wings, from bats—painted the rock, nature's arrow of sorts pointing to the crack. The powerful beam of the floodlight revealing a substance within the crack, Matt began edging it out with this jackknife blade, flakes of moldy, yellowed paper and green pieces of leather began coming out.

"I'm destroying what's jammed in there," agonized Matt as he worked with his knife. "I'll be right back."

Matt ran to the boat, returning with a spatula and a wooden utensil used to remove toast from a toaster. For a half hour they worked on the material within the rock crevice. At first, just larger pieces of paper fragments came out, then the nonrock material began to move. Finally, they were able to get a general movement along the whole of the crack. With great care they worked the intact contents of the crack free. It was part of the log of the *Carol K.*

Matt photographed all they did and saw. No more human items or clues could be found in the area, digging was a joke—the soil was only a few inches deep, when there was any soil. They carefully took the fragile log, placed it on, and covered it with, Matt's jacket. Moving it to the *Ferr Play,* they secured it between bath towels on the cabin table. Deciding that a rocking boat and 12-volt lighting made opening the log too difficult, they would to wait until they were ashore to inspect their prize.

Dark clouds loomed to the north, a front was trying to come down. While their wind still blew warm and gentle from the south, it was time to make the run to Munising.

26

Grand Island and Munising

unning at 20 knots, the *Ferr Play* rolled gently in the well-spaced swells. Viewing the shore to their south, Matt and Tanya silently watched from the windy helm, awed by the beauty of the fall colors, the white of the frequent sand beaches, and the breaking shore waves that splashed on each comma-like point and peninsula they ran by. Tanya sat on Matt's lap, she kept him warm in the 45-degree air they moved through at cruising speed.

Tanya pulled up her sweatshirt's hood, drawing it tight around her face, finally zipping up her down windbreaker. "It's more beautiful than the Keys—but I can't feel my nose."

Nuzzling Matt's neck, she proved her point. They began kissing, their lips a little cold at first, soon working perfectly.

Matt came up for air, "I think we should find a protected cove—I was going to tie up at the Munising dock, but its all empty now. Let's spend the night alone in a bay—I think the weather will cooperate."

"I'll cooperate too," whispered Tanya.

Matt turned the helm chair slightly, checking the Garmin GPS: speed, direction, superimposed topographic maps, aerial photographs and the tracks of their previous travels all displayed on the small, bright screen. He had bought it for the boat a year ago—an extra 'thank you' to the Ferr brothers for the kind sharing of their boat. He paid nearly as much for the Great Lakes chip as the unit itself, but the information on their maps and pictures took the place of dozens of rolled up maps—hard to use on an open bridge.

Matt knew Grand Island well, he had friends who had a hunting cabin on the northwest side—a grandfathered arrangement with the U.S. Forest Service who owned the island. There was a protected cove on the northeast end, its sand beach and a picnic area made it a common port-of-call for boaters during the summer season. There would be no one there at this time of year, except a few hungry, prowling bear that overpopulated the island. They could anchor off the shore in good water, protected from all weather except a strong nor'easter. If the waves got bad, they would run around the point and head south into Munising harbor.

"We aren't expected at the dock to pull the boat out until nine o'clock tomorrow and your folks aren't meeting us until after 11:00. If we can get the cabin warm we can share a nice evening together," Matt said as he brought the boat slightly to starboard to follow the outgoing track shown on the GPS. "Another half hour and we'll be at anchor"

Tanya stood up, moved to the ladder, turned to go down, holding the chrome handrails. "I'll turn the generator on, crank the heater up and get our bunk ready."

She gave Matt a smile that was an invitation. He moved both engine levers forward an inch.

Curiosity about the log had been put on hold. When they tried to open the pages, the edges just crumbled or stuck together, so they agreed patience and thought would be the keys to unlocking its secrets. They put it on a wooden cutting board, wrapping it in multiple layers of paper toweling, finally putting the whole bundle in a plastic garbage bag, hoping that George could open it where they had more space and light than the boat provided. Also, Matt wanted to photo-document everything.

The cove, nearly glass calm, had 100-foot pines and hardwoods protecting it on three sides, the south wind entirely blocked by trees and hills. Matt brought the boat to the west side of the small bay. Dropping the anchor onto a holding bottom, he backed off plenty of line as Tanya helped pay it out and tie it off. Setting the GPS for an anchor watch application, he turned on the anchor lights and secured the bridge. One last scan of the area showing no human presence or activity except several wooden picnic tables stacked at angles against large trees—ready for winter snows. The rumble of the two large engines stopped and the wonderful silence of the secluded bay surrounded them, disturbed only by the muted below-deck hum of the generator. Matt went down to the aft deck to join Tanya. She turned toward the shore, he put his arms around her, she snuggled back against him. The late afternoon sun, its setting colors blocked by hills and trees, nevertheless turned the yellow and red leaves to flame around the cove. The regular hiss of gentle waves breaking on a low, sand beach became nature's only sound, until the high-pitched cackle of an eagle brought their attention to the east. They could see the straight line of body and wings that identified the souring eagle. It seemed to be stationary in the light southern breeze, the white head and tail of the mature bird clearly showing as it side-slipped, then dove toward the grassy area of the eastern cove edge, disappearing against the dark forest background.

"The cabin is warm enough. Would you like an hors d'oeuvre before supper?" whispered Tanya as she wiggled against Matt. "Maybe, Tanya pâté on a half bunk?"

Supper was very late that evening.

Sipping the last of a bottle of 2005 Mouton Cadet Bordeaux while the coffee finished percolating, Matt noticed the steam-covered cabin windows, even before the coffee pot had started its efforts. Feeling totally happy about themselves, they called Tanya's parents to tell them where they had anchored.

Anita went on about the bargains she had found—closeout sales on summer items, all of which could be worn as year-round dress in the Keys. George figured they would need to rent a vehicle to drive back to the Keys—their booty too much for plane luggage. Half kidding, he confessed they really might drive back to enjoy the fall colors in the Smokies and visit friends in the Georgia coastal low country.

Matt and Tanya had noted a change in Mrs. Vega over the last few weeks—she had stopped talking wedding at every evening meal, instead phoning Florida friends almost daily to ask about her home and yard. They thought the cold, northern fall with many gray days in the low 40 degrees, freezing nights, drizzling rain and occasional snow flurries had made her yearn for sun and warmth. She also didn't talk about the kidnapping or the gunmen or the fire. But, every day, she had seemed to pull more within herself. All the bravery, initiative and strength she had shown during their times of crisis had drained her. Tanya had had long talks with her, but they all ended with no answers, just sighs and silence. Anita and her husband had worked tirelessly to fix the damage and make the house ready for winter. With the house in shape and all four people healthy, everyone had expected Anita to be her energetic self again, but her moods and voice just got darker and quieter each passing day.

There is a time in the Upper Peninsula between leaf fall and snow fall where the world just seems to wait. It is a time to hunt, enjoy a fireplace, read, walk, end all outdoor projects, drain and put away hoses, plant winter bulbs, put stakes by your mailboxes and driveway edges so the snowplows know what they should miss—or hit, depending on the mood of the driver. Anita seemed not to understand or appreciate this hiatus. She was a two-season—not a four-season—person. Her husband George, always happy and busy, could always see and find work to do. He was much more adaptable.

On board the Silverton, Tanya and Matt listened to Anita and understood that the Vegas would soon be heading south—like the monarch butterflies and the Canada geese. Noticing the worry in Tanya's eyes, he said while pouring the coffee, "You're worried about your mom. I'll do anything you want to make her happy."

Matt thought, *Like buying rice and getting a new wedding suit...*

"I don't know what's her real problem," Tanya said as she finished her coffee. "She may not either—she just wants to go home now. She always gets strange when Webb is even mentioned—now he's in our lives again, calling us regularly. She's very grateful for his power and efforts to get me back—but there is some deeper something."

Wanting to break the mood and subject, Matt got their coats and brought Tanya to the aft deck. He flicked off the generator switch, ushering her out the cabin door. After turning off the anchor lights. The stars, with no competition from man, took their breath away—aided by 38-degree air. They cuddled against the side rail, with Matt again holding her in his arms while they enjoyed the beauty around them. On the northern horizon they saw lights flashing on and off like truck lights going over a hill. The flashes intensified then formed into bands that extended up across the northern sky—the aurora borealis slowly working its way into a magnificent display that ended in a rare crescendo of green and red streaks. Then, ebbing, it all became an indescribable memory, leaving the stars again on display.

"We are just a small part of something truly magnificent," Tanya whispered almost to herself. "Let's go in and enjoy being together."

The morning came calm and misty, low clouds forecasting rain or drizzle. The *Ferr Play* moved around the east side of Grand Island, almost reluctant to make waves on the glass-like water surface. As they passed an antique, wooden lighthouse on their starboard, Matt viewed the deserted harbor—colorful boats, noisy jet skis, boatloads of tourists at the rails of the sightseeing boats, green hills and leafy trees gone for the season. They glided by the deserted boat slips of Munising Harbor, past the high school and came to dead stop off the dock where the large blue Travelift waited to bring the 34-foot Silverton out of the water and onto its cradle—where it would be fitted with a blue, plastic winter cocoon.

They were 15 minutes late—no alarm clock and ever darker mornings would be their excuse. In reality, they had both been awake before dawn but had wanted to maintain their little world within their warm bunk for as long as they could.

"Bring her in," yelled the Travelift operator from the dock.

Matt maneuvered the boat into the narrow confines of the slip. At the same time, the Travelift began moving on its runway. Within minutes, the straps were tightened under the boat. Tanya and Matt, moving to land, watched while the boat was hoisted and brought easily to a crib where it would spend the winter. The blue, spiderlike carrier motored past the large glass-bottomed and excursion boats that brought the wonders of sunken ships and the magnificent Pictured Rocks National Park to thousands of tourists each year. Small by comparison, the *Ferr Play* finally hovered over its prepared supports, among sail boats and other powerboats of its size.

Two of the Ferr brothers were there with several of their workers from the mink farm. They all had their jobs. The boat was tilted with the bow high, the bilge plugs open, water draining, while a power washer moved around the boat, blasting the summer grime off the antifouling paint and hull—then the white Silverton was eased onto its wooden supports. Engines would be winterized and all drains opened, with the four engine batteries, the generator battery and any easily removed electrical devices boxed up and put into their pickup trucks. Matt and Tanya helped by removing their personal property and clothes and staying out of the way as the Ferr crew scurried all over the boat, moving up and down the single ladder.

Matt made a pile of their property under a tree, sandwiching the carefully carried log between layers of sleeping bags and blankets. Satisfied it was hidden in plain sight, along with the wrapped up M-16, he said, "Let's walk up and get some breakfast, they'll be two hours on this and your folks won't be here for at least an hour—even if your dad is early as usual."

They walked up the hill from the harbor and along the highway to a restaurant where they had a good breakfast, returning in a little over an hour.

"You bought us something new again?" asked Will Ferr—the youngest brother. "What's it do?" He held out a dark gray plastic device, about the size of two cigarette packs end to end. "I took it off the radio antenna—it's always smart to remove anything easy to steal before some kid helps himself and you don't know it's gone until spring. Is it for weather, GPS, a rescue signal?"

Matt took the device—dark gray and heavier than he expected with a small, one-inch antenna at one end and thumbscrew clamps. It seemed electrical, micro writing on one edge that Matt could just make out—Skyeye Technology. They were being tracked—he hadn't noticed it when they went over the boat in Marquette. If it had been a bomb, they would have had it. A cold hand gripped his heart. He turned to the group watching him, "I'll find out what it does. It isn't anything I bought—maybe your brother or dad put it on."

"No way, I'd know about it," said Ferr. "Dad thinks the boat is just a plastic hole in the water where you pour money. My brother doesn't even buy beer when it's his turn."

"I'll look into this and let you know what I find out," Matt mumbled as Ferr and his workers got back to the boat work.

Matt looked around—a district phone office was across the field from the boat works. Matt thought they might be helpful.

Three phone engineers looked at the little gray instrument that Matt placed on their counter. After everyone established it wasn't their equipment, they had no liability and this wasn't their job or responsibility, they surrounded the little box and descended upon it like Dr. Christiaan Barnard's team removing the first heart.

"It's a GPS device with a big battery—made in Japan. It's waterproof. This is the on and off switch, or you can pull the battery connections." That represented the collective verdict after 15 minutes of fine screwdrivers and lighted magnifiers. Their final observation—"It cost some money."

Matt and Tanya thanked them and walked back to the boat. After giving their report to the boat crew, Matt handed Will a several-hundred-dollar check to pay his part for winterizing and shrink wrapping. At the end of these activities the Vegas drove into the boat area. George helped Matt cram the pile of blankets, sleeping bags, towels, food and toiletries into the back of the package-laden Yukon, the rifle and the bundled log already carefully placed out of harm's way. Sam Ferr, who arrived while Matt and Tanya were at breakfast, finally came off the boat to meet the Vegas. After shaking hands with the Ferrs and their crew, promising to visit more at camp during deer hunting season, Matt took Highway 28 east toward home.

Matt drove while George looked at the device. Tanya and her mother poured over the sale items Anita felt she had practically stolen from Yonkers. George chuckled and said, "Anita got deals on deals with senior discounts thrown in—she was one step from them paying her to take some of these clothes."

Everyone laughed—but George still held the turned-off, gray device, meeting Matt's eyes. Neither man's look reflected the mirth of the moment.

The rest of the drive was dominated with talk of the clothes and great buys gleaned by their two days of big town shopping in Marquette. George had multiple pairs of cargo shorts—much more in style than his cutoff Air Force utility pants he had used for decades.

"These are Columbia—$49 shorts that we ended up getting for $5.95— you couldn't buy the buttons, zipper and Velcro for that," Anita said as she pulled great buy after great buy from plastic bags. Soon all laps and seats were festooned with super deals, never to be duplicated in the civilized Western world. They had spent many hundreds of dollars driving the collective merchants' profit margin to the pavement. The time and drive went quickly—they soon arrived happily at Matt's beautiful, secluded forest home.

All the way back Matt wondered where the little gray box was hidden on the Yukon. He knew he and George would be under and over the vehicle as soon as they carried in Anita's booty, hoping their last thoughts wouldn't be a blinding flash.

The Livingstons were not done with them.

27

Bugs and Log

Matt and George, after only five hours of sleep, greeted the women at breakfast. The previous evening, they had spent nearly three hours going over and under the Yukon and then moved into the house to look for listening devices. They tried to make searching a low-key operation, but failed. The tapping, opening, closing, over and under everything inspections sounded like large rodents rooting through the house, soon Tanya and Anita became as involved and disturbed as the men. When they found nothing, the women went to bed. Drinking several beers, the men kept thinking and looking. Previously communicating by notes—they had agreed not to mention the log, patiently waiting in its bundle on the garage workbench. With the new day their note passing seemed dumb, literally. Finally, they called Webb.

Webb told them they would have his phones via UPS by the end of the day. He would talk to them at length then with more news. His voice—corporate, indifferent—fanned all their glowing coals of fears.

Spending the rest of the morning and early afternoon with the logbook, George separated the pages and Matt took pictures. Tanya placed paper towel sheets between each page. Lights and a small fan dried the moisture from the pages. Their contents—usually short, inked daily notes of the ship's course, speed, location, maintenance and passenger and cargo movement—listed the dates, with the edge of the leather binding itself showing the year 1933. Although both moldy covers were intact, the last third of the log had pages roughly cut out. There was no interesting or incriminating information to be found, until they got past the ripped out pages—they found penciled printing crossing the neat, red lined boundaries printed on the previously blank pages that made up the last of the log.

Three pages of uneven lines and words—crude printing, broken sentences, sketchy details—by two authors chronicled a ship carrying dying and dead passengers, led by a crazed captain, on a portless plague ship, driven over the edge when his wife also fell ill with smallpox. Finally, the log detailed the opening of the sea cocks, the shooting of several crewmen, the captain's killing of his own wife and the abandonment of the vessel by the captain and two crewmen in the larger, sail equipped lifeboat. The second person's hand gave a description of a sinking ship drifting a whole, stormy day; the struggle of two weak men from an aft quarantined cabin, recovering enough to leave their beds, hearing shots and following blood trails, finding dead people, a dying ship, the large lifeboat with three identifiable men moving away. The history included the activities of two surviving men: releasing the anchor (probably to lighten the sinking ship and to turn it into the wind), failing to light the main boiler or to make pumps work. They did close one of the sea cocks and close all watertight doors, slowing the sinking. The two men took to another lifeboat with a few supplies and made for the rocky island they could see even in the black of the night. Pushed by waves and wind, the boat hit and swamped on the rocks. The men got ashore with some supplies, the lifeboat awash against a windward wall of rocks. The last paragraphs and the men's names and signatures were indecipherable on the disintegrating paper.

Scrawled on the last page edge were several sentences, so close to the edge they were destroyed, leaving only fragments and a few understandable words: *freezing, no wood, lifeboat* and finally—with printing again, in the first person's hand—a single word. *Treasure.* Candle wax had dripped on and ran down the page. An image of cold, desperate men huddled over this work in a dark, cold rock crevice filled their minds as they clustered around the workbench.

Matt could feel the despair, anger and fatalism in the printed and scrawled words of the unknown men. He had experienced the loneliness and cruel environment of the island. Only 12 miles to a port, yet the crashing waves, freezing air and water, fever weakened bodies, and a water filled boat, added up to a nearly hopeless voyage. The legend of Lake Superior says it doesn't give up its dead, leaving the fate of these men a mystery. Matt had researched the sinking of the *Carol K* from the Canadian insurance documents. The recorded sinking area wasn't close to Granite Island. Only one lifeboat and one story ever got to land. Matt considered the pages scattered over the powerfully lighted workbench—with the final hours of two lives displayed before him, he felt a powerful obligation to them. As if reading Matt's mind, George, with emotions welling up from generations of Latin blood, said, "We must avenge these brave men."

Tanya held her father's shoulders, leaned over and kissed his cheek. Her eyes wet, she glanced at Matt, adding her resolve to their unspoken pact.

Matt checked the quality of the pictures he had taken; he printed several pages from his printer by putting the CF card into the printer, setting it for highest quality and increasing the inking levels. The three most damning pages were clear and easier to read without the red lines and yellowed pages of the logbook. Replacing the card in the Canon, Matt ran the white USB cable to his laptop computer. He built a file of all the pages—named only by the date of the photographs. It would take someone going through all his picture files to find the log material. He would send the file to other people when he got to a high-speed Internet port.

The UPS truck arrived a little after 4:00 pm, driving through the season's first real snowstorm that actually left snow on the ground. The UPS lady, blond and vivacious, chatted—about the weather, the long drive in, how glad she was they were home, and her admiration for their new home—while they signed for the fair-sized box. She backed the brown step van out of the driveway then, while carefully avoiding potholes, drove away, leaving them alone again.

The box, opened on the kitchen table, held two large cell phones—big like the early phones of the 1980's. Two instruction books—printed in English, French, Spanish and in the flowing script of Arabic—introduced the owner to the newest cryptophone technology. Good anywhere on Earth, the phones didn't record numbers and didn't have call menus and no camera or fancy features. The manual mentioned it was a modified Iridium 9555 satellite phone with encryption. Each phone had a number tag attached—with instructions to guard the tag. There was another envelope, labeled OPEN ME.

Matt, with a flash back to some part of *Alice in Wonderland*, opened the envelope to reveal a single page in Webb's large, clear script:

> Don't say the phone numbers, memorize them, destroy the labels and this letter, call me outdoors at the number below.

Matt gave one phone to George, he and Tanya took the other. Each phone had a numerical keyboard, a screen, several function keys and a power switch. A thin charger lay in the plastic bag with the manual.

Matt turned the unit on, pushed in Webb's number, hit SEND.

The screen displayed the number as it was entered, flashed as it sent its signal into the sky and, in a few seconds, blinked a timer.

Webb said, "Hello."

Matt pushed a volume arrow up, a bar displayed on the screen—indicating the volume increase. Webb's voice could be heard by the three other people standing near the phone in the gravel driveway—in the middle of over 300 acres of wilderness.

Matt said hello, describing their location.

Webb got to the point. "Do you have the logbook and does it say anything?"

Matt reviewed what they had and what they thought. He read the three pages he'd printed on his Canon printer. He gave his editorial comments and described the words on the logbook's edge. Matt editorialized about all the disjointed words from the edge—the word 'treasure' made no connections. But they knew they were dealing with desperate, cold and hopeless men.

Webb asked a few questions for clarification. Then he paused, indicating a change of thought or new information coming. "The Livingstons are in information-gathering mode. They are investigating all of us. The GPS is just part of it. I'd assume you are being watched and monitored. They are planning something or maybe just desperate for anything we know. The bugs and computer software we put on their ship haven't produced much—a few names in Washington, nothing very useful. The brothers are very careful and seem to be well schooled in state-of-the-art surveillance techniques. They realize if they come after any of us, I'll retaliate. I want to get my hands on the log, it's a powerful lever. I've also investigated their influence peddling with judges and government officials in the U.S. and Canada. The Livingstons have had victories in several Canadian Parliament committees with their Nuclear Waste Removal proposal. The proposal has also been favorably accepted in several U.S. House Committees. Their stock is up over 60% so far, no one is talking and nothing has been publicized. I'm still working on the UN portion of their plot, it's hard to crack such a slimy nut. International politics makes international crime look like amateur hour. Anyway, their plan is going very well. You're probably going to be millionaires soon.

"I can meet you at the same place we met before at the Sault. Let's say three days from now—1:00 pm Eastern time. I'll fly Al and me over—if the weather is good—and rent a car. Once the log is securely hidden I'll have a little talk with the brothers Livingston and get them to mind their own business and make us money."

Matt interrupted, "I didn't think you cared about money, anymore."

Webb made a sound, as close to a laugh as he ever came. "Increasing one's wealth is always good, plus I enjoy intrigue. I never said money is a problem; it is cash that's a pain in the ass. It leaves a trail, it's bulky, hard to move around, attracts attention from governments and other crooks. Drug dealers have such volumes they weigh it instead of counting it. A million in hundred-dollar U.S. bills is 37.4 pounds, in fifties 74.8 pounds. The mobs can't get away from it, it's their tar baby. But stock options weigh nothing, electrical fund transfers move at the speed of light, Cayman accounts are above politics, and a good secret is priceless.

"Anyway, see you in three days. Come alone."

Matt moved closer to the phone's mic. "I think the Vegas will be going back south, we have snow on the ground. It'll be deer season soon, and Tanya will be a hunting widow for the first time. We'll let you know if there are any more developments."

The phone connection ended.

28

Snowbirds

"What you want to do with these?" George Vega held up two red cylinders, then placed the two incendiary grenades on the workbench. Both could easily be held in one hand and each contained enough heat to melt an artillery-piece barrel. "These scare me."

Matt picked them up. "Let's put some tape over the pin and put them somewhere safe. We could really start some brush piles with them..."

George had labored all morning in the garage, cleaning, oiling and packing away all his many tools in several multi-drawered cabinets. He covered all his larger equipment—grinders, table saw and radial arm saw— and left the usually cluttered workshop area clean and bare.

"Where should I put them?" muttered George, opening a bottom drawer of a cabinet where plumbing materials were segregated—the large drawer filled with various length plastic elbows, caps, traps and piping. Choosing two short, black plastic drain pipes, which the grenades fit in easily, he put pipe caps on both ends. The piping went back into the drawer, hidden like a tree in the forest.

"That should do, I can't see anyone getting into this stuff," Matt said. "Unless a trap breaks this winter—and that won't happen. I'll drain the toilets, put antifreeze in all the bowls and traps, when I leave for the winter. The heat stays on—set at 55—but just in case of an electrical outage, I'll make sure we don't come back to frozen pipes. I can't turn off the water pump—it needs to be on to make the boiler and floor heating work—but I've got antifreeze in the floor tubing and I can shut off the water lines to the rest of the house. I'll have some people check on the house—snowmobile friends—the road will have four or five feet of snow by February. I've got to remember to put a snow shovel outside so they can get the storm door open. It's hard to think of all the snow we will have—and it's a new house I almost hate to leave."

Tanya overheard his comment as she brought a tray of sandwiches into the garage. "But think about the warm sun, clear water and my bikini. I'll need lots of sun lotion rubbed on me."

Putting the tray on the work bench, she gave Matt a hug and kissed his neck, returning to the kitchen with a little extra hip sway.

Matt grabbed a sandwich and watched her leave. "She makes a strong case for being a snowbird."

Zipping up a canvas carryall, George put it into the back of the Yukon, whose doors were open. "These are just a few of my old tools I can't live without."

The vehicle was half filled with boxes, a clothes bar suspended across the back space held some clothes with more to come.

Anita, loaded with two plastic boxes, came out and slid them into the SUV. "That's about it for me—just our overnight bags and a cooler and we're ready. George, you've got clothes to pack, your suitcase is on the bed. Have you looked outside? It's really coming down—we're not leaving any too soon." She returned to the kitchen.

Matt peeked out the garage side window, seeing a world of white and worrying about Florida drivers going into winter conditions, "Keep the windshield brush and scraper where you can get at them. Your windshield washer fluid is full—you go through a lot if the roads are snow-covered and salted. You got good maps?"

George brought Matt into the kitchen where he had maps spread on the counter. "Got lots of maps, we'll go I-75 a lot, with a side trip east through the Smokies on 25 to Cumberland Gap National Park—we went there when Tanya was ten years old—we may stay in that area, depending on the weather, then pick up I-40 to 26—it's a beautiful highway that cuts right through the mountains in Tennessee and finally comes out at Charleston. We like the low country of South Carolina and Georgia; I've got a good friend that lives on St. Simon's Island— we'll stay with them a few days."

Matt looked over the largest map, noting the highlighter lines indicating their route.

George spoke while folding maps and pamphlets, consolidating them with a rubber band. "The only traveling problem is Anita's map reading—she has to have the map facing the way we are going—so when we are going south she can't read the words or numbers without flipping the map around all the time, and then you need to be careful when she gives you a right or left. We could get a GPS unit, but that would be too easy.

"Plus, I've seen those machines get all mixed up, run you around in circles; send you down a swamp road. Just between you and me, I think, at times, the little lady in the machine drinks!"

Matt and George went back to the vehicle, George put the map bundle in the passenger door pocket. Turning to Matt he added, "Oh, I've taken apart one M-16, now with a new firing pin—it's all packed in my tool bag with two magazines, just in case we met unfriendly folk on the way. We'll keep our eyes open for trouble. Your Yukon switches to four wheel drive and is a fine vehicle—we'll be safe in it, even if the curvy, mountain roads get tricky."

Supper consisted of fresh fish from Naubinway, baked partridge, their own handpicked blueberries rolled in tarts and a fair amount of cold Chablis from a gallon jug. Still, the conversation was a little strained, the mood a little sad—Tanya felt badly about her dad driving all the way, after Anita stubbornly announced she would not drive "that big truck," as she called the Yukon. George smoothed things by saying she hardly ever drove anyway. After dishes, the family gathered before the fireplace, the great room's large windows framing a beautiful scene of big flakes slowly coming down on the trees and fields to the northwest. Breaking the appreciative silence of watching snow fall, Anita began planning the things that would have to be done back at the Keys. Semi-ignoring her, George talked with Matt about the Yukon, travel locations and finally what they could be doing with his 26-foot runabout when he got down there.

"Maybe you can get some dry ice and bring some venison down," suggested George as he ushered Anita up to their bedroom.

Tanya was in the bed when Matt came to the room after closing the house for the night. Matt got into bed to find his partner very warm, naked and not ready for sleep.

After some very enjoyable time, Tanya lay with her head resting on Matt's shoulder. "You know, I'm worried about dad doing all the driving. I don't mind being a hunting widow, but we wouldn't be separated for very long—and that phone is a wonder. You can call me from your deer blind and I can tell you what I'd be doing to you if we were on a deserted island or watching the stars from the deck of dad's boat."

After some difficulty following the thread of Tanya's thoughts and more kissing, Matt accepted the wisdom of Tanya's plan changing, agreeing that George could use some help. Hating to be separated from Tanya, he still knew she was right. It would only be a few weeks and much of that would be hunting time. He could still be with her at Thanksgiving—their one-year anniversary—when she had dropped into Matt's life in a crashed plane with drug smugglers and gangster links that brought Webb into Matt's world. Matt's whole life had changed during those few days in a major blizzard that had brought down the plane and isolated Matt and Tanya for several days. Suspicions and fear had turned to love, a constant adventure had begun for Matt. Tanya, her parents, a Russian criminal mastermind—Webb—and his family all became linked to Matt.

He had spent his winter as one great dangerous adventure, and now couldn't think of his life without Tanya. She seemed to draw him and a new world of excitement, even danger, to herself. She made his previous life seem rather dull…however worthy and satisfying it had been.

Matt finally rationalized the separation and joined Tanya in sleep.

The next morning's breakfast announcement made Anita cry with happiness. The women spent all day in a whirlwind of activities: packing, making various dishes for Matt, leaving lists of to-dos, washing clothes and bedding, and lugging more boxes and bags to the vehicle.

George and Matt repacked several times—wondering about but rejecting strapping some of the boxes to the top luggage carrier on the Yukon. Finally, by putting part of the back seat down and folding versus hanging the clothes, they were able to seat three people, see out the back and close all the doors. The jackets and seasonal clothes were positioned for use as they drove from winter, to spring and finally to the year-round summer of the Keys.

Lunch consisted of all the leftovers in the refrigerator—the wonderful smells in the house from casseroles and breads teasing them—off-limits food reserved for Matt's hunting weeks. Matt wanted to assure them he was totally capable of cooking for himself, but the ladies continued happily with their plans and culinary accomplishments.

Matt called Webb in the afternoon to confirm their meeting for the next day and the exact casino door of the rendezvous. He was told of their new plans. Webb suggested they should fly, but when confronted with the list of material needing transport he just sighed, concerned with Tanya being on the road but didn't belabor the point. He had news of the Livingstons—they were back on their ship and on the Lake somewhere. The stock had gone up even further, the international certification being announced in several capitals and at the UN. Speculation buzzed through the market—all to the benefit of the Livingstons. Webb had called them several times without success. He had people watching their homes and families but his electronic bugging stuff wasn't functioning.

Concluding the phone call, Webb said, "Be careful. I don't like their disappearance or the lack of communication—but they are in the end game of their big project. Let's stay in contact. I can have people with you if you would feel better with guards."

Anita, listening behind Matt, shook her head. Matt nodded and assured Webb they would be careful and safe.

After the phone call, the Vegas went back to cleaning, packing and preparing a late, last-of-everything buffet.

Matt asked Tanya to bundle up and come with him for a drive down to the quarry and a little walk after that. They said they would not be back for some time and not to wait supper for them.

The van had no trouble with the five inches of light snow, no wind and 30 degrees wasn't unpleasant when Matt and Tanya started their walk from the quarry floor.

Holding Tanya's gloved hand allowed Matt to lead her up his favorite old logging road, finally stopping at a mound of earth and logs that was once a deer blind.

Kissing Tanya, then turning her to survey the view of the woods from the low hill, Matt began pointing out the cedars and pines that indicated the swamp area, the oaks and maples of the hardwoods and the old logging trail that ran below the hill between the two types of forests. "We are on the exact spot when I heard your plane going down. It clipped those pines over there. I heard the plane hit the ice."

Tanya, turning and hugging Matt, said, "I don't remember the crash, just seeing the white of the lake in the black of the trees. I didn't remember anything until you were putting a bag of frozen spaghetti on my wrist. We ended up eating that spaghetti."

"It was in the freezer of the hunting cabin—I didn't have ice cubes. I used snow in baggies too—you were all bruised up. We were snowed in for four days. It seems a lifetime ago, not just a year."

They stood for a few more minutes listening to the snow fall on the dry oak leaves and the leaf-covered forest floor. Tanya shivered; Matt hugged her close then led her back down the path to the quarry floor and the van. They drove by the old quarry shop building—that had the hunting cabin inside it. In two weeks, Matt knew the cabin would be filled with hunters, surrounded by cars, ATVs, and cases of beer stacked beside colorful coolers holding various foods each hunter contributed to the hunt—the tradition of the deer hunts in the area going back many generations.

Matt and Tanya had their supper while George and Anita, having already eaten, sipped coffee at the table. Placing a thick envelope on the table, George removed the state brochures and TripTik provided by AAA. He commented, "Triple A is a goldmine of information—I got all this with a phone call. I've been a Triple A member forever. They even note traffic problems, road closings…and here is a landslide on 40 at Asheville, North Carolina. All those steep rock walls—a beautiful road through spectacular country." George repacked the envelope and pushed it to Tanya.

They talked about their travel plans: routes, daily distances, time of day to travel through a city, times to be off traffic-plugged highways and the cities to avoid totally. George Vega figured they would be out of any snow by Grayling. They made bets on when they would see green grass. Tanya picked Lexington. Matt, feeling a little sorry he wasn't going along, comforted himself with the prospect of a week of deer hunting, renewing all his old friendships and seeing his son again—who was trying to squeeze in a weekend away from his busy life of family and job in Wisconsin.

Talking done, final packing completed, carry bags laying open for the final toiletries, the couples said goodnight.

They would be up early to get on the road at dawn. The snow storm, being localized and ending at midnight according to the local news, wouldn't be an issue.

Long Day

Alarms buzzed and chimed at 5:00 am. Finishing its last burps, the coffeemaker said more than the four people that scurried around the house—all within their own thoughts. Matt, the only one not packing and loading, stood at the electric frying pan making four pancakes at a time and keeping them warm in a metal pan in the oven. He also heated maple syrup in a pan of water on the stove. The bacon lay in strips in a special tray that would go into the microwave—not traditional and it never got crispy, but it was fast and didn't get grease all over the stove. When the Vegas finally got to the table, Matt served the pancakes and bacon—adding orange juice to keep the big mugs of coffee company.

Tanya uttered the first words as she came in from the garage—her final bag jammed into the vehicle. "Good, maple syrup!"

Matt, taking his seat, said, "You know we had a good summer, this house got built in less than six months—wouldn't have happened without everyone working hard. I sure appreciate all you did. I hope you have some projects for me at your home."

George, taking two more pancakes, said, "I'll think of something—I'll miss the saw dust, paint smell and woodworking—but we always have the boat to work on, maybe we can charter a bigger boat and head into the Bahamas, or fly to some white-sand island. Anyway, we won't be bored—and these Livingstons still will keep us on edge."

Tanya, picking at her pancakes, said, "I hope you have a good hunt and then get down to us soon. Say 'Hi and thank you' to Webb. We owe him a lot. I'll stay in touch with his daughter at school. Maybe we can vacation together again, she could be a good diver."

Anita got up and cleared her dishes away—her old, typical reaction to hearing Webb's name.

Tanya noticed, pausing slightly, and went on, "I'd like to look at that ship's log again before we give it to Webb, there's something about it. Those poor men, they told us so much and we don't know their names. I can almost sense them when I touch the log. I'm going to go over it one more time before we go."

Tanya and Matt went into the garage—the log being the only item on the now clean and empty workbench. Unwrapping the log, she began with the front cover—looking it all over, turning each thick yellow page slowly, the paper toweling now removed. The regular writing finally led to the gap left by the torn pages, then the pages with the printing. Touching the pages as though reading Braille, she traced the pencil strokes, reverently reading each word, included the last one she touched, the scribbled word on the ragged, disintegrating edge—"treasure." Her two fingers staying on the word for several seconds, she closed the log. She squeezed the back cover, then the front cover. With a puzzled look, she said, "The back cover is thicker, look at this."

She pulled the arm that brought the overhead light closer to the log, tracing the edge, showing it to Matt. "This is cut along the inside edge and sealed with candle wax—see? It's been smoothed, not like a drip, you'd never see it without strong light, and you wouldn't look for the cut unless you felt the extra thickness."

Matt studied the log. He could see the seam and feel the extra thickness of the back cover. The small blade of his jackknife opened the waxy slit, expanding the space it made. Two edges of a folded document could be seen. He reached into a fishing tackle box, retrieving an old hemostat he used for getting hooks out of fish. Carefully, he teased the thick, stiff document out of the cover.

It was a folded parchment or canvas, lightly penciled on it was a message:

"If you find this, I did not make shore. Here is my treasure, my grandfather's work. I hold Charlotte Amalie in my heart."

It was signed with a scribble that could be Saul or Paul and a final initial—a capital P.

Carefully opening the tightly creased material, a light seemed to come from the act of the unfolding. Matt and Tanya wordlessly looked at a beach scene with several palm trees, the yellow and gold rising sun touching windswept fronds, the sky a dull gray with clouds touched by bright gold, pink and purple. The sea flat, reflecting all the colors of the land and sky. The main work was in ink, the colors boldly applied over ink lines. The artwork put the viewer on a warm beach at dawn. You could feel the heat of the new day on your back, making your soul anticipate the golden world that will drive away the gray and purple remnants of the night. The artwork had a magical feeling, much more than a two-dimensional exercise of ink and color.

The work signed with a simple "C. P." and, below the initials, "1851."

"This is truly wonderful," Tanya said quietly. "It's like a Monet, but finer, more detail—the colors and perspective take your breath away. This is a great piece of work, Let me take it, I'll research it. I love a mystery—Charlotte Amalie is a port not a person. Don't give this to Webb."

Matt gave her a nod. She took a manila folder from a file cabinet in the garage, carefully inserting the folded painting, between three pieces of paper toweling, before putting the folder into her suitcase, already packed and which occupied a top position in the Yukon.

"I'll explain this to my folks when I know what we have. This is artwork by a master. My mother would fixate on it and it would become a problem we will have to live with for fifteen hundred miles." Pausing with a concerned expression, she added, "Maybe you should get some pictures."

Fearful the Vegas would come out while they worked, Matt and Tanya took her suitcase into their bedroom—without explanations. There Matt took several pictures of the painting and the printing.

The crease down the picture hadn't cracked the oil significantly, but would take some effort to correct. The bright colors showed an overall patina of tiny cracks, the edges showing rusty punctures from brads and staples that indicated a history of care and several framings. As they looked at the work on their bed, the painting seemed to carry its own light. Matt could understand why the sailor would treasure it—the palm trees and sea brought warmth and the prospect of a fine day, regardless of the reality in which he might find himself.

Tanya lovingly replaced the painting into her suitcase.

Back in the garage, the vehicle all packed, Matt and Tanya kissed again. The Vegas said goodbye, wished Matt a good hunt and urged him to fly down as soon as possible. George made sure all the rental car contracts were in order, so Matt could drop off the van at the Marquette airport. Anita was the first into the Yukon—nesting in and organizing her space in the back seat. George would drive until Gaylord where they would take a coffee break.

Tanya, last getting into the Yukon, put Webb's satellite phone on the console between the front seats. "I've got my own cell phone, too, so let's talk every evening—before you go to sleep."

While the garage door was opening, Matt gave Tanya a last, light kiss. The Yukon slipped into gear and crunched down the snow-covered driveway. One honk from George, a swirl of water vapor and exhaust from the newly started engine and they were gone down the lane.

Matt checked his watch—he had time to sight in his rifle, check out his hunting gear and then clean up before going to the Sault to meet Webb.

Matt's deer rifle, a Remington 700 in 7mm Magnum, had a 3x10 Leopold scope. It was more rifle than he needed in Michigan, but he liked its accuracy. It never varied from year to year—but to miss a deer or, worse, to wound a deer because he was too lazy to check its accuracy was unforgivable. Matt put the rifle, his packet of shells, a large paper target and a staple gun into the van, which was parked outside covered with four inches of overnight snow. He cleaned the windows with a broom, drove to the far side of the quarry floor—where someone years ago had built a wooden frame. Stapling the target to the gray wood of the frame, Matt walked 100 yards to a shooting bench made of an old Formica-topped kitchen table pushed up to a large flat rock used as a chair. He cleaned off the snow, rolling his coat up into a ball and bracing the rifle across it, loaded three shells, pushed in yellow, foam earplugs and slowly fired three shots. The powerful rifle kicked back at his shoulder—without the padding of a hunting coat, he could expect a bruise. The sound of the shots echoing across the flat quarry floor, off the rock banks and the surrounding forest made Matt feel lonely. He missed Tanya already. He leaned the rifle against the table. The barrel, hot to the touch, steamed in the 20-degree morning air. Putting his coat back on, welcoming its warmth Matt followed his tracks back to the target to check the pattern—two touching and one, the first shot, a half inch low but all in the bull's-eye, the 10 ring. All would mean a dead deer.

Back at the house, after cleaning and oiling the rifle, Matt sorted through his closet—the fire and cleaning had moved everything—to find his jacket, its liner, his woolen glove liners, his hunter's orange Kromer cap, his wool pants and his polypropylene socks. Matt spread the coat out on the bed and felt the shoulder and sleeve where the jacket had been professionally repaired—no trace of the knife cuts from a fight to the death he, wearing the coat, went through nearly a year ago. His Danner boots were in a tin locker in the garage. His Marble knife, Silva compass, Bic lighter, nylon dragging rope, plastic gutting gloves, Kleenex packet, small flashlight—all assembled in a shoebox waiting on the top shelf. Matt reminded himself to pick up some new batteries when he bought his deer license. More than once he had gutted a deer with the flashlight held in his mouth. Some friends had head lamps or LEDs that clipped to their caps— but Matt felt they were either too bulky or provided not enough light. He also liked to carry little Hershey Special Dark Chocolate bars or chocolate-covered coffee beans—for energy and to keep awake. He felt in the pockets of his jacket—some year-old candy was still there, discolored and crumbly but good enough. The camouflaged jacket still smelled a little smoky—he had not let them dry clean it, feeling it might ruin the waterproofing of the Gore-Tex or the insulation of the space-age fibers that held heat better than down and stilled worked when wet. He knew if you put polypropylene socks in a hot dryer, they would be ruined—the little fibers would melt and wouldn't hold air anymore.

Satisfied his hunting gear passed muster, he showered, deciding to catch a delicious greasy hamburger in Trout Lake—on his way to the Sault.

Matt put the logbook bundle in the van. Only half filling his insulated cup with the last of the morning coffee, he headed out, stopping twice for deer in the road.

Three hours later, still burping the onions he had heaped on his Trout Lake hamburger, Matt checked his wristwatch for the third time. He needed to pee. Waiting at the main entrance for over an hour, he observed every type of human the planet could offer—except Webb or Al. Calling the Canadian Sault airfield, charming the private terminal lobby receptionist, he had confirmed a white Skymaster was parked among the dozen private planes tied down on the parking apron. Another two hours had gone by since that call. Matt worried—punctuality being a virtue of Webb's.

Matt had used both phones trying to locate Webb—the Canadian number answered by the caretaker confirmed Webb and Al had taken the plane to the Sault around noon. The satellite phone rang or buzzed for sometime and then went silent.

Matt stood outside on the wide steps leading to the casino. Using his cell phone, he talked to his son, learning he could not make the hunt this year. There was real disappointment, but his family and business came first in his busy life. Matt felt frustration, blending his old and new life wasn't always easy.

Matt's kidneys finally won the conflict between standing sentry and leaving a gap in his surveillance. Gone for five minutes—he half expected to find Webb waiting with a grin and to be greeted with, "Glad to see you finally got here!"

But there was no Webb or Al—another hour went by. Matt had been on vigil for nearly four hours total. The security guards asked him if he needed help five times. They stood or sat at their desk, watching Matt more and more as the hours went by.

Finally, Matt called Tanya on the satellite phone—having stayed off it up to now, hoping Webb would make contact.

Answering the phone, Tanya's voice flooded love and excitement into Matt's sour mode. "Darling, I've got all kinds of news. We stopped at a library here in Ohio—I couldn't keep the painting secret. Dad knows St. Thomas, its main town is Charlotte Amalie. The painting is by Camille Pissarro. It is super rare—most of his early work was destroyed in Europe during the Franco-Prussian War in 1871. Almost all his remaining works are of Europe—not his St. Thomas life. He was born there, went to school in Paris, but went back to the island in his twenties for many years. In 1851, he was twenty-one years old—just starting to find his style. He was a founder of Impressionist Art—influencing and working with all the big names: Degas, Cezanne, Gauguin and even Monet. We are going into Cincinnati tomorrow and get it framed—we'll spend all day on it. I couldn't find out who the sailor is—Pissarro had several sons. Mother insists we get it in a frame with a good backing and glass covering it. She is guarding it like a pit bull. Dad has done all the driving. The Yukon is fine; we were out of snow before we stopped for coffee at Gaylord. Dad says we are getting 17.4 miles per gallon, and your speedometer is slow by two miles per hour, could be the tires. He likes the vehicle. The lady at the library really helped us—she was excited as we were. We told her it came from an old book we found."

Matt finally got a word in. "Webb hasn't shown up, and I'm worried. You be very careful. If the Livingstons come after us—they will have to take care of Webb first. The more I wait, the more I worry. Webb's plane is at the Canadian Sault—I don't think I can go to the U.S. side and make inquiries—it might get Webb in trouble and he likes to keep a low profile. I guess I'll just go home and wait."

Telephone goodbyes given to everyone, Matt broke the connection. The security guards were also outside—watching Matt using the large phone. Matt walked slowly back to the van, heading it back to the quarry.

30

Ambush

The Chrysler Town and Country van had lots of bells and whistles, could seat eight, rode smoothly, had plenty of storage room with some seats folded down, but Matt liked his GMC Yukon better. He liked to be sitting up and seeing over other cars, like in a truck, he didn't like every car's lights in his eyes. Blowing snow occasionally made a white-out of the road as he drove west on 28. He almost missed the sign and left turn onto 123 in the swirling white stuff. The temperature had fallen to 20 degrees Fahrenheit—with below-zero temperatures forecast for overnight. Dressed too lightly, Matt turned up the heater. This would be the second year in a row with below-zero cold and snow before deer season. The last two summers had set cold records in Michigan and Wisconsin—the deer numbers way down mainly due to two hard winters and late springs in a row. Matt thought, *Damn Al Gore, where's your warm weather?…and damn your whole Global Warming cult…all a scam, a power play by the UN and grasping, uninformed socialist politicians.*

As the side gusts blew against the van, the defroster's fans had to be turned higher to fight the ice and condensation forming on the outside and inside of the windshield. As the flakes came down, the headlights made each flake a moving sparkle, the van seeming to travel into a lighted, white tunnel. Lack of visibility forced Matt to slow the vehicle; although the cold kept the road surface dry and clear. Driving into the hypnotic, white flakes, global warming still boiling in his brain, cursing the legislative time spent on the subject by ignorant people, Matt mentally reviewed the best example involving his favorite author—the late Michael Crichton.

Literally a giant of a man—six feet, nine inches—super smart—creator of scores of great books and movies—castigated before a Senate Committee by Senator Hillary Clinton because he wrote State of Fear, *a novel about politicians using climate and environmental issues to gain control and hold power over people.*

Matt remembered the YouTube video of Hillary reading a very nasty statement, then leaving the hearing—not listening to anything Dr. Crichton had to say—insisting on being called Senator—while calling the author—Mr. Crichton. Matt knew that while Hillary was writing her senior paper at Wellesley College—about Saul Alinsky, a Chicago political agitator, organizer, socialist—Crichton, already Summa Cum Laude and Phi Beta Kappa in Biological Anthropology as an undergrad, was completing his M.D.—both at Harvard. Matt's ire boiled at the lack of respect, the lack of scientific background and data understanding that lurked in the hallowed halls of government.

The wind and Matt's emotions calmed down as he drove through Trout Lake—the temperature now 15 degrees. Matt noted with satisfaction that science was numbers, and numbers will eventually show the politicos for the manipulators they are.

The drive into the quarry showed more vehicle tracks than he expected. The deer hunters weren't due for another four or five days. The prehunting work by the locals had been done weeks ago. They didn't bait much—and then only during the season, just to slow down and direct deer movement. They hunted trails and swamp edges—they did drives and had few permanent blinds—most just points of concealment that responded to the wind and to the trails that showed activity for that season. Matt and all of his hunting friends, mostly relatives, would be here in a week, skilled hunters all—they used apples rubbed on trees and stuck on branches to draw curious deer, plus various deer smells and some corn and carrots. No one used huge piles of bait, everyone spent some time walking—good for them and an aid to others—moving deer around. They all knew where each would be and how they would hunt that day—a great map of the property, on the quarry cabin wall, would be all grease-penciled with marks by the end of the season.

Matt saw that the tracks going down to the quarry were days old and the freshest tracks led to the house. The blowing snow made an exact guess of time difficult, but Matt felt the tracks were several hours old—and they may have come and gone—a delivery truck, maybe friends. The driveway showed tracks coming and going, Matt didn't notice footprints.

Hitting the garage opener, Matt felt glad to be off the snowy road, anxious to call Tanya, and still worried about Webb. He closed the garage door, picking up both cell phones, and went into the kitchen.

The house felt different. Putting the phones on the kitchen counter, Matt went into the great room—a single light shown, circling a person in the big leather chair. His back to Matt, long legs crossed, bony hands resting on one of Tanya's art books.

Before Matt could say anything, a pistol barrel touched Matt's neck. Jared Livingston turned in his chair, saying, "Welcome home, Mr. Hunter. Do what you're told and your blood won't be spraying all over this pleasant room."

The pistol pushed harder against his neck to emphasize its presence. Another person moved from the opposite side of the archway—efficiently pulling Matt's hands behind him and snapping on handcuffs. Surprise changed to shock and claustrophobia as Matt was moved to and thrown upon the couch that completed the conversation circle within the great room.

Reaching into his jacket, producing a small cell phone, Jared speed-dialed and spoke, "You can bring the truck back now."

Face down on the couch, fighting for breath, his wrestler arms and upper body uselessly fighting the painfully thin handcuffs, Matt began working to gain breath and control. Grabbing his own hands to take away the control of the unyielding metal, Matt turned his face toward Jared. "Why? You won't get away with this. Webb will have you for breakfast."

Grinning like an evil scientist in an old black-and-white movie, Jared said, "Right now, Mr. Webb is up to his Russian ass in government trouble. We are the absolute last people he is thinking about.

"When my brother gets here—we will tell you our plans and your fate. You should have left old secrets alone. Now we will have new secrets, but the old ones will die."

Moving around on the couch, Matt got to a sitting position, his hands cuffed and numb behind him. Livingston's interest went back to the art book, ignoring the movement. The two men that captured Matt were in the kitchen, he could see one's back and hear them moving and talking. They were scurrying around on the kitchen floor. Matt could see a cordless screwdriver beside one of them. They were replacing baseboard electrical outlets, taking them from one box and putting the removed outlet and plate into another cardboard box.

Casually noticing Matt's attention, Jared commented without looking up from the book, "Microphones, throughout the house, micro technology—multiple channels, all going to a relay transmitter located in a tree outside the house. We knew every time you made a plan or made love. We have locators in your cars and boat. With a call to our ship I can tell you where the lovely Tanya is within a few feet. I believe they are in beautiful downtown Cincinnati as we speak. We have great plans for you all. However, I'll wait for my brother before I say more."

The satellite phone Matt had placed on the kitchen counter gave its trill of scales. One of the men in the kitchen picked it up and stood in the door way—Livingston made a slight turn, lifted his right hand and made a circular motion to indicate the man should continue. The other man came into the room, approached Matt, jamming a face towel into Matt's face—trying to make a gag. Matt fought him, and he finally picked up a pillow and said, "One word, I smother you."

The other man, walking into the kitchen, answered the phone. Matt could only hear parts of his responses. He said he was Matt's hunting buddy, Matt was down at the cabin. They planned to do some scouting for trails tomorrow all day. Matt would call her late tomorrow. Did she have any messages? He listened for a minute—made a note on the pad kept for grocery lists and said goodbye.

Sinking back on the couch, Matt felt lost. The Livingstons had planned very well. The conversation seemed plausible, and it was delivered very well.

The phone man came into the room, giving the note he had written to Jared.

Consulting the note, Jared said, "Your Tanya says to call anytime, she sleeps with the phone. They plan to get the watercolor print framed tomorrow and drive to the Cumberland Gap State Park in Kentucky for tomorrow night.

"That's good, all our plans are developing as we expected."

Matt took in and exhaled a cleansing breath, thinking, *Tanya wasn't fooled—she thinks something is wrong. The painting is ink and oil—not watercolor and not a print. If she doesn't get a call back she will know for sure there is trouble...what a woman.*

Matt strained against his cuffs, moaning in his helplessness. Livingston went back to his art study with satisfaction. Matt looking defeated but thought, *All I need is a half second, a free arm, you have a pencil neck like a sharp-tail grouse—I can snap it like a pretzel.*

The garage door opening broke Matt's reverie. Jud entered with a leather gym bag. He had the same superior smirk as his brother—and, Matt noted, an equally thin neck.

Looking at, then ignoring Matt, he reported to Jared, "Just off the phone with the ship. The Vegas stopped for the night, Webb is still in the Sault—at a federal holding facility. Washington is alerted and all over the situation. They're in a feeding frenzy at the U.S. Justice Department; government piranhas all wanting to bite a piece out of him."

Moving to Matt, Jud turned him face down on the couch again, checking the cuffs. "I told you we couldn't have marks—look at this."

Matt couldn't see what was happening but heard the bag opening, cellophane wrapping rustling—he felt a pin prick in his shoulder. Jud rubbed the spot then ordered the cuffs removed.

Matt's hands were free, but didn't seem like they belonged to him. Watching with interest as ice bags were applied to his wrists, he fell asleep.

31

Down the Creek

Tanya held onto the mast, smiling in the sea spray, her wet bikini blending with her suntan, giving the effect of nudity: so beautiful. Matt thought, *Damn these sail boats, always wet, slanting, uncomfortable—wet feet, water in your face, fighting for balance. I'll turn into the wind, lower the sail, start the engine, dry the boat out.*

Matt couldn't move his arms to wipe the water away, spray hit him again and again. It was cold, not salty. He felt sick. Tanya gone, a long white face looking at him, more water came from a plastic cup.

Matt woke up—the face was Jared Livingston, a black knit sailor's cap covered his long white hair. He looked younger, crueler—still with a nasty grin—and inspected Matt like he was a specimen pinned on a wax-bottomed dissecting pan. No pins, just ropes—half-inch braided nylon—bound him like a mummy from ankles to shoulders. Matt thought he must have used 20 feet of the stuff.

Finally focusing, Matt lay on the bottom of a flat-bottomed boat, his feet over the middle seat, his shoulder and head jammed against the bow seat. Jared squatted next to him, dipping water with a leather-gloved hand, carefully gripping the lip of a large plastic cup with his thumb and fingers. The water came again—cold, mind clearing.

Jared spoke. "Wake up, there's lots to do this morning. You're sleeping away the best part of the day." Slapping Matt lightly, he then brought him to sitting position—against the bow seat. Matt noticed he just used one hand—strong for an old guy.

Sitting up, Matt took in the surroundings—a square-bowed john boat, 14- maybe 16-foot—on a small river or creek. Cold out, morning, breath condensing—big man at the stern with an oar, holding their position against the current. They must have a bow anchor out. Matt couldn't turn to see upstream. The shore was snow covered, ice building on the shore edge a foot or so. There was an electric-motor screw clamped to the stern transom—pulled way up, looking dumb. Then he felt the cold: wet feet, wet face, gloves sodden on his hands—wet from the bottom of the boat, water pooled where he sat.

"Where are we?" asked Matt—his voice, but it didn't feel like he was talking. His lips and cheeks didn't want to move. He felt out of sync.

"We are on your little river, only three miles from your cabin. You are out scouting for deer signs—before the season starts. I'm afraid you've had a rough time and fell into the water, got all wet. Bad thing when it's minus 8 centigrade—for you that's 18 degrees Fahrenheit. Quite refreshing.

"Notice your boots are gone. They are making their way here as we chat. Your vehicle will be at the beginning of the tracks—a little over a mile up the trail. You might be able to get to the car, start the engine, put on the heater and get nice and warm—it's a challenge you see. You've got all your hunting gear: jacket, knife, and rifle. I'm afraid your cap got swept away in the river—it's down there somewhere." Gesturing downstream, he continued, "Hans, show Mr. Hunter his rifle."

The man at the stern lifted Matt's rifle out of the water by its sling, leaning it, glistening with ice, against the gunwale.

"I'm afraid we dipped it like an ice cream cone into chocolate—several times. It's loaded and you've more shells in your pocket—also your lighter. We put a little grease on the wheel, so it wouldn't rust. Here's your fancy cell phone—only your fingerprints on it—I'm afraid it fell out when you fell in." Jared brought the phone from a bag at his feet, looking at it for a few seconds, then tossing Webb's phone into the water—out of Matt's line of vision—commenting, "They don't float, do they?"

Matt strained against the ropes—lots of slack. He brought his feet off the seat and pushed himself upright—he could see around. He knew where he was, several miles north of his property. They had done some good map study or scouting to find this remote place, but Matt had a lifetime on the swamp trails and the river. The only place a hiker could leave a vehicle would be several miles to the northwest— rough walking—a 50-year-old logging trail with 20 years of uncleared windfalls. That's why the man wearing Matt's boots was behind their schedule—maybe he'd broken a leg.

"Webb will kill you, you know," Matt muttered—talking through lips that didn't want to.

Jared smiled, "We put $100,000 of unregistered, cancer-fighting isotopes in his rental car. No small trick, I'll have you know. He put the nuclear monitoring machines at the American border crossing on their pegs. They can pick up a single person on isotope diagnosis. He was lucky not to be shot on the spot—too bad really. Someone had also alerted the U.S. Justice Department to the threat of massive iso-tope smuggling due to the lack of Canadian medical shipments and the scarcity of the materials needed to treat U.S. cancer patients. We were hoping he would be using a fake passport—but he, unfortunately for us, used his own. Nevertheless, there are many unresolved issues from Mr. Webb's last incarceration by U.S. federal authorities. He and his muscle man will be charged tomorrow with smuggling, and soon will have an avalanche of other charges brought by your ever-vigilant and publicity-hungry federal prosecutors.

"You see, after all, he is a gangster, a blackmailer, smuggler, even a killer. His comeuppance—profiting from sick people's need for can-cer treatment. Only shooting a little puppy dog would put him in a worse public view."

Matt had trouble understanding all the logic behind Jared's words, but he knew it was bad for Webb—therefore bad for him and bad for Tanya. Tanya...Matt worked at making another statement. "Leave Tanya alone."

"Tanya and her parents will have an awful accident I'm afraid, the rock cuts through the mountains can be very dangerous. We have a powerful GPS in your vehicle—hidden in a heater duct, under the dash…too clever for you and the very mechanical Mr. Vega. There are two fellows in some kind of truck that will do the job. They don't know us, just our money—lots of money—before and after. I'll supervise the coordination and communication from our ship. You see, Mr. Hunter, if you want things done right, you do them yourself, or at least inspect what you expect. I want you to know I'm very much enjoying being right here, right now."

Jared's last words, totally lost on Matt's brain. The cold flowing into his body began to be countered with another force—hate. Hate so strong it focused thought, and energy, taking away fear, remorse, discomfort, pain. Matt had to live to save Tanya.

Matt thought, *they aren't going to hurt me, just let cold kill me. They want me to try for the car—I can't accept any of their directions or suggestions. Focus on getting warm when they leave. What if they give me another shot? No, my dying by exposure wouldn't fly with a lot of my folks—they'd do an autopsy. Shit, I'm thinking like I'm dead. Think actions—build a fire—cedar and white birch all over, gun powder… Tanya, Tanya,*

Tanya, some rotten-toothed, smiling micro-cephalic in a dump truck, more lug nuts than IQ…Can't let it happen. How long between Cincinnati and the mountains—can't work it out—a day's drive? No fancy cell phone, but two other phones in the car—I know the numbers by heart…I'll remember them when I need 'em.

Matt heard someone coming down the trail, an instant hope it might be a friend, dashed when the smaller of the two men came to the edge of the river. Pushing the boat next to the bank, Jared and the big man helped the sweating new arrival climb clumsily into the now-crowded craft. He sat on the middle seat, back to Matt. Taking several diving weights out of his jacket pockets, he asked for water. As he unlaced the Danner boots he commented, "That's a lot of shit to go through."

Jared broke in, while handing another pair of boots and a plastic bottle of water to the man, "Do you have the car keys? We want Matt to have a chance of getting into it, starting the engine and enjoying the heater. He has his own tracks to follow back, doesn't even have to think about it: just one foot in front of the other. I bet you make it, Matt."

A lot of activity happened next. Matt's ropes came off, his boots went on—first dipped and drained in the river—keys got shoved into his pants pocket, the rifle was thrown onto the bank. Before Matt could flex the stiffness from his unbound arms and legs, he was rolled into the water—only two feet deep, but enough to soak him. Matt worked up the bank on his hands and knees, globs of black mud and frozen snow sticking to his wet, wool glove liners and dark green, heavy wool pants.

Looking upstream, Matt saw the little boat passing under overhanging cedars and tag alders—the hum of the electric motor, water going over and around rocks, snags and icy edges the only sounds. At the motor's tiller, the big man stooped under a cedar branch, having to stand because the shaft came up very high, the motor's propeller working only a few inches below the draft of the olive brown, aluminum boat. Sitting in the middle seat, a grinning Jared gave Matt a last salute.

32

Cold Hate

Just standing up seemed to take forever, brushing the snow and mud from his knees and gloves took his full attention, working in slow motion. Finally standing upright, Matt began surveying his location. The old trail ended at the river. He stood in a small clearing, an old logging yard, cluttered by two long ago fallen trees, mostly low weeds, terrain gently sloping to the water. Fifty-foot cedars and swamp brush surrounded him. Up the trail, taller trees—birch and pine. No wind, a gray sunless day, five inches of fresh snow, ground frozen, temperature in the teens. Clothes wet, no cap, very cold hands, leaden shivering legs, nausea.

Matt took off his sodden, wool glove liners—his standard hunting gloves. He usually carried another pair—checking his pockets, none there. Wringing the gloves out hard, Matt wished his hands were around Livingston's pencil neck. The wringing and hate gave him some warmth. He had to get back, phone Tanya, warn her. *Hard to think. Too cold.*

His hair wet and uncovered—first thing, cover head, survival 101. Reaching back for the hood of his hunting jacket—gone—just the raw edge of the zipper that once held it to the jacket. Every winter hunting jacket Matt owned had a hood—most detachable—and they had detached this one. *Rotten bastards.* Matt had his knife and could make a head covering—maybe cut out a pocket. No good, the pockets of the jacket were all built in. Going around the jacket Matt found the game-pocket zipper on the rear right. Not used for game—but a big pocket for lunches, rope, whatever. It ran across the small of the back. Matt reached inside. It was there—a blaze orange net vest, almost no weight, Velcro closure in front—only used when walking through areas that might have other hunters. Adding more orange than just his Kromer. Pulling it out—tearing the Velcro fastener open, spinning the vest into a scarf, wrapping it around his head—he fastened it around his neck like an orange babushka. Feeling the warmth immediately, Matt scored one for the home team.

He went through all his pockets, finding an old wet doe tag from last year, compass, packet of Kleenex—opened and wet—three 7 mm Mag shells, Bic lighter—that wouldn't spark. *What did Jared say he did to it?* No candy. He had his sheath knife. Scanning around, he found his rifle in the snow—looking like it had been flocked for the Christmas season.

Brushing off the snow, trying the bolt, he found it immovable. The rifle felt like a solid piece of metal—a glazed coating of ice all over it.

Matt started to shiver. Running in place, holding the rifle like a recruit on some punishment exercise, his body began to heat up, his system purging the drug they used—at least he could feel his legs and hands again. Looking at the boot prints as he exercised, Matt almost felt that he should try for the vehicle. But that's what Jared had suggested several times. Maybe the drug they gave him was meant to make him suggestible.

They guessed wrong. My weight, more than they thought—the walking man, late for the rendezvous. I bet they expected to drop me over fifteen, twenty minutes earlier. Their biggest mistakes—telling me about Tanya and underestimating my power to hate them.

Life came back to his legs in the form of pain—pins and needles in the big thigh muscles and cramping in the calves. Matt ran through it. He knew feeling—even pain—meant he was fighting hypothermia. The workout would be good for him. Over 20 years of coaching high school football and wrestling meant being on a field or in a gym for eight months a year—lots of effort and muscle would give some payback now. His mind warming with the rest of his body, he had to think of a way to build a fire—dry out before going for the van.

I can't assume the van is a safe haven—I've got to survive right here.

The thumb of his wet, left glove froze to the rifle barrel. Matt thought it was like a kid sticking his tongue on a flagpole. He needed to pour water on the glove; keep from pulling the glove apart, even wet wool would keep in heat. Matt went to the river to free his glove and—with more luck than brains—solved the frozen rifle problem.

Matt held the rifle in the water—the river water had to be in the mid-40s, maybe 30 degrees warmer than the air. The water certainly felt a lot warmer than the air to his immersed left hand. The glove came free. Matt held the rifle in the water by the sling. In the cold air, his left glove and hand began to freeze. Pulling off both gloves with his teeth, Matt kept the rifle in the river for a few minutes more, alternating his hands in the relative warmth of his jacket pockets. Pulling the Remington out, lifting hard on the bolt, it slowly came up. More pulling, the bolt started stiffly back, then quickly, it came free—*damn* —he stupidly ejected a shell into the water. With the bolt back, he lifted and reversed the rifle—looking down a bore of shiny, spiral rifling, wet but clear. Slamming the bolt forward, chambering a shell, Matt pushing the safety forward, pulled the trigger.

Ker-Pow—the sound, deafening and delicious, bounced off trees and water. The kick, like life itself. Matt pushed the bolt release button above the trigger. Pulling the bolt out, he shoved it into his shorts— it was as cold as everything else down there. He took the Kleenex package, found some just damp, not sodden, and wiped the breach and slide—the rifle action had been as damp and even colder during other hunts and it still had worked. Matt half-hoped Livingston had heard the shot and would come back—*I'd field dress 'em, leave them for the wolves.*

Working the magazine release, the flap opening, two shells dropped into Matt's bare hand. They went into his pants pocket. He took the three other shells he had in his jacket pocket, and they joined the others—damp, about as much dryness and warmth as he had to offer. He had five shells and a rifle that would fire them. He now needed a fire—badly.

Matt had a lifetime of building fires in the woods—wet or dry, hot or cold, rain or snow, windy or calm. Every condition brought different techniques—but they all called for dry tinder and starting wood. Leaning the Remington against a tree, Matt went into the woods and found a large, leaning cedar tree. Using his sheath knife, he cut the bark back and scraped the dark brown under-bark—it formed hair-like bunches. He scraped enough to form a large ball of the material. Next he went to a fallen white birch, large pieces of its bark forming curls. Picking dry, unmoldy pieces, Matt formed a large cone, stuffing it with the cedar fiber, adding some thin pieces of white birch from living trees—thin, dry, crackly. Shoving the pieces in among the cedar fibers, he left the woods.

Shivering stopped, his fingers didn't hurt anymore—Matt knew these actually were bad signs. Matt's mind started to wonder. *I've been cold before—I've been wet before, I've been hot before, I've been dry before...I've seen fire and I've seen rain—Stop singing—focus. Think— Tanya. You die, she dies.*

Picking a flat area against a two-foot diameter fallen log, Matt scraped a patch clear of snow and leaves. Laying down his cedar and birch bundle, he gathered "Squaw wood," dead branches on live and dead trees—off the ground, always dry. In a minute he had an arm full.

He put a layer of sticks on the ground, constructing a tiny, log cabin of larger sticks, placing the birch cone inside the little square construction; he made a cabin roof of the driest small twigs. His work now just needed a match. Nine pounds of flame-shooting Remington would do the trick. Having seen many rifles fired in low light or occasionally in illegal—no light—situations, Matt knew a lot of flame belched out of a rifle barrel. He needed just a little of that flame.

Retrieving the rifle, Matt fished out the bolt—happy to remove the metal from his private area. The bolt went into its slide, he worked it back and forth several times—the action closed and opened. Taking a single shell from his pocket, he dropped it, bending to pick it up, his leg muscles working in slow motion, fumbling to place it in the box magazine, Matt's brain clicked off two hypothermia signs: clumsiness, lack of coordination. Shoving the bolt home and locking it down, Matt put the barrel into his carefully constructed wood cabin, nestling the barrel above the cedar material.

He pulled the trigger.

Another satisfying *Ker Pow.*

His cabin, the stack base, all the birch and cedar tinder instantly disappeared. *Shit—too much firepower...If I wasn't freezing to death, it'd be funny. Be patient—start over. Focus.*

Getting down on the ground—ears ringing—he looked for a spark or something smoldering, seeing instead his careful construction scattered five feet in every direction. He found his birch cone empty, the scorched cedar ball a foot away. He should have known the magnum power would be too much for a little cabin. *Poor decision making—next comes apathy—who cares about apathy—ha, ha.*

A stray thought about the second shot came to him, one shot in a swamp or woods was hard to judge for distance or direction—a violator's mantra. A "Speed Beef Merchant"—someone shooting a deer illegally—was always careful to get the job done with one shot. Matt had shot twice—and would need to shoot again. Could the Livingstons hear him? Probably not—not much wind, lots of trees. He was shooting up his shells to start a fire—depleting his ammunition he'd need if they came back, or he met them again. No way around it—he needed to have a fire to live. *Focus—stay on task.*

His fingers reddish, opening and closing only with effort, the shivers came back. *Think, act, focus...make a fire.*

Matt jogged a few clumsy jumps: *waste of time.*

Back on his knees, the cabin rebuilt—noticing the last twigs were placed with shaking hands. *Think, think, one more try—take your time—do it right.*

Moving the little sticks aside on the cabin's roof—pulling the cedar cone, stuffed with cedar bark and crumbled pieces of the birch bark. He unlaced a boot—cutting a foot-long length of lace. Matt bound the thick curl of stiff white bark—tying a knot took three tries.

The reinforced fire core went back into the little cabin.

Taking another large cartridge from his pocket—another idea came to Matt. He needed less powder. Take the cartridge apart—pour out some powder.

Now the hard part—taking the bullet out of a cartridge without tools, using fingers and a brain that didn't want to work well. Matt got on his knees with the rifle between his legs, barrel on the log. By the numbers: one, hold the cartridge; two, pull back the bolt a half inch; three, put the red plastic-tipped bullet into the opening; four, push hard and hold the bolt against the bullet; five, wiggle the cartridge, prying the lead against the copper neck; six, more pressure, wiggle the shell, more pressure, pull, wiggle, pull, pray. The bullet showed an eighth inch of shiny copper. Pull, wiggle, a quarter inch of the beautiful untarnished metal. Wiggle, pull, the cartridge came away, a few pieces of powder fell out, the neck of the cartridge showing no deformity. The bolt action would be able to shove the cartridge back into its beveled breech.

Think, one time, has to work.

Matt watched with interest as his shaking fingers poured over half of the powder onto the cedar-fiber ball. Turning the cartridge up, he used it to tamp the little black logs of gun powder down among the tinder. *It will burn not blow up.* Another thought—*the lighter.* Resting the precious copper cartridge between two large sticks, then finding the little plastic lighter and poking a hole in it with his knife, he sprinkled half of the liquid onto the hair-like cedar.

Now, load the shell—STOP...

The powder would all pour out when he aimed the rifle down...close call. *Not totally stupid yet...*The primer needs some powder close to touch it off. Keep the rifle pointed up or level—like a powder-filled black powder gun without wad or ball. Matt's now numbed fingers slowly pushed the cartridge all the way into the breach. Using some extra force, his arm muscles slow, needing conscious effort, Matt—with consummate interest—watched his gloved hand, first pushing, then closing and finally locking down the bolt. Staying on his knees, Matt aimed the rifle at the pathetic little stick cabin that probably meant life or death to him.

He stopped again, the blast needed an exit or everything might again be blown away. Matt turned the cedar bark tinder cone sidewise, with fingers and a stick created an opening, pushing it against the log as a back stop, he braced it with two larger logs so it couldn't move easily. He brought the rifle barrel up to the opening, making sure the barrel was positioned level or slightly upward.

Matt's numbed mind conjured a vision of his prayer-like posture—kneeling on frozen ground in the midst of wilderness, his blaze-orange wrapped head bent in supplication in front of an altar of sticks and bark. Holding the barrel's muzzle six inches from the tinder hole, grasping the rifle's grip and trigger, Matt had one thought—*Please.*

He pulled the trigger; the firing pin hit the primer, the result—a muted, sickening—*POP.* The primer didn't even blow the gun powder out of the barrel; no rolling tongue of life giving flame…just a little fart of a pop.

Ejecting the shell casing with disgust only fouled the breech area with little black logs of gunpowder. *Have to clean the breech, take another cartridge apart, shit, shit, shit.*

Needing a swab, Matt cut a piece of his undershirt, split the end of a stick he gathered from the fire material, with shaking hands and numb fingers, he removed the bolt again, carefully cleaning the chamber and breech area of little gun powder logs. Then replacing and working the bolt proved everything was cleaned again.

Need another shell pulled apart—don't think—do it—get it done. Kneeling again, praying position, locking the bullet by the bolt pressure, prying the big shell, wiggle, pull, wiggle, pull—there's some copper color—more—more—careful—don't spill the powder—done!

Matt thought or maybe said to himself. *This has to work. I shot black powder with the guys, we were setting fires in the grass—all the time—burning wadding on the dry September grass—had to stomp out fires—all the time—all the time.*

New idea—gunpowder in the wadding—the swab he had been using already had gunpowder on it—*pour in some more, roll it up. Pour some powder onto the tinder, push the swab into the shell casing—don't drop it—done. Looks like a real blank cartridge with the wadding flat across its copper neck. Now, lock and load.*

Resting the loaded rifle on the log, Matt knelt to organize the tinder and little cabin for the third time, sprinkling in the last of the lighter fluid. He jammed the bundle of bark and tinder against the large log, so the rifle blast would go into it and not just blow it out of the way.

Cramps hit his legs and lower back, even the arches of his feet. Matt had to stand, the pains easing. Looking around, Matt saw a pile of old logger cans and oil bottles. Rummaging proved futile—no oil or anything flammable, however he found an old crushed two gallon pail. He pried open the rusty, mostly bottomless piece of junk, then shoving his tinder bundle into it, he placed it against the log, hoping the metal would contain the blast and flame. Matt could smell the lighter fluid, he could see the powder mixed with the tinder. He looked at the sky—maybe for a prayer—no sun or he would have broken the telescopic sight for its lens.

This has to work!

He picked up the rifle. Bringing the barrel within an inch of the tinder, safety off—*stop shaking, you're making me nervous, pull the trigger, visualize flaming gasses coming down the 7 mm bore—this time pushing a wad of burning cloth.*

Bang!

The cabin and sticks again became a shambles...a wonderful burning shambles. Matt, from his knees, began pushing the pile together—with hands that couldn't feel the heat yet—to centralize the burning materials. With trembling fingers he added more twigs, some more white birth, more twigs, bigger sticks, more sticks, then two larger—wrist thick limbs. The limbs on two sides effectively holding the fire together, more branches...not neat, but truly a blaze, the heat feeling wonderful.

Matt ran—more like hobbled with his stiff legs—into the woods and returned with an armful of white deadwood. The fire, burning happily against the big log, accepted and burned the added wood. Soon the fire produced flames that rose two feet into the gray, cold day.

Four trips into the woods and two up the hill produced an assembly of logs and branches. Matt dragged a deadfall treetop back to the fire—it would be his clothes rack. He started another fire against the log, five feet away from the first fire. He sat between the two fires. He had his rifle warming, bolt in and open. His last two cartridges lay on the log—warming, but safe from the fires.

Rummaging through the pile of logging trash produced only one useable aluminum pop can. Matt cut the top back with the can opener on his knife, put two holes at the top—with his leather punch—put a stick through the can, rinsing, then filling it with stream water. Soon he was able to put steaming, warm liquid inside him.

Listening to the river and the quiet of the place, Matt gave a prayer of thanks—but a darker emotion followed quickly. He had to get to a phone, warn Tanya, then kill the Livingstons. *That smile of Jared's saved my life—the hate made me strong—kill me, but don't smile while you're doing it.*

The two fires burned happily, his jacket open on the impromptu drying rack, his boots upside down, opened, hanging by their laces tied to branches resting across the setting log, like fishing poles with a strange catch. Matt moved and turned them to maximize the fire's drying ability. He left on his shirt, wool pants, socks and underwear. His long johns—two-piece WinterSilks—would dry on him, the thick wool pants wouldn't dry completely for a week. His shirt wasn't one he would have chosen for hunting—it was red-checkered cotton, and Livingston must have felt it looked like a hunter's outfit. Matt liked wool or polar fleece—zip up high-neck or turtleneck shirts under his hunting jacket. His old polypropylene socks were almost dry already—while Matt had rested his feet on a small, dry log he had pulled up for a foot rest.

Working with the blaze-orange mesh vest—his babushka—Matt allowed his hair to dry. He had to have head covering—half a person's body heat will wick away from an unprotected head. Matt figured he'd probably be better off with a hat than pants in a survival situation. Matt cut the tail off his shirt to form a head-covering piece of heavy, checkered cloth, put it into the mesh and rewrapped his head—now he had his head and ears warm and comfortable. Red checks, orange mesh—an interesting fashion statement.

Matt's muscles and fingers let him know they were not happy with his treatment of them. His big thigh muscles felt like someone had hit them with a ball bat. His fingers tingled and the ends actually hurt. Matt lowered his pants, pirouetting on a little stand of sticks to get heat to his butt and legs. The pants, inside out, because he had pulled them down, were drying some. Matt wondered what a picture he must be.

Watching his wool glove liners steaming on sticks near the fire—like his pants they wouldn't be completely dry, but dry enough—Matt sat figuring when he would be ready to make the trek out. He wouldn't even try to carry fire—going over and under windfalls and hiking several miles would make it too hard. Besides, he had no time to spare for another fire.

Another 20 minutes, by his wristwatch, found Matt redressed, boots dry and effectively laced. Taking a final canful of hot river water and rewarming his hands as he held the hot can at the now single fire— that wouldn't go anywhere—finally placing the can by the dying fire, Matt headed up the trail.

33

Back Trail

T he trail lead up from the swampy river bottom to a level pine plain. Matt made good time on the trail north, knowing it would eventually loop west, going back toward the river bottom and swamp land, full of small tributaries and meandering loops. As a National Forest area—great pains were taken by the U.S. Forest Service to keep taxpayers off it. The only easy-to-walk old logging roads had bulldozed berms across them. ATV paths had been quickly attacked and closed with fanatical zeal by government hordes. If there were not enough deadfalls crossing every useable trail and path—the forest service would cut a hundred trees down in order to save the forest. Their logic absurd, far beyond a normal person's ability to fathom, and their actions criminal and malicious, if they were taxpaying, common folk.

Walking easily, loaded rifle slung over his shoulder, Matt studied the boot tracks on the trail back, recalling the weights being placed on the boat's seat: new, price stickers still on unmarked plastic covering. Matt thought, *The Livingstons had everything worked out—the person had to be my weight, including carrying a rifle. They tied me so I wouldn't have rope burns. I can see a corporate check list with every action and contingency listed. Three coordinated attacks—fun and sport to the Canadians—but I'll do my best to take the fun out of it.*

No longer cold, his boots and socks dry—his toes happy, his fingers cool but serviceable in damp wool gloves. The large muscles of his legs felt stiff, even tired, but they worked just fine. His jacket stayed zipped up until he felt warm. Ready to break a sweat, he unzipped it to his belt line. Stopping at the top of the hill overlooking the line of tracks that came up the hill from the tangle of thick cedars, Matt noticed the tracks getting close together, even shuffling and tripping at times. Remembering the man complaining about going through a bunch of shit, Matt made a decision. He would stay along the ridge and walk through the pines. Much faster and easier than a gauntlet of deadfalls, snags and muddy bottomland. He knew where he could pick up the trail again. The Livingston route must have come from an old U.S. Geological Topographic map that showed a nice trail. They couldn't have used a satellite photo—it would have shown the ridge as a better alternative for walking to the river clearing. Having hunted in this area for many years, Matt knew the bottom trail as a place you didn't want to drag out a deer. He checked his compass, just in case he got too far away from the ridge edge and lost sight of the cedars. His watch showed nearly 11:00. Gray flat clouds, no wind, no sun, still in the teens—a good day to have a compass if you went to walk in the forest. He would head north for a half hour or so, then work west—there was a road running north and south that he couldn't miss. Unless he came too far north—then he would cut the man's trail first, saving a mean scramble through creeks, bogs and cedar swamp. The old logging trail the man had walked cut through the swamp. The van would be parked along the road or more likely in a clearing once used to yard logs—the trailhead.

Easily walking through mostly tall red pines, with no understory to fight, Matt let his thoughts return to Tanya. He had carried both cell phones into the house—he was fairly sure—and Jared had thrown away the big one—Webb's, if the other wasn't at home. He'd drive to the nearest house toward Rexton. Urgency meant picking up his pace—his breathing came a little faster—and sucking more cold air into the nose and lungs. Realizing he had been stressed and nearly taken by hypothermia, Matt slowed the pace to avoid sweating and allow him to breath comfortably through his nose—warming the air he took in. Getting hot and tired wouldn't help the situation.

Twice tripping over fallen trees, realizing he couldn't lift his legs as high as normal, Matt stopped for a short rest. Zipping up his jacket, dusting off a fallen tree, Matt sat. A plan began to enter his brain— he had to warn Tanya, number one priority—but if he couldn't get in touch—perhaps phone problems in the mountains—he'd go after the ship, their communication center. Whether they loaded the boat on the pickup or not, they still had some miserable two-rut roads to drive out on, and if they went back to Matt's house, did some cleaning up or more searching for evidence—whatever—they wouldn't be back to Marquette until late afternoon, more likely evening. There was a good chance they wouldn't leave until the next morning. Several of Lake Superior's deadliest rocky shoals lurked just underwater between Marquette and Thunder Bay. Even with radar and GPS, a prudent captain would wait for daylight. Matt wondered how he could attack a ship with at least five men on it.

Matt checked his watch—he had rested ten minutes. He slung on his rifle and headed through the pines. He worked north—aided by compass and occasional glimpses of the cedar bottomland. Matt knew the river would be flowing almost north through here—the ridge skirted the meandering valley formed by the main river and its many tributaries. The river would eventually cross M-28 then disappear into uncharted swampland, reorganizing into the Tahquamenon drainage, coming out in Lake Superior.

A growling stomach reminded Matt he hadn't eaten in almost 24 hours—the thought of the Trout Lake burger danced in his head. He felt a little lightheaded, but he'd been through a lot. His breathing and muscles all seemed fine.

Webb came to Matt's mind as he walked. For some reason, Matt couldn't see anyone or anything defeating Webb for very long. Matt smirked. *Sooner or later the Livingstons wouldn't live long enough to appreciate the man they had taken on.*

Matt noticed the pines now went a fair ways to the right of north, time to head west—hopefully cross the trail and get to the van. Another half hour, half of it in swamp that was getting more miserable with each anxious step, he crossed his distinctive Bob-sole boot tracks, lots of little holes in the snow—very happy with himself for having saved time and avoided the difficult swamp country, he picked up his pace.

Another 40 minutes of easy walking brought Matt to the van, parked in the corner of the old logging yard, unseen from the gravel road. Large snow flakes started to fall as the prospect of setting down, getting warm, getting to a phone, and just being alive made him jog across the open area.

Scouting around the van, Matt noted one set of tracks from a man who had gotten out and walked away. The key beeped the lock open; Matt got in the vehicle, put the key in the ignition—and stopped, thinking, *If I move, will it show on Livingston's ship? They'll know I'll come after them, warn Tanya—shit, what to do. Think. Focus.*

Starting the van while standing outside it with the door open, Matt slowly exhaled—no bomb—the heater did work and did feel great. Two hard, dry granola bars and three Chinese fortune cookies were in the glove compartment —carbs are carbs to a starving man.

Ten minutes of chewing the old bars, wishing for a beer, minutely inspecting the heating ducts ended with success—one duct cover had been scratched, and was loose on one side. Matt didn't mess with the side that had the holding screw—he pried the cover off with his knife and fingers, the screw pulling free of the plastic. The exposed tube held the GPS—held in place by a wrapping of double-sided tape.

Matt took the plastic GPS unit and, finding thick brush near the van, placed it under the largest bush. He piled leaves and snow over the unit— hidden to all, unless someone or something tore the bush apart.

The drive back didn't do the van's shocks any good. The rutted road and several one-lane bridges bounced the van, the washboard corners fishtailed it, but Matt soon found the quarry road and home.

Stopping a hundred yards north of the house, Matt entered quietly, rifle loaded and locked. He circled around three quarters of the structure and entered the far garage door—unlocked, no car, driveway with a dusting of snow. Old tracks of a truck or a large SUV: a careful entrance and search confirmed no one home.

Matt found his cell phone and dialed Tanya—the rings followed by phone mailbox instructions. Matt tried three more times, finally leaving the warning message. He next tried George Vega's number—same lack of success—and again left the warning message about the GPS and the road ambush, hoping George wouldn't have another anxiety attack.

Matt went through the house: M-16 gone, no logbook, the Canon's flashcard totally erased, the PC hard drive reformatted. Matt felt sick—a lot of pictures and memories gone—maybe a red flag to a police investigation but no ghost images or hidden files to worry about. The whole house showed nothing broken or messed, the floors clean—Matt bet there wasn't a fingerprint on anything. The only good part of the inspection—his realization that they had spent a lot of time on these thorough efforts. They had to still be in Marquette.

He drank two glasses of milk, ate a cheese and hard salami sandwich. Starting a pot of strong coffee, he got into a hot shower, leaving the cell phone on the counter set on its loudest ring. Matt let heat seep back into his muscles. His thighs still felt strange—heavy and painful.

Twice he turned off the shower, imagining he could hear the phone ringtone. Matt keep listening, thinking about Tanya—and at the same time making plans for his Marquette trip.

34

Armed

Afterr dressing in his old, soft, dark-camouflaged bowhunting clothing, Matt found his fall hunting boots—eight-inch Gore-Tex Jackals by Danner, waterproof but not insulated. Perfect for quiet work. The clothing and boots went over heavy, black poly-propylene underwear, thick insulated socks, and a navy blue, British military, wool turtleneck. A black knit cap that pulled down into a face mask completed his stalking outfit. On the kitchen table lay his Browning semi-auto shotgun, loaded with #2 magnum three-inch shells touched only by his rubber-gloved fingers. They were from the time when you could hunt geese with lead shot: the deadliest shells he had. Matt still had a half box left after loading five into the shotgun. He had a Browning Buckmark .22 but rejected it: size, portability didn't outweigh the power, intimidation factor and untraceable shot of the shotgun. Also on the table, not much bigger than the shotgun shells, lay the two red Haley and Weller incendiary grenades—retrieved from George Vega's tool cabinet. Matt had spent an hour trying to figure a way to set them off while being elsewhere.

Rubber bands of various sizes and thicknesses—scattered from a bag labeled "variety pack"— lay before Matt, also string, yarn, nylon cord, candles, various sized cigars.

The bomb worked by pulling a ring that secured a cotter safety pin, which released a spring loaded handle—the handle would be held down until the grenade was thrown or jammed down an artillery piece barrel or rigged as a pressure release booby trap. Matt didn't know the time after the handle came up to the bomb's detonation—but figured it would be a few seconds. The pin could be wired to be pulled out with a trip wire.

He discovered that a rubber band would crush the softened candle as it burned down, putting it out and not making enough slack to let the grenade's handle up. Yarn tied to a rubber band didn't work, and the candle smelled. The even smellier cigars went out when they got to the constriction of the rubber bands or yarn, which didn't burn through. Matt had no cigarettes.

All his fuse ideas lead to failure and none were what Matt wanted. He wanted a time-delay system. He couldn't really test the spring on the handle—because it would set off the device—and their kitchen had already been burned out once. He just hoped it had enough spring to fight through a very loose rubber band.

Looking at several water puddles on the table, Matt got a dish cloth and dried off his working area. Ice cubes had been one of his first ideas. He had hoped they would release a rubber band looped around it as they melted—but the cube was too small, the bands slipped off too soon and the pressure of the bands cut into the ice cube, eventually freeing the band, allowing the handle—hopefully—to pop open. Ice seemed a good idea, and nearly on the verge of working, but it meant too much fussing and was too delicate to set up.

As Matt's mind went on idle, out of ideas, the cell phone trilled.

Matt ran to the counter and opened the phone—seeing Tanya's number filled him with relief and happiness. He never got out a hello.

"Matt, Matt, are you all right?"

"Yes, Dear," Matt said.

"I'm in Detroit, getting on a plane in an hour for Marquette—best I could do to get back to you. I knew something was wrong when I talked to that man who said he was a hunting buddy, he had a Canadian accent.

I left my folks in Cincinnati. The painting will take several days to get done—no one would frame it fast. They are staying downtown in the big city. I couldn't get to Webb either. What's happened?"

Matt could hardly breathe, his brain went on overload. Starting with Webb's no-show and ending with coming out of the swamp to find the van, he detailed his last 24 hours. Tanya only interrupted twice, with sighs of sympathy and surprise.

"What are we going to do? My parents plan driving south tomorrow. Dad may or may not call in—he doesn't leave his phone on." Tanya said.

"We have to stop your folks from driving south. You need to forget about the plane and get to your folks—they could be calling you. You keep trying them—maybe get them through the motel they are in, or the art store."

Matt thought, *I don't want you around what I'm going to do. I'm going to Marquette and take on the Livingstons alone. I'll either shoot off or burn off their death head's grins I can't get out of my mind. I don't care about bribes, contracts, agreements, understandings, stock options, or Christian forgiveness. If we want to live—they can't. We can't rely on Webb to do all the dirty work, or any of it now that he's in federal custody.*

Tanya's voice broke through his thoughts, "Matt what about Webb? He was set up, maybe Edward—my former handler with the DEA—could help. I can get to him—Edward worked out the deal that got Webb set free before. He has to know what's going on. I can tell him we can verify the setup with the rental car. We need to help Webb and Al."

"Ok, call him, Make sure it is a private conversation—tell him everything that happened, hold nothing back. See if he can help Webb. After all, Webb gave the DEA good information before, naming names and supplying evidence in exchange for a plea bargain and immunity, so Ed should help him. A deal's a deal. Webb's involvement started with rescuing you, he shouldn't be prosecuted for saving an American's life.

"Stay overnight in Motown to make your phone calls. Your folks come first, then Webb. Ed owes you a lot. Miss your plane tonight—don't cancel ahead of time—and rebook for tomorrow. I'll explain why later. Just trust me on this. Call me with tomorrow's flight info—on this cell phone. I may not answer, so talk to the mailbox. I'll meet the earliest plane from Detroit to Marquette tomorrow. I'll be waiting for you with warm clothes. Also, stay by Webb's phone—mine sleeps with the fishes. Webb or Al may get to make a phone call. You have your little .22 with you?"

Tanya sighed. "Not armed—just have my carry-on bag. Dad has the .22 and his black rifle—after we couldn't get in touch with you or Webb, he put his rifle together. It's wrapped in a car blanket to keep it ready on the front seat. Mother covers it with her coat. We went to an ATM, got cash and got into a motel without using a credit card. The painting won't be ready until tomorrow afternoon or maybe the day after—everyone that sees it treats it like wood from the true cross. I'll get to Dad somehow. "Are you sure you're OK?"

"I'm fine. Really."

"Get some rest. I miss you, I'm worried about you. I'll see you tomorrow. I love you." An expectant pause.

"I love you, too."

Matt heard the smacking sound as she threw him a kiss before hanging up.

Matt sat at the table—as happy as he had felt in days, actually only hours. Gun and bombs lay before him, murder weighed on his mind mingled with love in his heart for Tanya.

Looking again at the two bombs—balloons and ice cubes came to mind. Fill a balloon with ice cubes and water, poke a tiny hole in the balloon. As the ice melted, the balloon would lose a lot of size, the water flowing out—the rubber band would free the arm. And voilà— 4,000 degrees of Fahrenheit heat would say hello to the diesel tanks of Livingston's yacht.

Eighteen hundred gallons of diesel fuel should cook their Canadian gooses.

Matt didn't have balloons. He would buy some on the way, somewhere. He made up a package of the bombs, heavy rubber bands, duct tape, a small Maglight, a short fat LED flashlight he had been using as a substitute for the bombs and his extra shotgun shells. He put ice cubes into the cooler, added cans of diet pop and beer, poured a thermos of hot coffee, made four sandwiches and put it all in the van. He gathered an armful of Tanya's winter jacket, sweater, insulated boots, stocking cap, gloves, slacks and heavy socks. Adding his own winter jacket, Matt threw all his gatherings into the van, covering the shotgun on the back seat and—still thinking of water balloons—Matt added a gallon jug from a lineup of water-filled jugs stored on the garage floor—bought for the hunting cabin where the pumped water smelled like dinosaur farts. Then another idea came to him. The hunting cabin had cases of half-liter plastic bottles stored outside the door—they would be frozen like big ice cubes. He would pick some up on his way out.

At the hunting cabin in the quarry, the van's headlights lit the doorway and the stack of water bottles—left there from fall hunting by the grouse hunters. Matt took four bottles, handling them with gloves—they were frozen solid and he duct-taped them to the van's luggage rack to keep them frozen.

As he left the quarry area—his cell phone played its tune.

It was Tanya. "I had to talk to you again—I know you are up to something. You're going after the Livingstons, aren't you? Please let Webb deal with them—it's his type of work."

"We can't—they might have Webb tied up for months or years. Sooner or later, the Livingstons will get to us—they are too well organized, financed, and intelligent. We won't be lucky every time. I'm alive because of deadfalls in a swamp, the policy of the U.S. Forest Service to never clear a trail, and an underestimation of my outdoor skills. You're alive because of an 1851 painting, a shipwrecked sailor and a conscientious picture framer. We can't rely on fate to overcome cunning and preparation. I believe in offense over defense. I can't tell you my plans—you won't have to lie about actions you don't know about.

"You know we don't have any real evidence against them. If they looked at the pictures I took on Granite Island, they will probably go there and destroy the rock scratches. They probably have U.S. government contacts that can even get rid of Webb—he has a lot of very powerful enemies that would like to see him dead."

Tanya, pleading, said, "Matt, wait for me, I've had some training in dirty tricks. I've dealt with gangsters—we can work together again."

Matt listened to more reasons, some intellectual, some just based upon worry, all founded in love. He responded, "I've got to go now—they planned for my death. Everything they do is on a corporate check list: analyzed, prioritized, tested to a consensus conclusion. They wouldn't understand a totally spontaneous attack within hours by a dead man.

"I've probably said too much already...I know you'll worry—but I'd rather be alone. I must be alone. I wouldn't have enough guts or hate if you were with me, I wouldn't be mean enough. I'll give you the best kiss either of us ever had when I see you at the airport. I can't answer the cell phone for the next few hours. Just know I love you."

"Me, too."

"Did you get through to your folks?"

With a hint of defeat in her voice, Tanya replied, "Yes. My Dad will find the GPS if he has to take the whole dash apart. He'll turn it off. He has the other one, too.

"And I've got calls into Ed at the DEA—just to secretaries so far. I'm not privileged enough to warrant his voice mail. But I know he'll call and help."

Matt and Tanya said their goodbyes. Matt turned off the power to his phone before he closed it and put in into the glove box.

He gassed up in Naubinway using a credit card. Turning on his cell phone again, he checked his phone mail before heading west to 117, then north to Highway 28. Two sandwiches later, and most of the coffee consumed, Matt was west of Munising. The Lake Superior shore passing on his right, several parks and beach entrances offered good areas to pull off the road. He was getting to Marquette too soon. He pulled into a parking lot just past the Au Train River bridge. It was paved and off the road enough to not attract attention. Matt wanted to do some more experimenting. Taking one half-liter water bottle from the luggage rack, he used the small lithium battery flashlight as a substitute for an incendiary grenade. He became satisfied he had solved the timer problem. By cutting and breaking off one side and the bottom of the plastic bottle he could expose a big, thick ice cube. He secured the bomb to the remaining plastic side and upper part of the bottle with thin pieces of duct tape and used a medium-size, fairly thick rubber band that seemed strong enough when around the bottle, but loose enough if the ice melted away. And it looked like a solid system. He just had to place it so the handle could spring free when the rubber band released it. The timing would depend upon the room temperature where the bomb was placed. Like a nice hot engine room.

A car slowed down coming from the west. Afraid it might be the law, Matt acted like he making a cell phone call. The vehicle—after checking if he was all right or maybe just looking for a romantic place to stargaze—sped away.

Back on highway 28 he reviewed many plans and contingencies. His worse-case plan had him shooting all aboard and taking the ship out, sinking it and getting back with whatever lifeboat he found. The "A" plan would be sneaking in, placing the bombs and watching the ship motor away—soon becoming just a blazing pool of diesel fuel. Variables abounded—a night watchman, a locked cabin door, the location where the ship was moored, the activity in the harbor...and the greatest question—did he have the guts to shoot men in cold blood?

The snow stopped, the clouds moved on, the star-filled Lake Superior sky spread to his right, visible above his low beams. Counting on surprise, audacity and enough resolve to see him through to dawn and a reunion with Tanya, Matt drove on.

35

Boarding

The deserted lower harbor at Marquette lay before Matt. Steam rose from the freezing water around the pilings, slush made a rustling sound as it worked against wood and concrete. One 20-foot, center-console fishing boat sat with snow on its canvas covering. No other boats were in the slips. The 82-footer appeared out of place because of its size and whiteness in the harbor lighting. Moored against the far inside breakwater—commonly used by cruise ships or large research vessels—it was in a good location to be boarded from the far, dark side of the harbor. The dark background of the steep hill behind the harbor revealed the ship had no lights at any portholes—just an anchor light atop the strong tubular metal mast, above a forest of antennas and communication dishes.

Pleased that the boat was there and in a favorable mooring, Matt drove away from the harbor—heading for Northern Michigan University's campus to search for an all-night, drive-up restaurant. He wanted to use up a few hours—making his move around three in the morning. Worrying about the activity of police and drunks at bar-closing time, he didn't want to be on the road at 2:00 am. He feared going into a bar or a major restaurant in case some former student recognized him. He found a small burger place, used their bathroom, washed his face and got more coffee and a burger to continue stoking his furnace from going more than a day without food. Then he drove around to the Coast Guard Station area. Finding some parked cars just before the curve to the marina, he nestled the van among them. He would eat and drink slowly, then ready himself for the boarding.

The temperature on his mirror read 11 degrees—no wind, little snow where there had been wind. Matt put on rubber gloves before bringing in all the frozen water bottles. He removed the plastic from the bottoms, and all but an inch of one side from two of them, and attached the little red incendiary grenades, using thick, dark blue rubber bands and neat, narrow strips of duct tape. They looked efficient, whether they would work or not. Rolling each into a dark plastic bag he placed one in each large pocket of his heavy hunting shirt. He added several shotgun shells to his pants pocket and turned off the inside light. With the shotgun resting against his right leg, he sat, breathing and thinking. Almost 15 minutes went by. Matt finally turned off the vehicle. It cooled quickly inside the dark van, his hunting clothes were made for fall hunting—not winter weather. A final check, no cars had passed for 15 minutes—the time was 3:15 a.m.

Matt had his hand on the door handle and put the keys on the cup holder between the seats. His heart racing, images flashed through his mind: the Livingston's death's head smiles...the hopeless loneliness of being in the dark a hundred feet underwater trapped and stalked by killers...the image of a killing crash of fenders on a mountain road... the desolation of having Tanya taken away while he was helpless... the words on the log and scratches on rock by men soon to die...the kitchen fire and a man trying to throw another bomb...and the final thought that would stay with him forever, or at least get him through the night—the salute thrown to him by Jared as he left him freezing to death in a cedar swamp.

His hate boiling, his resolve steeled, Matt stepped from the van. Holding the shotgun under his arm against his body, he walked slowly and upright down the road edge. Crossing the road at the curve, he walked on the road that ran along the marina. No cars, no movements, only a reddish city glow in the cold haze that surrounded the harbor. Matt walked to the marina entrance, staying on pavement and sidewalk to avoid tracks in any drifting snow. He heard a truck coming behind him. Ducking behind a trash barrel, Matt hid until it went past and up into town. Another hundred steps brought him to the ship, secured with many lines. A wooden ramp with poles and rope hand line connected the stern to the shore. Crossing it, moving carefully over the deck, Matt came to the heavy weather-tight salon door. Amazed that warships didn't seem to need locks on their doors, slowly opening it outward, he stepped in, carefully shutting it behind him.

A dozen red eyes were staring at him. The unblinking, rat-red eyes came from various pieces of office equipment. Matt's eyes also picked up a few greens and yellows.

The main ladder to the below decks was softly lit. Ambient noises came from fans, heaters, a pump turning on and off, a freezer or refrigerator cycling below deck. The thick carpet swallowed all his noise as he moved to the ladder. Shotgun at the ready, Matt stood listening for several minutes, pulling down his special black watch cap—making it a two-eyed, small-mouthed ski mask—he slowly went below deck.

Matt imagined what a startled crewman sitting at the galley table sipping coffee would think when a camouflaged clothed and booted, face covered man with a shotgun, came sneaking down their ladder. He was pleased to get his eyes below deck, seeing an empty galley space and passageway.

The galley area had its own overhead nightlight, another lit the hallway. Matt didn't need to use his flashlight to orient himself. The port and starboard fuel tanks were like thick walls separating the galley space from the aft area of the engine room. Placing the shotgun in a corner by the steep steps, Matt began unrolling one bomb. Sorry for the plastic bag noise, he carefully placed it between the freezer and the aluminum wall that was the side of the fuel tank. The over-800-gallon tank ran from the ceiling to below the deck floor. A hole burnt in the aluminum would flood the below-deck space with hundreds of gallons of diesel fuel. The grenade rested against the metal wall, its handle free to pop upward, the dark plastic bag providing support and concealment. As the ice melted the device might move a little lower but not tip over. Matt nodded in satisfaction with the placement—in a five-inch space between the fuel tank and the stainless steel of the freezer, the heat would be directed against the very meltable fuel tank. Pulling the pin carefully, Matt stood up.

Looking across the galley area, Matt saw a series of shelves fronting the starboard fuel tank. He moved into a far corner behind the mess table, a cramped group of shelves and drawers formed a small closet area; it seemed a good place to find a home for the second bomb. Below the seaworthy, dowel wood fronted, higher shelves were two cupboards with doors. Opening the doors Matt found towels and linens, the back of the cupboard showing the shiny metal of the tank—another perfect place.

A sound of a door latch froze him. His shotgun stood across the mess space. He crouched behind the mess table, keeping his head and eyes down. Looking below the table, he saw stockinged feet silently shuffle from the port stateroom, enter the bathroom, close the door, the sound of urination, no flushing, water running at the sink, door opening, shuffling back into the room, quietly closing the door. Matt didn't believe he had taken a breath during all this time—now breathing again—he waited several minutes for the man to get back to sleep.

Standing, returning to the still open cupboard, he unrolled the icy bomb, quickly, carefully, placing it behind towels, pulling the pin, Matt closed the door.

Looking around—retrieving his Browning, Matt was amazed at all the noise in the sleeping ship—Matt had a fleeting notion of just going into the staterooms for a final assurance that the Livingstons lay in the bunks and maybe finishing these rotten people then and there with messy, untraceable number two shot. Plan "A" and good sense won out, and he slowly moved back up the ladder to the main salon. Standing at the top of the stairs for several minutes, then finally moving to the door, Matt slowly opened the door and stole off the ship, checking for foot prints—the windswept, metal deck, free of snow, showed no tracks.

Getting caught going away from a crime foils many an evildoer. Matt felt like throwing the shotgun away—as it marked him out of place and out for no good. Although it was the end of the duck hunting season, not even the densest of lawmen would believe he was stalking mallards. Matt left on the same path and sidewalk he came in on and put the shotgun against the trash barrel he had ducked behind previously. Without a shotgun, and after he had pitched the two grenade pins into the dark harbor water, he walked comfortably back to the van.

In the van, he removed his rubber gloves, which snapped sweat as they came off. Matt, wet with perspiration, drank from the gallon jug of water. The van fogged until the fans and heater defeated the condensation. After several minutes, he drove the van back to the marina, pulling in by the trash can, slipping on his winter leather gloves, quickly disposing of the plastic bottle pieces and the trash from his sandwiches. Seeing no one in any direction, Matt brought the shotgun back, covering it in the back seat, vowing to empty it as soon as he could do it unobserved.

Every mile Matt put behind him made him breathe easier. He had no destination. Four patrol cars of various enforcement agencies passed him from one way or another. Each quickened Matt's heartbeat. Without thought, Matt headed to the airport, driving carefully and damning himself for the sandwich papers he had left behind that had his fingerprints on them.

No returning to the scene of the crime, he reminded himself, Perry Mason shows not wasted on Matt.

The Marquette airport, many miles out of town, was a former SAC base—the runway seemed to the horizon. The terminal was open and deserted. Someone must have been somewhere—but Matt's calls went unanswered. He walked to the ticketing area, a bulletin board listed the day's flights—the same flights for every day it seemed. The first flight from Detroit came in at 10:36 am. Matt had about six hours to wait, and nearly four hours before daylight.

Returning to the van, Matt drove slowly back toward town and pulled in to the only open business he could find—the Holiday Station at Harvey. After killing time checking out every row of food and merchandise, he bought a large hot chocolate and two packages of Twinkies—enough caffeine and sugar to keep his clock wound very tightly. Back in the van, he unloaded the shotgun, disassembled it, rolling it in a car blanket and storing it with the box of shells in the floor locker behind the back seat.

His thoughts were a jumble of possibilities—melting bottles of ice, someone going into the cupboard for towels, the grenades just going *pop* and farting a small black puff of smoke, a handle coming up and being stopped by the wall, the Livingstons flying home in their helicopter. Checking his watch for the fourth time in five minutes, noticing the total blackness of night all around him, Matt made a plan—watch the sun rise from Sugarloaf Mountain.

The mountain—really a thousand-foot rock promontory, nearly 500 feet above lake level, provided an excellent panorama for miles around. From its rock ledges a hiker could view all of Marquette to the southeast, hills and forests to the south, Lake Superior with several islands to the north, a rugged coast line to the northwest. Matt had not been there for 20 years, and that was during the summer. He wasn't sure the trails would be open, but the thought of watching the Livingston ship for a long time from a safe distance made a seven-mile drive and a mile hike uphill in the cold seem worthwhile. Beside, he had to be somewhere, doing something, while water drops from melting ice became metaphors for the bloodstained sand grains in the hourglass measuring the Livingstons' lives.

36

Sugarloaf View

Carefully weaving through Marquette, Matt turned onto Presque Isle Avenue, eventually found CR-550 and drove west. A few miles of uphill, empty road brought him to the parking lot with a sign for Sugarloaf Hiking Trail. Three inches of snow showed human activity from the previous day, and the lot, now empty of cars, had no gate across the entrance. Matt pulled in and parked. He had his winter parka with a hood, a wool Kromer and Thinsulate-lined leather gloves. His boots weren't heavy enough for standing, but fine for hiking. Pocketing his 8x23 Steiner hunting binoculars and picking up a Maglite flashlight, Matt locked the van and started up the trail.

The cold hurt his nose. Pacing himself, moving carefully and slowly behind the flashlight beam, Matt reminded himself to walk slowly—avoiding a major sweat. The trail was listed as "moderate" for difficulty, but in the dark with drifts of snow the upward trail proved taxing. Appreciating the presence of the guiding tracks, Matt guessed three people had made the trek up and back since the last snow. Groups of steps made the effort much easier than the trail Matt remembered from two decades earlier.

Thank you, county park people.

Although at times slippery, the wooden steps were much better than the worn dirt and rock path. Stopping several times, Matt opened this jacket to keep cooler. He wished he had brought a bottle of water. He envisioned the nice cool drops coming off his frozen half-liters on the ship—and licked his chapped lips. After 20 minutes of climbing and cold air, Matt brushed off a bench and took a break. The stars sparkling, no wind coming through the trees, the glow in the eastern sky came from Marquette not the rising sun. A few minutes to get back to regular heartbeats and breathing, Matt started again. He could see farther into the trees on either side of his low-held light beam, as dawn approached. Two more steep series of steps and he came to the rocky area that marked the summit. His flashlight beam made a white obelisk jump out from the background of black sky—a Boy Scout monument to a past scout leader killed in World War I—signaling the end of the climb and standing as a tribute to the effort of one of the oldest scout troops in the nation. Walking across the deck area above all the surrounding hills toward the limitless lake and sky felt like flying. The stars brilliant—Orion the Hunter lay low on the eastern horizon, the Big Dipper's pointer stars lined to the North Star—out over the black inland sea that held ten percent of the world's surface freshwater. Getting his breath back, Matt basked in the beauty of the place for many minutes. Walking around the deck, using his binoculars on the sky and city to keep his mind off his cooling toes, Matt used up another half hour. Finally while looking east and south of Marquette's city lights, he could just make out a faint glow marking the horizon— dawn approaching.

Touching the obelisk at 7:15, the sun made the rocks glow against the still-dark northern sky. It wouldn't shed its light on the shore for another quarter hour. Scanning the city with his binoculars Matt could easily see the power plant's twin chimneys, working right—south—he could pick out several landmarks and estimate where the lower harbor should be. Headlights identified streets and the movement of people going to their jobs or classes. He couldn't see the harbor due to sunlight defusing into the city's morning haze and condensation.

Another cold hour went by, passing faster than Matt expected because of the breathtaking view of pink, yellow and orange colors of the ever-changing vista. At 8:20, Matt identified a light on a moving mast, rounding the point high above the mist-shrouded water, as the spot of light headed north. Magically, the whole white ship appeared in Matt's circle of eight-power optics. The relative warmth of the water compared to the air made a looming effect; Matt could see the ship and its ever increasing bow and stern wake. The sleek, white craft made a beautiful picture against the dark water.

Mat thought, *How long will the rubber bands hold the handles down? The steel hull and metal of the fuel tanks must conduct a lot of cold from the forty-degree water. No heaters or fans pushed warm air into the cupboard, the towels would even keep the ice cool against the metal, the bottle by the freezer might get heat from its compressor— but how hard does a freezer need to work in a cold ship? That really is a fine looking ship—too bad its run by people that want me and mine dead.*

"Isn't this just beautiful?" spoke a winded man behind Matt.

Matt jumped and would have gone off the platform except for its rail. The man—carrying equipment in both hands and wearing a headlamp—looked like a cyclops porter.

"Sorry to scare you—I'm a photographer. This is my favorite place, but I'm running a little late," said the man as he set up his tripod and attached an elaborate, white lens—several feet long—that he lifted from a padded metal case. Attaching a digital camera—a Canon several levels better than Matt had been using—he panned against the colors of the rising sun. Matt began looking at different views—trying to impart a general interest in the panorama, not his real fascination with a white ship that was the only moving object on the water.

The photographer was good and bad news to Matt. A person that could place him in Marquette and also verify he was miles from what he hoped was a pending disaster.

Matt moved closer as the man focused on the reddish dawn breaking over the snow-covered hills. He lamely ventured a statement, "I came to pick up my girlfriend at the airport—and found I was several hours early. I got the take off time mixed up with the arrival time. This is a great place, even in the cold."

The man moved his setup to the far side of the deck, panning east again, the shutter sound clear in the cold, quiet air. After a dozen shots he spoke. "I sell these at art fairs and some off the Internet."

Watching the photographer for a few minutes, Matt finally moved away to check the Livingston ship's progress through the binoculars. The 82-footer—more than half way to Granite Island—seemed at full speed with everything shipshape.

The sun, now totally above the horizon, cut through the morning mists, announcing a sparkling day. The photographer, screwing on a different lens filter and staying at his task, jumped quickly behind his camera, clicking away as the light changed with each passing minute.

The ship was swinging westerly, its nearly six feet of draft didn't want anything to do with the shallow waters on the south side of the island. Suspecting they planned to anchor where Matt had placed the *Ferr Play* in September, he brought up his binoculars again. The lake being very calm, the air very clear, Matt appreciated the smooth curve of the wake. A change in the stern froth and the spacing of the wake waves, indicating a speed change, confirmed Matt's theory. Another ten minutes had the ship at dead slow, then stopped, followed by an anchoring procedure. Matt couldn't make out crewmen at first, then careful focusing brought dark specks moving on the bow and aft deck area. They were working with the center boom and the whaler secured on the deck.

Suddenly a black billow of smoke enveloped the foredeck. Matt couldn't see people. He held his breathe as more and more black smoke boiled from the white craft. There was very little breeze, and the cloud of smoke surrounded the ship.

"What's you look'n at?" said the photographer.

"I think that ship's on fire or they really burnt their breakfast toast," quipped Matt.

"Holy shit…let's get the big lens on that." The camera and its large lens quickly and expertly moved to the north side of the deck. For 15 seconds the photographer remained totally engrossed in the cranks and handle of the tripod, the zooming and focusing of his equipment. "Son of a bitch—they're in trouble—fire is coming out of the hatches. You got a cell phone?"

"Mine's in the car," said Matt.

"Mine too—I have to carry enough shit up this mountain. We need to call the Coast Guard or something."

"Look at the smoke—lots of people can see it. What do you see?"

The man took a dozen pictures and stepped aside for Matt. "Check it out."

Matt moved to the eyepiece—the telephoto lens had to be in the 20 or 30 power range, more magnification and a bigger field of view than his binoculars. He saw the ship belching black smoke, tongues of flame jumping in the salon and above the forward hatch. Matt figured someone opened the hatch to get out of the forward stateroom and made a wind tunnel. As Matt watched, an explosion came from the stern. A flash and material flew into the air, the sound came later as a rumble; had to be gasoline or maybe a propane tank in the hole.

The man pushed Matt aside. "I gotta get this." He fiddled with the lens and camera dials, clicking away, commenting, "I have two hundred more shots on my chip—but my battery is going down fast because of the cold."

Matt checked his watch, almost 9:00, he felt tired, sad.

A helicopter rushed over the city, heading for the burning ship. Matt thought, *Good. Fan the flames.*

The helicopter circled the ship, blowing smoke away, exposing the spread of oil and some flames. The ship couldn't be seen—the black cloud rising almost straight up for hundreds of feet. The chopper made dents and swirls in the smoke column. A boat came around the point, white with the orange stripe—Coast Guard. It rocketed across the calm water.

Matt got behind the photographer, hoping he could get another look. "Can you see anyone in the water? What's the helicopter doing?"

"The smoke is too thick to see anyone on board, can't see anyone in the water. Funny, I thought I saw two shapes on the island—maybe they swam to shore—but now they're gone. Here, look for yourself."

Matt could clearly see the billowing smoke, some flames, no heads in the water, the ship settling by the stern—maybe the explosion opened a seam in the hold or shaft space. Matt panned back to the island— the helicopter hovering over it, pushing the smoke away from the ship, brought the blackened bow into view. It was empty and rising— exposing its antifouling paint.

Matt moved away, the photographer anxious to record all the action.

The Coast Guard vessel neared the burning wreck, stopping a significant distance away—the spreading oil now on fire. Matt could see the flames with his binoculars.

As the ship lowered in the water, the oil spread increased—encircling the ship on all sides. There would be no swimming away from its burning grasp.

Matt had seen enough. He folded his Steiner optics and put it in his coat pocket.

Twenty minutes went by as Matt watched the photographer, who mumbled while he shot.

"She's going. I got all of it, water over the back area, there she goes—her bow is just bobbing now. Can't see anyone around her." He clicked another dozen shots. "I can still see the bow—come on, my battery is about done. There it goes—gone—yes, got it all."

"Would you like help getting your equipment down the hill?" asked Matt.

"I'd really appreciate it. I think it's harder going down—easier to slip. I'm going right to the paper, then the TV station—although I think that was their chopper."

He offered Matt the folded tripod; he carried the metal case with the camera and lens. They went slowly, not talking.

Back at the van, cramping leg muscles forced Matt to stand and lean on the vehicle. The photographer, not noticing Matt's distress, hurried out of the parking lot, bound for the newspaper.

After some bending and stretching, Matt eased behind the wheel and headed for the airport.

37

Information

S till early for Tanya's plane, Matt checked on international flights
of private planes or helicopters—there hadn't been any for three
days. At the main terminal he checked on flights to Thunder Bay
on commercial flights—he found you couldn't get there from here. No
one had any records or reasons to share information with him.

He used his cell phone to check his mailbox—Tanya's tinny recorded
voice magically changing his sad mood and filling his heart with expec-
tation. She would be on the 10:36 flight.

An office had local television on—the ship fire had made the news,
the helicopter had carried a local TV news cameraman. Several people
blocking Matt's view only increased his curiosity, he couldn't go behind
the counter and he couldn't hear the narrator. Matt caught the name
"Livingston" and glimpsed a Coast Guard officer with a microphone
shoved in his face, the burning ship sharing the split screen.

Trying to use the uncomfortable waiting room chairs only brought
back his leg cramping, so Matt paced until the 10:36 plane came in
at 11:10.

Looking like a teenager coming from college, Tanya ran to Matt. The kiss made Matt's ears ring and focused all his attention on her lips, her smell and how soon they could be alone. Opening his eyes, he saw travelers passing by with "get a room" looks and a few grins. He didn't care—Tanya now safe in his arms made the scene on the television he viewed over her shoulder well worth the risks.

She began her report, "My parents are fine—they're staying in Cincinnati another day. They aren't going to the Smokies but heading directly south. Dad wouldn't say what route or their timetables over a cell phone. Mother is fine—focusing on *her* picture. Dad said he would check in every evening with a phone card from a motel or payphone.

"I heard from Edward finally—he can't talk in detail about Webb but is helping him. They're investigating the rental dealership with the RCMP inspectors. The consensus seems to be the isotopes had to be planted, Webb wouldn't be so stupid to drive through a boarder crossing with a car full of radioactive material. Still, we have government people seeing Webb as big publicity, a way to play partisan politics, and he has a lot of Washington enemies that would like to see him swinging slowly in the breeze."

Matt's attention strayed from her animated beauty to the TV in the office off the reception area. Tanya followed his glance, also seeing the screen and a flash of the smoking ship—enough for her to speculate what the news was all about. Before she could say anything, Matt took her bag, his arm around her shoulder, and escorted her out of the terminal.

They didn't talk crossing the parking lot—Tanya's clothes and shoes too light for the temperature. Once the heater and fans were going, Matt looking at Tanya, her eyes both full of questions and begging for answers.

Matt began, "That's *Sleeping Giant* in the smoke. They had a fire and sank just off of Granite Island. I don't think anyone got off—but I'm not totally sure the Livingstons were on her. We need to get the news. How about staying in Marquette tonight?"

Her eyes still searching his face, she took his hand in hers. Absorbing the information shared and Matt's reluctance to explain more, tears welled in her dark brown eyes. She put her other hand to his face. "Oh, Matt—are you alright?"

"I'm fine—just cramping up from almost being an icicle in a cedar swamp. Frankly, I feel worse about a fine ship going down than its crew. We need to know who all was on the ship. I think local TV news and papers will know as fast as anyone. Plus, we could both use some extra rest."

"I know how to help you fight hyperthermia, and maybe even let you get some sleep. I want to know everything—step by step from them waiting for you at the quarry. I'm so glad you're OK. Let's find a nice place and celebrate being alive."

Matt drove to the expensive Landmark Hotel—out of the price range of most hunters coming to the area for the rifle deer season, opening in a few days.

They got a bay-view room with a fireplace and a sitting area in the turn-of-the-century decorated hotel. While Tanya organized her few items from her carry-on bag and the clothes Matt had brought, Matt sat before the television. Searching for local news, finding nothing of interest, he went to the bedside radio—again nothing of interest.

Looking at himself in the mirror over the fireplace. "I need some clothes. I look like I just came back from a search and destroy mission..." Matt held his eyes on his reflection in the dark, camouflaged clothing—so out of place among the polished furniture, overstuffed upholstery and chinch curtains—thinking, *I did search and I did destroy—now I need to know how many I destroyed.*

"Let's get some lunch, go shopping—we're in the big city, twenty thousand folks—then come back here and stay in our room the rest of the evening," Tanya suggested as she finished changing to wool slacks and a heavy sweater, with a down vest completing her outfit.

Gone for over two hours and after surviving the busy, confusing roads between the Red Lobster and Yonkers, Matt and Tanya got back to their room in time to catch the local television news—featuring the burning ship and an interview from the local Coast Guard station.

The Coast Guardsman said, "We had been on the ship earlier this fall—it was a converted 82-foot cutter—used in the '60s and '70s. The Livingston brothers were very happy to show us their makeover— several bulkheads and watertight doors were removed to make easier movement and larger spaces. They put in newer engines—less horse-power than the military but a lot more efficient. They removed much of the military fire control systems—pumps and hoses and such—still complying with all regulations, however.

"They both had master's papers—their ship was their office. They were semi-retired but still ran some of their business as they cruised. They usually only had one or two crewmen—the ship's engines are all controlled from the helm, like you find in a much smaller boat."

"How many were aboard," asked the announcer.

"We've recovered two bodies—neither seem to be the Livingstons. Their corporate office had them on the ship last evening. We have people and equipment coming that will let us do an underwater search with sonar and video, if the weather lets us. We should get more information in the next few days."

The interview went on for some minutes without any more facts coming forth.

Tanya stood by the bathroom door, holding out a paper bag containing aerosol shaving foam, razor, toothpaste and toothbrush. "Get thee to a shave and shower."

Matt obeyed. Later, Tanya came into the shower to make sure he had soaped thoroughly. Matt never enjoyed hygiene more. They loved and snuggled away the afternoon, falling asleep for several hours.

With his new slacks hiding his hunting boots and wearing a dark turtleneck sweater, Matt looked civilized. He took Tanya to an Italian restaurant for a late supper. He picked up a paper on their way out of the hotel—the burning ship occupied the front page and the banner announced "Canadian Yacht Burns and Sinks."

Tanya read parts of two separate articles as they drove to the restaurant. No names of the crew or number of victims, but a quote from Forbes about the Livingstons and quotes from several Coast Guard crewmen, all with a local writer's byline. A lengthy listing of the Livingston's business history—from the AP wire service—filled another column. She carefully folded the paper, stuck it between the seat and console and, with a look, silently announced the ship would not be table conversation during dinner.

Their dinner at the long established Italian restaurant began with a basket of hot, buttery garlic bread, and a wicker-bottomed bottle of imported Chianti went perfectly with their entries, both savory perfections. While sharing bites of each others choices, the darkened room allowed the candlelight to soften Matt's mode, increasing his appreciation of Tanya's beauty. They drank the whole bottle and talked about everything except burning and sinking boats. Webb came up one time, and Tanya said they would cover him later.

Deer hunters surrounded them, all dressed in outdoor clothes—at several tables, women accompanied their men. Matt noticed Tanya observing the mixtures at the various tables.

"Do you want to hunt?" asked Matt.

"I don't want to break up the good old boys' club. I'm not so possessive I'd make you give up time with your friends. A man should have time alone and with men—it's kinda tribal. I think I could shoot a deer—but I don't want to clean one. I catch and clean some big fish—but they are cold and somehow different to me than a deer. Maybe it's something we could think about next year."

Matt alternated between sips of his coffee and the last drops from his red wine. "We've had dads bring their daughters to camp twice so far—it keeps our language cleaner—and no one objected. We hunt hard—up early, in the field all day—and bed time comes soon after supper. We could sleep at the house—joining the bunch just before we go out—eat supper at the cabin. You might like it—you know most of the people. A couple of college kids will be there—good for dragging deer out of a swamp. I don't think any girls are planning to come this year, but I know everyone would love you there."

"No, I think I'll wait until next year. Getting the right clothes, shooting a rifle, figuring where to hunt—I want to do it right. I'll be very happy to keep the house and bed warm for you this year."

Full and happy, they drove back to the Landmark. Finding their pillows, they were grateful for each other. Matt had brought in and put the folded paper on the coffee table—tomorrow would be soon enough to study it and watch the TV news.

The morning came with a room service breakfast. Juice, coffee, assorted bread rolls and western omelets—Matt ordered it on a slip he had put out the night before. He didn't know the cost, but gave the college student that delivered it four dollars—then noticed the gratuity was already on the bill and the smiling kid already gone.

Breakfast was accompanied by the local TV news—the same film and interviews as the night before. The local paper would not come until early afternoon. Tanya discovered the best newsflash while looking out toward the harbor—several boats of the trailerable, 20-plus-foot variety headed out into a gray, cold day on the fairly calm lake. One was white and green—labeled EPA in large red letters. Another, with writing on the side she couldn't read, carried student-aged people. All were met by the Coast Guard vessel and escorted north—out of her field of vision through the window.

"There should be more news when those boats report their findings," Tanya suggested while standing with a cup of coffee and a dry croissant.

Tanya's cell phone chimed—it was her parents: heading south, nice weather, not to worry. Tanya told them about the excellent hotel and that they would stay another night before heading back home for deer hunting. George Vega didn't give his location or plans before he passed the phone to Anita, who chatted for a few minutes, promising she would check in the next day. Then the call ended.

On a hunch, Matt used the Webb phone Tanya had. Surprisingly the "Hello" came from Al. Matt had never talked to Al on the phone before and made sure it was really the big ex-cop and bodyguard before asking what happened.

Al brought them up to date, "Two days in separate detention rooms—good cops, bad cops, government badges, waves of three piece suits. Threatened us with smuggling, terrorism, intrastate transportation of stolen goods, four or five charges concerning nuclear material. I was driving, not carrying, and we just told the truth—we didn't know squat about carrying isotopes. The whole thing being a big frame—Webb had three lawyers here by that evening who fought with the U.S. Justice Department officials. Brought up planted evidence being used on Webb two other times—had court and Department of Justice findings to offer, had bench judgments critical of planting of evidence and the appearance of planting of evidence. The breakthrough came when we were screened with very sensitive radiation detectors—came out clean, so we couldn't have loaded the van. We had to rent a van, the only option at the rental desk. We absolutely could not have loaded it unless we used hazmat suits and had gone through a series of decontamination procedures. I just got released and given back my stuff—including this phone. Webb is still behind closed doors with federal people. I only talked with him for a few minutes—we couldn't say anything, knowing we were being recorded and watched. I also think the Canadians smelled something fishy with the rental people. I'll call you when I know what's happening. Webb may want to see you, or he might fly back to the cabin, it depends on what he feels like doing. Again, I'm not sure when they will be done with us."

Matt didn't tell him about his adventures with the Livingstons. The phones had been out of Al's and Webb's hands, no telling what federal communication experts could do to them or with them.

Matt finished the call on a light tone with his real message in the middle. "We'll be back home by afternoon tomorrow—the Vegas are driving south. Why don't you come and stay with us—lots of things to talk about...Maybe you could get a rifle deer license and come hunting. You'd enjoy the break—get some fresh, cold air. We've got clothes to fit you."

Al listened and didn't comment for a few seconds, then said, "We'll think it over." Then they finished the call with the usual, "Good to hear you again, take care."

Finishing breakfast, Tanya and Matt bundled up and walked across the street to the impressive city library. Matt paid to join the Friends of the Library Association and got access to a computer and the Internet. Although the Canadian papers were following the sinking closely, nothing new was gleaned, except some bland quotes from the sons and the corporate media VP. They went back to the hotel hoping for a local news break.

The evening TV news and the local paper provided a mine of information.

The Coast Guard and underwater experts from two local universities found and identified Livingston's ship—using sonar and tethered, powered video cameras. In their efforts they also found another wreck lying close to the *Sleeping Giant*. Interviews with students, professors and Coast Guard personnel promised pictures when they could be processed from the recording equipment used aboard the ship. They identified the second wreck as the *Carol K*.

A student of marine archeology described his exciting experience: "We could see this big anchor chain leading away from right under the *Sleeping Giant*, so we followed it down a rock face—right to the hawsehole of a big ship or, at least, the bow and part of a forward cabin of a big ship, in good shape. The rest of it is scattered wreckage, going deeper than we have cable. The anchor chain seemed to hold the bow area against the rock ledge—the ship's name on it—easy to read, clear and clean—jumped right out of the dark, like it just went down. *Carol K.* We'll look it up—it's an old ship—from the '20s or '30s.'"

Matt felt like he couldn't take in enough air. Tanya sat beside him squeezing his arm. When the Canadian press and the insurance company got this news the world would change for the Livingston family.

Moving to another group at the dock, the handheld video camera zoomed to a tall individual—a professor somebody, who led an environmental impact group. Their interest centered on any oil contamination effects on the flora and fauna of the rocky shore biome. They also reported a discovery of prehistoric petrographs found on granite outcroppings, probably depicting a hunting story based upon the clearly identified arrow drawings. They would go back the next day and continue working the shore and the rock drawings.

Matt whispered to Tanya, "Wait until they find the scratches spell out *Carol K*—real smart cavemen."

The *Mining Journal* newspaper brought more news and pictures from the mountain: two half-pages with six pictures of varying sizes showing the progression of the tragedy. Matt could see the open front hatch with black smoke coming out as though from a chimney, the increasing intensity of the smoke, then flames on the water surrounding the black mass of smoke—no ship visible—and finally the blackened bow just before it slipped below the surface. Matt also noticed the shore on one of the early pictures—a fairly wide shot—and felt he could see two figures standing there watching the burning craft. He pointed this out to Tanya, who said it was just swirls of smoke or a trick of light.

Matt thought, *I wonder what the specters of Paul or Saul Pissarro and his friend felt while watching the ship burn. All the deadly secrets of the Livingstons will soon be known. I hope my secrets will be the only ones to remain.*

Matt, suggesting a short walk before an early to bed and an early to rise, gained agreement from Tanya.

38

End Game

Breakfasting quickly on the drive back, Matt and Tanya enjoyed dry roads and made the trip to the quarry in less than two hours. They followed a number of tracks into Quarry Road. After the initial mile, while they went straight, many tracks turned left into the quarry floor—hunters going to the hunting cabin.

Matt noted, "I'll need to get down there to see if anyone needs anything. I'll also let them know I'm not sleeping there this season."

A car parked off the side of the driveway. Two sets of tracks led through the snow to the front door of the house, then back to the garage side door—which was unlocked.

Stopping in the driveway, reassembling and loading his Browning, Matt had Tanya push the garage opener while he stood, shotgun ready, in the driveway—no one in the garage. Matt entered the garage, calling for whoever was in the house to come out. The door from the kitchen opened slowly, Matt's trigger finger touched off the safety. Al's smiling face and large body filled the doorway, and Matt lowered the barrel as he again clicked on the safety. Webb came out behind Al.

Tanya drove the van into the garage and closed the door as Matt shook hands and hugged his visitors. Both Webb and Al looked tired and older than when he had last been with them at Webb's cabin. Matt unloaded the Browning, leaving it and the shells on the workbench.

The house felt damp and cold. Explaining their decision to come to them instead of going back to Canada, Al followed as Matt turned the heat up and quickly kindled the fireplace, leaving Tanya and Webb hugging and talking in the garage. The four rejoined around the kitchen table—occupied by a large brown bag, from which Webb quickly produced a large bottle of Russian vodka, several tins of sardines and oysters, two wedges of cheese and a box of Scandinavian crackers.

Webb, settling heavily at the head of the table, started the conversation. "No caviar in the big store at the Sault. Let's drink and talk. I have news, you have news. Who starts?"

Al stood by the sink, behind Webb, quietly opening the door that hid the plastic trash bucket—lifting up an empty, round half liter of Russian vodka for Matt and Tanya to see, then letting it slide silently back into the trash. So, Mr. Webb was into his Boris and Natasha act brought on by one of the few times he drank more than a glass or two. Matt was glad the fireplace had closed glass doors; he hoped the boisterous Russian would be able to see the doors and would not throw his glass into it.

Webb produced four juice glasses, tore the foil top off the big vodka bottle, put two fingers of the clear liquid into each, pushed a glass to each person and uttered a Russian toast as he emptied his glass. Al, Tanya and Matt obediently, but more slowly, drained their glasses. The instant each person's glass touched the table, it was refilled.

"Slow down," said Matt, his throat burning "We need time and control of our tongues to share our news."

Tanya, moving behind Webb, touched his shoulders and gave him a quick kiss on his cheek, then brought plates, utensils, napkins to the table. "I'll put a casserole in the oven, we had it ready for Matt's week of deer camp."

While she fussed with lunch—Webb began, "The Livingstons did me a great favor—out of the mess they got me, us, into came an agreement. My lawyers cleared up many issues with the U.S. government—I now can see my daughter and watch Western football games without fearing an arrest at the stadium.

"The Livingstons made two big mistakes—they didn't put radioactive material on the steering wheel, they didn't pay and frighten the rental car people enough."

Al added, "The boxes of normally closely regulated serial numbers of medical isotopes were too untraceable—only $700-an-hour lawyers can make a case pointing toward the Livingstons because the materials must have come from a source supplier, not a warehouse or delivery service. It became a case of too clean a history—like a pistol that never had a serial number or a proof stamp on it. They argued it was incongruous that a smuggler clever enough to have untraceable material would be so careless as to drive it himself across a radioactive-monitoring border crossing. And the Canadian investigators got the rental car people to admit they limited the choice of available vehicles to a single van and may have allowed people to 'inspect' the van earlier in the day. We never mentioned the Livingstons—it would have helped get us off one hook, but onto several others. Their name came up, but we both denied any knowledge of them, totally confused why they would set us up."

Matt thought, *That must have been Edward of the DEA's work, helping make the radioactive material connection.*

Webb, chewing greasy fish on crackers and washing it down with vodka, swallowed and added, "What happened to your phone? It cost a lot of money, you know. We couldn't get to you, Tanya either didn't know what you were doing or would say nothing."

Matt took milk from the refrigerator, poured a glass, sat at the table—slowly drinking half the glass and carefully putting it down to provide time and establish a theatrical moment to focus the attention of all on his beginning statement.

"The Livingston brothers and two henchmen were right here in this room three evenings ago. They were communicating with a fifth person on their ship moored in Marquette's harbor. Overpowering me when I came back from our non-meeting at the casino, they knocked me out with a needle induced drug, I woke up in a flatboat with Jared splashing water in my face…"

Matt went through the whole story to the point of watching the ship go down from his viewpoint on Sugarloaf Mountain. The only interrupting came from Webb's three "son-of-a-bitch!" exclamations and Tanya moving to the chair next to Matt.

Al asked, "Did anyone see you coming or going from the ship? Would the photographer recognize you? Did you buy gas with a credit card, or meet any friends while the ship was in port? Can anyone tie you to the Livingstons when they were here?"

Answering all the questions—and a few more—in the negative satisfied Al's police intellect and confirmed that he had not left a ready trail from the Livingstons or the ship to himself.

Tanya, silent until now, explained what they knew about the sinking, adding the discovery of the *Carol K* and the rock writing.

Webb laughed and, pouring another splash from the now half-empty bottle and slamming the glass on the table, exclaimed, "Bravo, better I couldn't do…The government assholes that kept us two days—without even a phone call—are my alibi…

"Two ships resting together, a killing drawing killers, everyone dead, like an ending in a Greek play."

"There is more," Matt said. "I don't know if we got the Livingstons. There should have been five men on the ship—only two bodies have been recovered. Eighteen hundred gallons of burning diesel fuel inside a metal wind tunnel wouldn't leave much. The news should tell us—the Canadian government and their Department of Transport will be all over this investigation. The Kaisers would have loved the log—maybe the words on the rock will give them some proof. We have firsthand observations, the copies of pictures I sent to my friend in Gladstone and the back of the painting to give proof and provide at least one name with the evidence—but we can't get involved without implicating ourselves. We'll have to wait and see what happens."

"Don't forget the old pistol—I still have it," interjected Webb—about thirty seconds behind the flow of the conversations.

Tanya took his statement as an appropriate time to serve the now-reheated casserole, adding some bread and butter to the table. Picking at and carefully separating the casserole into various parts: noodles, mushrooms, water chestnuts and hamburger chunks, Webb ate from the segregated groups on his plate. Everyone at the table watched him while they ate and talked normally. Finishing, with slower and slower movements, Webb asked to be excused and retired to the leather chair in the great room. While Al served himself a large second helping, Webb's soft snores could be heard.

Al, listening for a few seconds, spoke, "I need a handgun. I left mine on the plane—darn good thing as we had enough trouble. They might have shot me if they saw a pistol. I never saw so many guns held in shaking hands—like six Barney Fifes all round our vehicle.

"All I have is a .22—but it is a fine pistol, 10 shot magazine and very accurate," said Matt. Getting up, he went into the main floor master bedroom, returning with the semiautomatic Browning Buckmark—fairly large with a dull black finish, walnut handles and a gold trigger. He also had a second magazine. Al took it, ejecting the magazine, opening the breach, letting it close on an empty chamber, sighting, then testing the trigger pull. He noted the hollow point shells, replaced the magazine, pulled the slide to chamber a shell, put the safety up and, tucking it in his belt behind his right hip with the extra magazine in his left pocket, went back to cleaning his plate.

"Thanks, now I feel like a bodyguard again," came after his last mouthful.

A honking from the driveway preceded a group of happy and loud hunters entering the kitchen—led by Will, the youngest Ferr brother, announcing, "We're out of ice cubes and could use a can or two of cream of mushroom soup. Having partridge for supper—we've got enough for an army. You're coming down, aren't ya?"

"Yes, and I'll bring Tanya, if you all promise to look but not touch."

After Matt introduced Al and explained that Webb was Tanya's family friend—Webb was still sleeping off the half bottle of Vodka in the other room—the group gathered ice cubes, found two cans of soup and didn't mind toasting the coming hunt with the rest of Webb's bottle. Matt's refrigerator nearly depleted of beer, the group left as they came, happy to be at deer camp—expecting Tanya, Matt, and Al, and Webb too if he felt like it, around dark. Some of the hunters were still out scouting around.

The limited TV coverage from Matt's satellite dish only had a brief mention of the Livingstons—that on the business and stock channels, with their nuclear waste program sparking more interest than their possible demise. Up until then, Matt had enjoyed the isolation from the constant, petty reporting of the never-ending string of talking heads wishing to show how clever they were. He couldn't phone anyone without tipping their hand. So he turned his attention to hunting.

While Tanya took a nap and Al switched through the news channels, Matt checked his rifle—the Remington had come through its dunking with no serious issues. Its bolt and receiver showed no scratches from being used as a vice to hold the bullets while Matt had pried off the shell casing. Matt had previously taken the stock off and removed the butt pad to make sure everything dried well—after a good oiling, the rifle was like new again. The waterproof scope came through unscratched and not cloudy. Matt did some bore sightings across the north field—and the cross hairs lined up perfectly. Too late for a shooting check in the area where they would hunt.

At dusk, Matt and Tanya bundled up to go down to the cabin—taking some cheese and their last six pack of beer. Matt assured her there would be plenty to drink and eat.

The cabin was all warmth, good cooking smells and steamed windows. A black bag in a plastic garbage can half full of beer cans, multiple liquor and mixer bottles cluttering the table and kitchen counter indicated a serious party. Plates and platters with multiple choices of cheeses, sausages, chip and dips covered the kitchen table.

The cocktail hour lasted two hours—the snacking migrated to a sit-down dinner, with those not able to get to the table using the coffee table. The main course came from a large pan of partridge and chicken breasts wrapped in bacon and covered with mushroom soup, grated cheeses on a bed of dried beef. Garlic bread and salad completed the offerings. Multiple cakes and pies—sent by wives—weren't touched, the men so full they needed a walk around outside before they could turn in. All agreed to a 5:30 breakfast call—Matt to be there at 6:00— and everyone out by 6:30 or 6:45 depending on how far they had to go.

Matt and Tanya returned to the house to find Webb in the guest bedroom while, in the great room, TV news droned softly, drowned out by Al snoring loudly on the big couch. Tanya covered him with a light blanket and turned off the set.

Matt got his gear laid out in the heated garage, made the coffee ready to switch on and happily slipped into bed with Tanya after setting his alarm: experiencing a wonderful sense of pleasure to be back in his home with the woman he loved and all the folks around him safe. The vision of the ship's bow disappearing below the water kept flicking through his brain while he tried to think about an opening day big buck peeking across a shooting lane.

Turning the alarm off one minute before it buzzed, gently easing out of bed, Matt tucked the blankets around Tanya and left their bedroom. In the kitchen, he turned on a small counter light, pushed the coffee machine switch, left a note to Tanya—"See you at noon"—and went into the garage to get dressed for the woods. He checked to make sure he had two Bic lighters. Adding a camouflage face mask and a three-by-six-foot piece of light camo netting, several clothespins and an insulated seat to a pile next to his jacket, he felt ready. After a large mug of coffee and two buttered plain donuts, he put on his coat, covered his head with a blaze orange stocking cap—missing his Kromer—and loaded the Remington in the light of the garage. He headed into the darkness—taking the road to the quarry and the hunting cabin.

The three-quarter moon had set, the woods were black, but the snow covering made the road easy to see and to walk. As he came down the final grade to the quarry floor, the lights from the cabin made the old, huge shop shed windows look like a candlelit church. The crunch of the snow, the cold air, a sky full of stars all made for a perfect opening day.

The cabin had everyone in boots, pants and underwear tops—finishing their last cup of coffee, some packing lunches. Not moving during the noon hour was a proven deer hunting strategy that Matt would ignore today. Matt didn't carry a lunch, planning a dawn sit and a slow stalk along the upper ponds—working around the north and east back to a lunch with Tanya and, hopefully, Webb if he stayed the morning. After his unaccustomed vodka drinking, he would be slow and dry in the morning. Matt quietly sipped some coffee in the busy cabin, he felt a disconnect with his friends and the season, his mind still churned with the events of the last few days.

With Matt, there were eight hunters total—they each marked their blinds and strategy for the day's hunt and coordinated their movements. The stalkers would help the concealed blind sitters. It was cold enough to make the unheated blinds uncomfortable after several hours. The rut was mostly over—the colder weather had brought it earlier this season. The big bucks would be holed up with their does—afternoon and evening hunts would see more deer. But opening day was a special time, looking over a rifle barrel at dawn, a tradition. They weren't just hunting big bucks—several does would be taken, even some fork horns, all by agreement. Passing on all does and filling tags with only the largest breeding bucks would be poor deer management, and over time would diminish the size and quality of the deer population.

After everyone wished everyone else good luck, Matt stepped into the darkness and walked across the quarry and up the north ramp— stopping to enjoy the lack of light pollution and the last of Orion the Hunter diving into the wooded horizon. Matt heard a couple of 4x4s droning to the east and south. One set of hunters would low gear a truck down rutted two tracks, then have a slow, hard walk into swamp blinds where shooting a deer was not as big a challenge as dragging it out. The rest would melt into the woods, silently fanning out within a mile of the cabin, mostly along the swamp edge, thick cover and lake area: a brotherhood of friends, each experiencing the familiar and new adventure of an opening morning.

Matt eased up the quarry ramp and walked slowly into the woods among regular poplar-covered mounds, on a trail that, at one time, ore cars filled with overburden had traveled on tracks, leaving exposed the nearly pure limestone mined aggressively for 30 years. Several hundred yards later, Matt came to an opening that ran generally east and west containing low brush and grassland, bordering a flooded beaver stream. He stationed himself with the light north wind in his face, by a fallen tree, kicking the snow and dry leaves from under his feet, clothes pinning the camouflage netting across a small bush and a limb from the fallen tree. Placing the insulated pad he unhooked from this belt on a tree stump, Matt made himself comfortable—waiting for first light.

Three hours later—nose, fingers and toes cold—Matt had enough of watching an empty field, listening to crows and seeing only one skinny fox. Around 8:30, he heard three shots—two from the southwest, the swamp area, and one far to the north, probably not from their group. Enough sitting for a cold morning with nothing moving, Matt quietly rolled up the netting, rehooked his seat pad and began working his way back, east to Quarry road then south to the house.

Approaching the house, looking at tracks, with the rifle slung on his shoulder, Matt saw a large sedan in the driveway—black, shiny with no coating of dirt and salt stains. Not a Yooper vehicle.

Matt went back into the woods, out of sight of the house, working around to the garage side door. Loud, angry voices and his intuitions calling for caution, Matt shrugged off his coat: rifle at the ready, thumb on the safety. Just as he ducked to avoid exposure at the kitchen door, there were several gunshots. Bursting into the kitchen, crouching in the doorway opening to the great room, Matt came upon a tableau of statue people looking at him.

A man was sprawled face down before Matt, Al sat on the couch with blood showing on his left arm, the Browning .22 in his right hand. Webb curled across a footstool, holding his stomach. The side table and now shadeless lamp scattered on the floor. On the left, by the French doors that lead to the patio, Jared Livingston stood holding Tanya's upper arm—a small black pistol in his other hand touching her neck.

Looking like the deranged fanatic he was, he spoke in manic bursts. "Webb killed my brother…no court will convict me for shooting him… they were resisting arrest…I have a right to defend myself…Anyone move, I shoot her!"

The bright kitchen light behind Matt made him an easy target against the relative darkness of the north-facing great room. Moving into the hallway leading to the bedroom—keeping the rifle low but pointed at Livingston—Matt spoke. "Webb didn't kill your brother— I did. You're next."

Recognition dawned on Jared's face, mixed with incredulity. "You're dead…you have to be dead…we killed you."

Jared brought his pistol away from Tanya and toward Matt. Tanya spun away, diving behind the large leather chair.

Jared brought his arm and pistol up to fire at Matt.

With Tanya out of the line of fire, Matt crouched to be a smaller target, while lining up his rifle for an off hand shot. He knew he was too slow, he saw the pistol aiming at him, the black eye of the barrel at the end of Jared's outstretched arm. Time broke into separate bursts of impressions as he pushed the safety off and his finger fumbled for the trigger. Bracing for the impact of the bullet he knew would hit him, Matt concentrated on lining up his awkward, unpracticed shot. Jared's pistol flashed and banged.

In the same a part of a heartbeat, Matt and Al both fired into Jared. The noise a painful cacophony of the .22's sharp cracks and the rifle's single pressure wave boom. The smell of powder came with the ringing in Matt's ears. The ringing sound joined and continued by the vibration of a heavy crystal vase on the mantel, a shell casing hit the flagstones of the fireplace and bounced off the metal heating vents. Matt's bullet went through Jared and out the picture window. Al had fired four times. While waiting for the pain and shock of a bullet wound to reach his brain, Matt chambered a new round—no need, the air was all out of Jared. In a split-second he went from being a crazed billionaire to a bag of old bones in a dark suit.

Matt stood up, no pain, no leaks—Jared had missed a shot from 12 feet.

Checking the neck pulse of Jared's man on the floor—and finding none—Matt rushed to Tanya. They both went to Webb. Breathing shallowly and looking white, he still gave a brave smirk, "I've been shot worse places by bigger bullets."

"What in hell is going on?" Sam Ferr's voice boomed, his younger brother Will's head bobbing over his older brother's shoulder—both had rifles leveled. "We saw you cross the road and came for hot coffee. Looks like we got a war."

Sam crossed the room, with his 30-30 Winchester he poked Jared's body, "I don't suppose you got a license for this?"

Without waiting for an explanation, they began helping Webb and Al. The brothers had seen a lot in Vietnam, stepping over the prone gunman, ignoring the pile that was Livingston, they went to the wounded.

Al had a clean wound in the upper arm—more a deep gash—and Will and Tanya took him to the bathroom to clean him up. Sam Ferr and Matt got Webb to the bed in the master bedroom—his wound showing as a small hole just above his left hip bone. It oozed blood, the bullet still inside.

The Ferrs didn't ask any questions until two bodies lay wrapped in plastic tarps, cooling on the patio. The thermopane window, literally and figuratively shot, was sealed with duct tape inside and out.

Al, sprawled on the couch, gave the story to Matt. "We didn't hear their car, we were watching news—TV had a whole segment on the Livingstons and their ship sinking, showing their kids and grand-kids talking about having a memorial. They got behind us with pistols drawn. Jared, totally crazy, wanted to kill Webb himself—with his toy of a pistol. Tanya tried to talk him out of it and got between him and Webb. While they yelled at each other, Jared's man, with the big pistol, looked away from me and toward Tanya—I shot him three or four times before he got one into me. I think he couldn't believe he was being shot—the .22 is no stopper." Al took a breath, wincing as he tried to shift his position on the couch, "I thought I'd draw Livingston's fire, because I had the pistol and was shooting, but he grabbed Tanya and shot Webb, I couldn't get a clear shot. Then you came in."

"Did they say why they weren't on the ship?" asked Matt.

"No, but they were looking for Webb—didn't say much more than I told you."

The Ferr brothers fussed around the room—cleaning what they could—and heard everything said.

Later, beer cans, shot glasses and a brandy bottle shared the kitchen table with the intruders' guns— a large Smith and Wesson 10 mm semiautomatic and a tiny Ruger LCP .380. Webb made two cell phone calls—a doctor and a chartered helicopter would be heading out of Detroit within an hour. Vicodin and vodka were the medical treatment of the day. Webb and Al were in beds, Al's wound cleaned and bandaged, but needing stitches. Webb's wound was much worse— oozing as Webb breathed or moved, his shirt and sweater showing that material had been carried into the wound along with the bullet. Infection would be in a race with the helicopter, but Webb insisted he would be fine—he wasn't dizzy or lightheaded and internal bleeding probably would not be a short-term issue.

Matt explained the Livingston story to the Ferrs—initially omitting the home attack by the two men, only to have the brothers see through the omission. They returned to the mysterious fire—no one ever really believed it was an accident—and made Matt admit to the attack. They didn't question what happened to the two attackers—maybe another day, another bottle.

Will Ferr brought up the big problem. "What you going to do with the bodies? We could put them through the big grinder—mink don't give a shit what they eat, long as it's mostly meat."

Sam almost choked with the offer, but didn't say anything.

Matt thanked them, "No, no—It might poison the mink. I think Webb and his helicopter will be going back over Lake Michigan."

Chopper and Whopper

Wearing gloves, Matt went through the black limousine—Canadian registration, corporate insurance and registration. Jared was on some kind of business trip. On the big driver-bodyguard, he found a poorly adjusted shoulder holster and several gasoline receipts—Duluth, Marquette and the American Sault. He had a cell phone—Jared didn't. There were two overnight bags, containing one or two nights of clothing. The news, and their sons, still claiming the older Livingstons went down with their ship, so Jared's trip seemed a mystery to their corporation and to Matt.

Matt went back into the house—where everyone was gathering in the master bedroom, Webb holding court.

"All can work out if we do smart things. I got a doctor to fix us up, a helicopter to get us to a medical facility. I had them also send a person to take the black car away—we put the bodies in the car, since too many people might be watching the helicopter to put them there, and it makes a complexity with the charter pilot. Al and I fly out of your lives in a few hours. Tell people I had an appendix emergency, if they ask.

"The chopper pilot will call when they are gassing up—we'll need a clear area. You can give the directions—GPS numbers would be best. It might be dark, so we'll need some lights on the field."

Sam Ferr spoke up. "What are we going to tell the gang?"

Webb looked at him, "gang" to him didn't mean the men at the hunting cabin.

Matt intervened. "Relax. He's talking about the other hunters—they will be back by dark. The appendix emergency is good, Al can get into the helicopter without drawing attention—Sam and Will now have a secret to keep."

"Can you two keep a secret? "Webb asked the Ferrs, giving them a hard look. "What does it take to buy your silence?"

Sam Ferr snorted and turned his back to Webb. Will Ferr looked hard right back at Webb. "Matt bought our silence with thirty years of friendship. We've shared many a hunt and fishing trips. We may tell lies—but never secrets. I heard the old man say he killed Matt. I heard Matt's story—that's good enough for us. The old fart had to go. We'll help you pull this off. Sam, let's get back to camp, we can use our truck and get some of the ATVs running. I'll come back with a GPS."

"I've got a little Magellan—it will give coordinates," said Matt. "If it doesn't work, I'll come down."

Al, who had been standing, carefully sat down in a bedside chair. "Let's get the limo into the garage, load the bodies and drive over the tracks a few times."

The group broke up. Matt and the Ferrs carried the bodies, Tanya moved in the limo—the big trunk held both bodies. Al took the Smith and Wesson, returning Matt's .22. Matt kept the tiny Ruger. While moving items in the trunk, Matt found several manila folders with string closing flaps—signoff lists printed on the outside showing several unidentifiable scribble signatures. They contained various pages of sales numbers, personnel changes, news and magazine clippings of the nuclear waste project, and year-to-date itemized budget projections and actual expenses. All corporation information for Jared's review—the driver must have been a messenger, delivering printed material to the ship. He might have been armed from the ship. The ill fitting shoulder holster showed it had been on a larger person, the leather folds and holes indicating for some time. Matt thought of the large man that had manned the tiller and helped Jared dump him into the river. Luckily, the new wearer was slow to react and not a great shot. Jared must have been using him to get to the Sault for some reason— maybe to check on Webb's situation or the car rental people, or some whim he needed to pursue personally. The important thing being that the Livingston HQ didn't seem to know about Jared's travels. The messenger's cell phone didn't show any outgoing, or unanswered, calls for the last 24 hours.

The Ferr brothers left, walking back to the quarry cabin. The helicopter had not called yet. Matt put two new AA batteries in his yellow Magellan eXplorist 200 as he went outside and walked down to the large, treeless field northwest of the cabin—formed by the original limestone pavement with little soil over it. He took several readings— writing them on a note pad. By avoiding a few larger rocks, neither snow depth nor grass height would bother a 4x4 or a four wheel drive vehicle moving in the field.

Returning to the house, Matt waited another half hour, while sipping coffee with Tanya, before the call came to Webb. The helicopter was at Pellston's airport—refueling. Matt gave Webb the paper with the GPS coordinates. Webb, tiring, handed the phone and paper back to Matt, motioning for him to continue the conversation..

After reading the coordinates, Matt began answering questions about the landing area, surrounding power lines, towers, landmarks, temperature and wind. Matt added he could get lights on the field and asked their arrival time.

The pilot, pausing for a few seconds, answered, "Fifty miles flight distance, ten mile per hour headwinds, we are here for maybe another twenty minutes—let's say an ETA of 5:15. Keep a phone at the field, and I'll call if we have a problem finding you."

Matt repeated the ETA to the group, again assembling around Webb, and handed the phone back.

Webb spoke to the doctor and the man that would drive away the limo, everyone knew their roles.

Missing his Yukon, Matt put on his coat and hat and walked toward the cabin, surprised at how fast the helicopter had gotten from Detroit. The hunters wouldn't be coming out of the woods until 5:30 or even 6:00, which was good because of the audience and questions the chopper would attract—but he needed lights. The Ferrs had a good four wheel drive truck, one old 4x4 ATV and two snowmobiles were also at the cabin.

Arriving at the cabin, Matt heard the snowmobiles running, and saw Sam Ferr pulling on the starter cord of the old 4x4.

"Battery dead," he snarled. "Piece of shit won't start. We got two Indy's and the truck—should be enough light—maybe we can make a fire, too."

Matt got on one snowmobile, Will on the other—Sam drove the truck.

Bringing some wood and gasoline from the house, the three men drove their machines to the field, the snow machines breaking paths and making a big circle in the field. The truck unloaded two piles of split wood—arranged on the far sides of the circle, they would give light and wind direction.

Ready—standing by the truck—they heard the chopper. Tanya held the cell phone—looking beautiful in a fur-lined parka. Sam, in love, had just promised her some mink-lined earmuffs. Lighting the fires and turning on their lights—directed toward the circle—the four watched the dark gray sky as the sound got louder.

They saw the bright lights coming over the trees before they could make out the machine. No calls came in, but the craft slowed, flared and landed very quickly. Blowing snow, engine and rotor sounds drowned sight and talk, until the twin turbines began winding down, and they heard the slowing whish of the four long main blades.

Two men came out of the helicopter—each carrying a bag.

Introducing himself, the men just nodding hello—no names given, Matt ushered them to Sam's truck—Tanya drove, Matt rode up the hill in the truck bed. The Ferrs came up on the snow machines.

The game plan, assuming the doctor thought Webb could travel, was to get loaded and away ASAP.

Guessing wrong, Matt took the older, most intellectual looking man to Webb. The smaller, shifty-eyed younger man—who Matt thought looked like the bag-man driver—followed along. However, once in the room, the little guy moved directly to Webb on the bed, began examining the wound. After some pushing, probing and questions—followed by two hypodermic shots and a covering bandage—the doctor ordered Webb helped to the helicopter. He also asked for a cartridge from the pistol that shot Webb. Turning to Al's wound—peeking under the bandage—he said, "I'll deal with you on the trip back."

While Al went to get a cartridge, Matt and Webb's man carefully lifted and carried the heavy Russian, their hands efficiently linked under his back and knees, and moved him to the truck. Webb inhaled sharply a few times, when lifting his arms around his bearers, but didn't complain. Matt drove the doctor and Webb to the chopper, Al and Tanya rode down on the snow machines driven by the Ferrs. The limo man went to his work in the garage.

Aft clamshell doors opening on the helicopter exposed a well-lighted area—including a gurney, medical paraphernalia and several jump seats. After quickly securing Webb on the bed with covers and strapping, Al and the doctor sat facing him on small jump seats. As the doors closed, a loudspeaker boomed "Clear the area" over the field.

Turbines wound up, the main and tail rotor blades began spinning— in less than a minute, the large craft began to lift. Blinding lights and snow masking the departure, the chopper accelerated over the southern row of trees before all the blowing snow had settled.

The Ferrs returned to the cabin—no other hunters came to the scene, but they all must have heard the chopper. The camp would be eager for information.

Matt and Tanya went back to the garage. The limo man had changed license plates and had done something to the car's OnStar system—and stuck thin plastic signs on both front doors, each with a large green and white pine tree in a circle and the words ACME Environmental Research Corporation.

The man made a final walk around; satisfied, he got into the vehicle. His parting words: "Let me out, and forget you ever saw me or this vehicle—drive over my tracks from the garage to wipe them out."

Matt had the van in the garage before the limo's taillights disappeared.

Truly alone for the first time since the bay on Grand Island, Tanya and Matt kissed and held each other. Holding hands, they moved back into the kitchen, exhaustion creeping in, adrenalin rushes ebbing, thankful to be alive.

Matt held her again. "I hate to say it, but we need to put in an appearance at the cabin—talk about the appendix emergency. Give your friend Webb a heart condition and note that he insisted on his Detroit specialist. Tell a whopper, and stick to it. Two drinks, a couple of deer stories, and we excuse ourselves."

Matt and Tanya bundled up and drove the truck down to the hunting cabin—they met two 4x4s at the curve that they let precede them down the sloping road to the quarry floor.

At the cabin, every light was on, including a Coleman. Two large bucks hung on an old swing set surrounded by hunters—each holding a beer, grinning, happy to welcome them. Tanya's tight Levis quickly became more interesting than the dead deer. Matt's cousins, Dick and Billy Lameroux, had both got bucks in the swamp—they recited their adventures, describing the shots, how they tracked them after they were hit and the grueling efforts of pulling two big animals out of a thick, cedar swamp.

Matt and Tanya listened to every hunter's tale—from sightings to miles of walking that produced nothing but great beer thirsts. The helicopter had been heard, but most thought it was the DNR being obnoxious—using hunting license money to screw up and spy on honest hunters. The Ferrs, with no deer stories, filled their story time with the helicopter med-evac tale.

When T-bone steaks began being slapped on the sizzling grill of the big Webber, it became the appropriate time for Tanya and Matt to excuse themselves and hike back up the road to home.

No stars or moonlight came through the evening's overcast, the well-traveled road presenting no problems. Matt held Tanya's hand as they crunched the half mile back to their house. Matt thought to himself how perfectly Tanya blended with the group, she had naturally said and done the right things about the deer: inspecting the killing wound, noting the fat deposits and the size of the antlers, listening earnestly to the tales, drinking her beer. She didn't try to clean up or do any cooking. Matt had told the group about his morning hunt—what he hadn't seen. He finished with the news that he was sleeping-in the next morning—which brought universal grins from the men, now mostly on their third beer.

Back at home, Tanya began working on two plates of food, while Matt made a fire, opened some red wine, and made a place before the hearth. The great room was lit by several candles flickering on the mantle, combining with the heat and flames of burning logs created a soft, warm atmosphere—an outside light from the patio shown on the snowy slope and trees to the northwest. The room retained none of the violence that it had experienced just a few hours before.

The food hardly touched—the wine sipped down only an inch—Matt held Tanya in his arms. After speculating about Webb's injury, the Vegas' driving progress, their individual luck and skill in overcoming threats and killers, kissing and enjoying each other's touch and warmth, they finally blew out the candles. Putting the uneaten food away, they went to their bed, freshly made after Webb's use.

The Second Week of Deer Camp

Hunting in the afternoons—although not very hard—Matt was happy prowling and standing. Twice he took Tanya out just to enjoy her company amid the beauty of the woods. They tracked, built warming fires, ate sandwiches while talking about their future and sipping blackberry brandy from a plastic flask; they saw several does and yearlings. Once, two wolves sat on a snowy bank, arrogantly watching them moving along the swamp edge, disappearing into the trees only when Matt brought the scope up to get a better look.

Calling twice the third day after his med flight—while Tanya and Matt tramped the woods—Webb left phone mail messages, increasingly upset that they weren't more worried about him, that they didn't have his expensive cell phone unit with them.

Back at dusk, around the kitchen table, putting the cell phone on speaker while listening to the mailbox, Tanya said, "Webb must be on the mend—he's feisty."

They called Webb—he had news. "I'm fine—just lost some blood and abdominal muscle—thank you for asking. Al is fine with twelve stitches—actually clamps—which should make a very manly scar. I've been sitting around, getting information from a dozen sources about our mutual interests.

"The Livingston Corporation may be spinning the news—claiming the bow of the *Carol K* drifted while it was sinking. There is nothing about the writing on the rocks getting into the papers or on TV. The sons may be paying off the researchers or the press. There's rumors of memorials, scholarships, research grants—lots of money going to people associated with the wreck. I'd say this indicates they know their family history and they are as concerned with the wreck as their fathers. They are known as hard working, honest businessmen—unlike their cantankerous and malevolent fathers. There will be no more diving now, or through the ice later. We can discuss this when I see you both. Secrets and cover ups are very complex. The next dives on the wrecks will tell us a lot about the posture that the sons will take. You should be fine. They will assume I somehow arranged everything that happened. Their fathers had to be doing all they did under the highest secrecy. It is very possible the sons knew nothing of the murderous plots—Jared and Jud kept their own counsel. Most everything they did was very well planned, but the last visit had to be off the script— spontaneous—stupidly emotional, most likely never communicated to anyone. Do you understand what I'm saying to you?"

Moving close to the large cell phone held by Matt, Tanya answered, "Yes, we follow the argument—this situation isn't over, but we are probably not on anyone's radar screen. Will you be alright?"

Matt thought, *Webb eats this kind of intrigue like popcorn—he'll squeeze money and power from it like it's an orange...I must be hungry.*

"I'll be fine, I'm playing with a lot of trump cards. No matter what happens, we are in a good position—rather, I'm in a good position. You two love birds should just go south and play in the sand and sunshine. You would be wise to assign the stock to me—I will front for you. Depending upon how much information sharing took place between fathers and sons—facts we can deduce by their actions—all their angst should be focused on me. I have no problem with that. They can never prove or even develop a logical speculation explaining how I could have been in government custody while arranging foul play—certainly not through highly reputable lawyers—my hands are totally clean.

"The Nuclear Waste program is driving up their stock. Our initial stock value has gone up over 60 percent. We might sell, take a short position, get the pictures published, which also lets out the major secrets—eliminating the need to kill over them. Make a lot of money, get out, rebuy if their technology overcomes the bad publicity. I've got people that will handle all that stuff. The Canadian stock market has some different rules than Wall Street."

Matt glanced at Tanya—her eyebrows went up—and thought, *Here we go, Webb can't do anything entirely on the square—his life is one big chess match, and his pieces don't always move within the rules.*

Matt still decided to risk his opinion. "I say let's do it—they can't hide the fact that a ship doesn't drift fifty miles and end with an anchor and chain draping like they were over rocks We have a whole set of ship and body pictures—including the very incriminating rock writing. The newness of the explosions will raise questions, too."

Webb didn't wait for Matt to finish. "Good, get me the pictures. I'll have someone contact you with the papers needed to move the stock. You both will make a lot of money and stick it to the Livingstons, too. If anyone connects the pictures with your diving, lawyer up—not unusual for diving discoveries. We'll be careful there are no fingerprints or trails available from the pictures we send. Take your vacation, be real snowbirds for the winter, I'll have it all working in a month or so—the various school teams and the State Police divers will get on the wrecks in the spring."

Webb said he was in Birmingham, outside Detroit, for the time being at Al's home, and Matt agreed to get the pictures with a trip to Gladstone after deer camp—then they would close up the house and head south, stopping to see Webb and Al. Webb talked to Tanya, asking about her parents and the picture. He said he'd like to run a yacht charter again with everyone on it—just to show his new scar. They chatted about Carla and Karen—making promises to visit and talk on the phone. Webb ended the conversation with his usual bravado about having everything under control and his looking forward to any challenges life could throw at him.

After five days of hunting, Matt got his buck—watching a trail and an active scrape for two evenings netted him a good shot and a smallish eight-pointer. By the end of the week, the camp had a deer of some size hanging for each hunter—the last two due to several hard drives through stubborn cedar swamps and thick marshlands.

Matt retrieved his pictures in Gladstone, making a few visits and venison promises to friends, then drove Tanya another 60 miles to do some Christmas shopping in Marinette, Wisconsin. The Vegas phoned from their home on Islamorada nearly every day—reminding them of warm weather and green waters.

Tanya tore up and burned the Livingston's card with the special number for the repayment of the fire damage. Thinking aloud while she and Matt watched the little pieces burn, she said, "We don't need any more links to the brothers. Eventually the dive and the contract for our silence will link them to us—but it will be months—and if the sons are as publicity shy as their fathers, maybe we will never be bothered by them."

"Having Webb as a barrier and protector isn't all bad either," said Matt.

By the second week of deer camp Matt had the house all winterized, caretakers lined up to check on the lamp he had put in the kitchen window—plugged into a small Honeywell device that turned on the light if the internal house temperature fell below his setting of 45 degrees.

They drove to Marquette, turned in the rental car and picked up their tickets to Detroit, planning to stay overnight with Webb and his wife Karen before continuing on to Miami where the Vegas would meet them. Matt had arranged for a local meat processor to send some selected frozen venison—packed in Omaha Steak boxes and dry ice—to the Vegas. Hunting friends would put a few pieces into Matt's freezer, and see that the rest fulfilled promises in Gladstone.

After a half hour of shoeless check-in searches and screening procedures, Matt and Tanya joined one other passenger to board the small commuter plane that would take them to Detroit. In the cold plane, they cuddled together on the right side of the narrow aisle.

Matt whispered in the nearly empty cabin, "You realize this is our anniversary—we have been together just one year. I hope this plane does a better job than the one you were on last November."

"I don't remember the crash, but I'll never forget the wonderful Thanksgiving we spent snowed in. We've had a year full of adventures and love. I've never been happier—how about you?"

Matt squeezed out of the narrow seat, rummaging in his leather carryon bag in the overhead, and sat back down with a small box. Handing it to, Tanya he put his arm around her. "This is to go with your other ring, you can wear it on the chain until you want me to put in on your finger."

Opening the white jeweler's box, Tanya took out a plain band on a fine chain and held it in her hand. Looking at it for a few seconds, with tears in her eyes, she turned to kiss Matt. Putting it over her head, tucking it into her sweater, she kissed Matt again. "I love you. I'll wear it now—we'll talk dates when we get to Florida."

"Would you like to charter a sleek fast boat, do the Bahamas again— enjoying long boring days of sun and fun—just the two of us?"

Tanya gave him another kiss, hugging his arm. "Yes and yes and yes."

The pilots finally entered the plane, bumping Matt as they moved to the cockpit. An attendant moved to the front and began her instructions, Matt and Tanya very courteously paying rapt attention.

The plane took off into a hard north wind—making a wide turn over the blue gray lake. Matt and Tanya held hands, looking at the forming ice, catching a brief glimpse, through scattered gray cloud wisps, of Granite Island—lonely and cold in a lake lonely and cold...

Matt took the folded newspaper article with the picture of the burning ship and the smoke-shrouded figures on the island. He held it near the window as the plane banked. "I think I'll share with Webb a story about ghosts."

Tanya whispered, "Let's take that painting to its home in the Virgin Islands and let the artist's relatives know how a brave man lived and died."

The End

Acknowledgements

Many people helped produce this novel. Most of all, Ann, my wife, reading every word, discussing plots and people, ever amazed at my spelling creativity. My son, Ben, offered good critiques, boating techniques and information about the Marquette, Michigan, area, including his hikes to the top of Sugarloaf Mountain—saving me great effort. Walt Shiel's expert editing, counsel, and literary skills honed the words, while his wife Kerrie's wonderful cover art graphically conjured several story images. Completing the Shiel family contributions, their talented daughter, Lisa, took time from writing to produce and maintain my website.

Historical ship information came from David D. Swayze, *The* expert on Great Lakes shipwrecks and a very friendly source of historical information. Also, the *Shipwreck Journal,* produced by the Great Lakes Shipwreck Historical Society, offered facts and inspiration. The 82-footer knowledge came via schematics and from men who served on the sleek Point Class vessels.

Diving techniques took a year of research. Advice and diagrams came from Jim Bruns during several visits to the Scuba Station on Fernandina Beach, Florida. Steve Bolek, a former teaching colleague and still an expert diver with the Delta County Sheriff's department, read and advised on the diving scenes.

The 34-foot Silverton is a real boat, the *4 Reel,* owned and operated by Warren Frank and my best buddy, retired USCG Master Chief Archie Davies—terror of the inland sea, off St. Joseph, Michigan.

Granite Island is real in location and structure. It is a private island with a wonderfully restored lighthouse. Its history and documentation are worth a web search for Granite Island Lighthouse. It has ghosts.

The nuclear waste project used in the story is the brain child of Father Frank Lenz, PhD. Father Lenz is one of the smartest people I've ever met. I pray the world will take advantage of his ideas.

Lastly, a coaching point: starting a fire with a rifle isn't easy. I pulled nine projectiles from their casings, pulled the trigger on my Remington as many times and produced only two fires, both of which needed the tinder in a bucket to hold the blast and flame.

About the Author

Born and raised in Michigan, John (J.C.) Hager earned a B.A. and M.A. in Biology and Science Education from Western Michigan University, taught high school science and coached football and wrestling. He retired from IBM after 27 years on quota. He and his wife Ann live in Michigan's Upper Peninsula on the shore of Little Bay de Noc. They have two grown sons. John dilutes his writing time with hunting, fishing, boating, traveling, and providing laughs and lost golf balls at the Gladstone Golf Club.

The Matt Hunter Adventures
by J. C. Hager

If you enjoyed *Hunter's Secret,* you won't want to miss the debut novel in this exciting series.

Hunter's Choice

With the sound of snapping pine tops and tortured metal skidding across a frozen lake, a peaceful deer hunt becomes a rescue mission. Hunter's choices quickly become life-and-death decisions as a barrage of life-changing events thrust him into a fast-paced, page-turning adventure.

"A powerful and intelligent thriller!"—Steve Hamilton, author of the Alex McKnight novels

Looking for the perfect gift for an outdoorsman, a fan of high-adventure thrillers, or someone looking for the perfect "summer read?"

The Matt Hunter Adventures can be purchased at:
- Your local bookstore
- Most online book retailers
- Direct from the author

Be sure to visit J. C. Hager's website to learn more about:
- This exciting series
- The author
- What's in store next for Matt Hunter

www.JCHager.com

You can also purchase autographed copies of one or both books at special discounts.

Both are available in a variety of eBook formats, too!

CPSIA information can be obtained at www.ICGtesting.com
Printed in the USA
LVOW11s0141240714

395786LV00003B/151/P